THE ADVENTURES OF
ROBIN HOOD
& HIS MERRY OUTLAWS

Greenwich House Classics Library

Robin turns butcher. (CHAPTER III)

THE ADVENTURES OF
ROBIN HOOD
& HIS MERRY OUTLAWS

RETOLD FROM THE OLD BALLADS BY
J. WALKER McSPADDEN AND
CHARLES WILSON

WITH ILLUSTRATIONS BY HOWARD PYLE
AND T.H. (THOMAS HEATH) ROBINSON

AND A FOREWORD BY
PATRICIA BARRETT PERKINS

Greenwich House Classics Library

Greenwich House
Distributed by Crown Publishers, Inc.
New York

This 1984 edition is published by Greenwich House,
a division of Arlington House, Inc.,
distributed by Crown Publishers, Inc.,
One Park Avenue, New York, New York 10016

Manufactured in the United States of America

Library of Congress Cataloging in Publication Data

McSpadden, J. Walker (Joseph Walker), 1874-1960.
The adventures of Robin Hood & his merry outlaws.
(Greenwich House classics library)
Summary: Twenty-four tales of Robin Hood, Little John,
Will Scarlet, Friar Tuck, and Allan-a-Dale, and the
merry adventures they have while defying the Sheriff of
Nottingham and other authority figures in and around
Sherwood Forest.
1. Robin Hood—Legends. [1. Robin Hood. 2. Folklore—
England] I. Wilson, Charles. II. Pyle, Howard, 1853–
1911, ill. III. Robinson, T.H. (Thomas Heath), ill. IV. Title. V. Series.
PS3525.C58A67 1984 398.2'2'0941 83-27494
ISBN 0-517-43602-7

h g f e d c b a

CONTENTS

LIST·OF·ILLVSTRATIONS:

FOREWORD

As a child, I remember seeing the movie of Robin Hood. I remember the colors, the actors, the scenes; and I remember carrying those images with me throughout my childhood. But at a certain point, I put the images away, as one does with childhood toys. What a pleasure now to pick up this book and find that what I had considered merely a young reader's story was so filled not only with those fondly remembered episodes, but also with such powerful imagery that its prose brings to mind the passages in Hardy's *Tess of the D'Urbervilles* which are so sensuous as to make one smell and taste and feel the richness of country life. So much of this story is like a fondly remembered camping trip, where we come, perhaps for the first time in our young lives, face to face with the wonders of nature.

The main intention of the author, J. Walker McSpadden, was to weave the various old ballads of Robin Hood together to form a continuous narrative, while maintaining the spirit and accuracy of the originals. And this he certainly did. But how was he to know that the atmosphere of today's world, with its diminishing natural resources and untouched settings and the threat of a nuclear holocaust would result in transforming mere description into poetry?

Robin Hood & His Merry Outlaws

So he set forth upon his way with blithe heart; for it was a day when the whole face of the earth seemed glad and rejoicing in pulsing life. Steadily he pressed forward by winding ways till he came to a green broad pasture land at whose edge flowed a stream dipping in and out among the willows and rushes on the banks.

A simple little description, but it takes on new significance when placed beside the morning newspaper.

And so does much else in this rediscovered treasure. The Middle Ages may well have been a time of cruelty. Undoubtedly the ballads were an attempt at social statements since many of the episodes show Robin and his band robbing and killing representatives of authority; in particular, there are his encounters with his most frequent enemy, the Sheriff of Nottingham. Yet, even amidst the inhumanity of the villains and the lack of respect for life of Robin himself (many of his band are men he first encountered in a one-on-one life-and-death battle), it is disarming to have the battles waged with quarterstaffs, which are young saplings pulled from the ground at hand and used with both hands on the staff about two feet apart. The staffs remove the element of physical contact from the contest, and at the same time make the battle seem almost like a sport or game—which it often turns out to be. The use of nature in this specific way makes one heave a sigh of longing for how sensible man's instincts were at that time, in contrast to the caveman's stone or modern man's nuclear fission.

The skill at archery as a test of man's worth is another memento of a forgotten time. Although archery is still a skill today, it was

Foreword

such an integral part of the daily life of Robin Hood's contemporaries that to take it away would be like taking away our cars or TV sets. What would we do? In no other story set in medieval times are the customs and necessities of sheer basic living and survival brought so vividly to our awareness.

But these are by-products. McSpadden's style of writing is one of immediacy. He brings the reader into the story and involves him constantly by speaking directly to him. This maneuver accomplishes two things: first, it creates a relationship between the author and the reader, and secondly, it makes the reader unwittingly carry on a dialogue with the author and thus become more involved. When McSpadden spends pages describing a character new to the story, and by his description we are able to guess quite soon that it is no stranger, but Robin Hood in disguise, our response to "Side by side with Rob—for it was he..." is to say, "I know that." For the young reader, it provides an opportunity for self-praise and a strengthening of self-esteem (How smart I was to figure that out!). For the older reader, it provides a chance to laugh along with McSpadden at his tongue-in-cheek guilelessness. But for young and old alike, it removes the tales from the realm of "a story about" and brings it into our space, whether we like it or not. And I think we like it!

This is indeed easy reading. The action moves swiftly; there is just enough mystery to keep you reading each chapter to the end; and the fact that each chapter is a little story in itself makes it

Robin Hood & His Merry Outlaws

possible to put it down and pick it up at one's convenience. A-chapter-a-night for bedtime reading or straight through on a train trip—either way it is tailor-made. Although we care that the ballads of Robin Hood were born out of a social impulse, more important to us are the gifts we have inherited and in which, due to McSpadden's labor of love, we may all share. For the romantic, we have romance; for the historian, we have a vivid historical document; for the youngster, an action-packed adventure; for the naturalist, it is almost a medieval Thoreau; and for anyone, it is a beautiful piece of work that may make the day a little brighter for having spent a few hours in the lush greenwood of Sherwood Forest among all those merry men.

PATRICIA BARRETT PERKINS

Baltimore, Maryland
1984

A contest of quarterstaffs. (CHAPTER XV)

ABOUT THE ILLUSTRATIONS

The beautiful line drawings in this book, complete with decorative panels, are by Howard Pyle, the American artist renowned for his interpretations of the children's classics. The illustrations in this edition have been selected and carefully reproduced from the first edition (1883) of *The Merry Adventures of Robin Hood*.

The remaining illustrations are by T.H. (Thomas Heath) Robinson, an English artist who flourished at the turn of the century. He is noted for his illustrations for Thackeray's *Henry Esmond* and *Cranford* by Mrs. Gaskell.

INTRODUCTION

SONGS and legends of Robin Hood and his merry outlaws have charmed readers young and old for more than five hundred years. They are among the earliest heirlooms of the Anglo-Saxon tongue, dating back to the time when Chaucer wrote his *Canterbury Tales,* and the minstrel and scribe stood in the place of the more prim and precise modern printing-press. The present stories, then, are but the retelling of old tales whose charm and interest, nevertheless, make them ever new. The old tales were in rhyme and ancient spelling ; they were hid in out-of-the-way places ; and they were more or less disconnected and obscure to our modern thinking. For this reason the adventures are now put into a continuous prose narrative in the hope that they will make some readers acquainted with one of the most attractive heroes in all story-land.

" Was Robin Hood a real person ? " will doubtless be the first question. It has been asked for many, many years, just as a similar question is being asked about the great Swiss hero William Tell, and many others whom we would much rather accept on faith.

The question of Robin Hood's flesh and blood cannot be answered by a brief " Yes " or " No," although learned men

9

have pored over ancient records and have written books on the subject—some saying that he actually did live in the greenwood and fight with bow and staff and sword ; others claiming that his deeds were but legendary stories relating to a group of men rather than to a single historical person ; and still others saying that he is but the embodiment of Maytime revels.

However that may be, Robin Hood has been the one great popular hero in England for centuries, and the accounts of his life are much more clear and distinct than those of many early kings and lords. His adventures are minutely related in numerous ballads, and his name is cherished as one of the first among those who stood out for liberty and equal rights to high and low. If ever a man has been loved by his country, it is Robin Hood. "It is he," says an old historian, "whom the common people delight to celebrate in games and comedies, and whose history, sung by fiddlers, interests them more than any other." In the sixteenth century an annual holiday was still set apart for him, and observed by all the people in the countryside. Bishop Latimer once visited a certain town, and announced that he would preach there the next day. But on the morrow when he went to the church he found the doors locked, and no congregation in sight. After he had waited over an hour for the key, a man came up and said : " Sir, this is a busy day with us ; we cannot hear you ; it is Robin Hood's day. The parish is gone abroad to gather for Robin Hood." The Bishop himself tells us of this incident, and adds with hurt dignity : " I was fain there to give

Introduction

place to Robin Hood." So he took off his robe, and went his way, leaving his place to archers dressed in Lincoln green, who played on rude stages the parts of Robin Hood, Little John, Friar Tuck, and even Maid Marian.

There is more than one reason why Robin has been a national hero. He was not simply a robber and brawler. We must not make too much of these traits in the turbulence and lawlessness of early days, when king warred against noble and noble against bishop, and all three oppressed the common people, to whom the law gave no redress. An outlaw in those times, when deprived of protection, owed no man allegiance. His head was forfeit if he were ever captured ; so his hand was against every man's, and every man's against his. And how easy it was to become an outlaw ! The shooting of a king's deer, or the incurring of some lord's displeasure, was enough to put a man's life in jeopardy.

This was the day, not only of oppression by Church and State, but also of the struggle between the Saxon landholders and their Norman conquerors. Robin Hood was, first of all, a Saxon who stood out for the rights of the people, waging war against knights, sheriffs, abbots, and money-lenders, whose sway was so heavy. But he was fair in war, a protector of women and children ; courteous, moreover, to noble and peasant alike ; kind to the poor and oppressed, with whom he shared the goods obtained from too heavily laden knight or bishop ; generous as well, giving to a bankrupt Crusader horse, clothing, and money to recover his estate ; a respecter of honest labouring men and tradesfolk, whom his men were forbidden to molest ; brave to rashness, proud and adventurous—ready to give blows as quickly as take them, and to defy the sheriff within his walled town ; skilled and adroit and resourceful ; finally, a man of frank, open countenance, singing among the lights and shadows of the good greenwood, and jesting in the face of death itself. This is the picture which all the singers and story-tellers give of him. Is there any wonder that the common people loved him ?

This love extended from him to all the members of his hardy band. " God save Robin Hood, and all his good yeomanry " is the way many of the ballads end. The clever archer who could outshoot his fellows, the brave yeoman inured to blows, and the man who could be true to his friends through thick and thin were favourites for all time ; and they have been idealized in the persons of Robin Hood and his merry outlaws. Stories of their deeds are the epics of the common people, just as the earlier stories of King Arthur and his knights are the epics of the courtly class. The striking contrast of these two classes is shown in the forest scene where King Richard meets the yeomen on equal terms. This and other parallel portraits of Richard and Robin Hood (or Lockesley) have been drawn in enduring fashion by Sir Walter Scott in *Ivanhoe*.

If Robin Hood really lived it was probably some time during the twelfth and thirteenth centuries. Joseph Ritson, who is accounted the first modern authority on this subject, found

Introduction

warrant for the supposition that he was born at Lockesley, county of Nottingham, about the year 1160—during the reign of Henry II. His true name was Robert Fitzooth, and he came of good family. By some writers he was reputed to be the rightful Earl of Huntingdon. He was a wild, adventurous youth, whose debts or other follies drove him to the forests of Barnesdale in Yorkshire and Sherwood in Nottinghamshire. Being declared an outlaw, he had no recourse but to remain in hiding until a new king should come to the throne, or other public event work in his favour. Meanwhile he mustered a picked band of outlaws, who became noted for their prowess and daring. They successfully defied the laws for many years, making other rough and ready laws of their own.

King Henry died in 1189, and his son, Richard of the Lion Heart, was hailed as King. But the government was then in a poor state owing to Richard's absence upon a Crusade and his brother John's weak regency. A history of the period by Mair has this passage : " About this time, as I conjecture, the notorious robbers, Robert Hood of England and Little John, lurked in the woods, spoiling the goods only of rich men. They slew nobody but those who attacked them or offered resistance in defence of their property. Robert maintained by his plunder a hundred archers, so skilful in fight that four hundred brave men feared to attack them. He suffered no woman to be maltreated, and never robbed the poor, but assisted them abundantly with the wealth which he took from abbots."

Robin Hood & His Merry Outlaws

When Richard returned to England it is said that he forgave Robin Hood, and attached his yeomen to the Royal Guard. But on Richard's death his successor, John, drove Robin again into outlawry, which continued until Robin's death. The ruins of a castle are still shown where the outlaw defied the King's men ; but there are also many hills, woods, rocks, and caverns which are spoken of as " Robin Hood's." The date of his death has been set down, doubtfully, as 24th December, 1247; but this would make him a very old man—too old to do the deeds of strength ascribed to him up to the day of his death. One of the earliest printed ballads gives Robin a later period, and asserts that it was not King Richard but King Edward (one of the first three) who pardoned him in Sherwood Forest.

Maid Marian also has been variously identified as a figure of history. She is said to have been a Mistress Fitzwalter, daughter of an earl, and a tomb is still pointed out as hers.

The earliest accounts of Robin Hood are found in ballads and songs which go back to the thirteenth century. As this was before printing was known they came down from generation to generation by word of mouth. Ballads of this nature were very popular at festivals and public gatherings. They were usually improvised by some chief singer, who found his theme in a well-known event, and all his listeners joined in the chorus, keeping time to the rhythm of the lines by patting their feet or dancing upon the village green. The popularity of the Robin Hood songs, and belief in this hero, are shown by the numerous

Introduction

examples which have come down to our own day, while songs on many other subjects are forgotten.

The first historical allusion to Robin Hood is found in a book called *Piers Plowman* (written about 1362), where his rhymes are mentioned as being well known. The next notice is in Wyntown's *Scottish Chronicle* (about 1420), where both Robin Hood and Little John are ascribed to the year 1283. In Fordun and Bower's *Scotichronicon*, a fifteenth-century work, the two outlaws are said to have lived in 1266. Mair, the Scottish writer of the first quarter of the sixteenth century—who is quoted above—is the next to mention Robin Hood, giving him, in the *History of Great Britain*, a period during the life of Richard I, which is now generally accepted.

Caxton introduced the art of printing into England in 1477, and one of the earliest books published thereafter was a collection of Robin Hood ballads (between 1489 and 1510) entitled *Here beginneth a little geste of Robin Hood and his meiny : and of the proud Sheriff of Nottingham*. The book was printed by Wynken de Worde. Toward the end of the sixteenth century Anthony Munday wrote his successful play of *The Downfall of Robert, Earl of Huntingdon*. This play and the doubtful epitaph quoted in the last story are the chief grounds for supposing that Robin Hood was ever anything more than a simple yeoman.

In 1832 the industrious scholar Joseph Ritson made the first anthology of this material in a book entitled *Robin Hood : a*

Robin Hood & His Merry Outlaws

Collection of Poems, Songs, and Ballads, which was prefaced by a Life. Ritson's book has been largely followed by succeeding writers. In 1853 appeared a collection of the ballads, with " A Historical Sketch of Robin Hood," by William W. Campbell. A later library of *English and Scottish Ballads*, edited by Francis James Child, presents a full collection of Robin Hood songs in connexion with other subjects. Professor Arber's *English Garner* gives the " Little Geste," as also does John M. Gutch's edition of these and other ballads.

In the present prose stories the old ballads have been followed for their spirit and main situations. The idea has been to weave them together to form one continuous narrative, making a complete, consistent picture of the great outlaw's life in the forest. Every story is begun by verses from the ballad upon which it is based, and frequently throughout the pages the exact language is used. Incidents are told more fully than could be done in the rhymed original, but always in line with what is naturally suggested between the verses. And if any of the appeal and charm of those original verses—their bubbling humour, simple gaiety, dash, swing, and the fragrance of growing things upon a fresh May morning—have passed into these lines of prose, the writer will feel more than repaid for a labour which throughout was one of fascination and deep interest.

J. W. M.

CHAPTER I

HOW ROBIN HOOD BECAME AN OUTLAW

List and hearken, gentlemen,
   That be of free-born blood,
I shall you tell of a good yeoman,
   His name was Robin Hood.

Robin was a proud outlaw,
   While as he walked on the ground:
So courteous an outlaw as he was one
   Was never none else found.

IN the days of good King Harry the Second of England—he of the warring sons—there were certain forests in the north country set aside for the King's hunting, and no man might shoot deer therein under penalty of death. These forests were guarded by the King's Foresters, the chief of whom, in each wood, was no mean man, but equal in authority to the Sheriff in his walled town, or even to my lord Bishop in his abbey.

One of the greatest of royal preserves was Sherwood and Barnesdale Forests, near the two towns of Nottingham and Barnesdale. Here for some years dwelt one Hugh Fitzooth as Head Forester, with his good wife and little son Robert. The

Robin Hood & His Merry Outlaws

boy had been born in Lockesley town—in the year 1160, stern records say—and was often called Lockesley, or Rob of Lockesley. He was a comely, well-knit stripling, and as soon as he was strong enough to walk his chief delight was to go with his father into the forest. As soon as his right arm received thew* and sinew he learned to draw the long bow and speed a true arrow ; while on winter evenings his greatest joy was to hear his father tell of bold Will o' the Green, the outlaw, who for many summers defied the King's Foresters, and feasted with his men upon King's deer. And on other stormy days the boy learned to whittle out a straight shaft for the long bow, and tip it with grey goose feathers.

The fond mother sighed when she saw the boy's face light up at these woodland tales. She was of gentle birth, and had hoped to see her son famous at Court or abbey. She taught him to read and to write, to doff his cap without awkwardness, and to answer directly and truthfully both lord and peasant. But the boy, although he took kindly to these lessons of breeding, was yet happiest when he had his beloved bow in hand and strolled at will, listening to the murmur of the trees.

Two playmates had Rob in those gladsome early days. One was Will Gamewell, his father's brother's son, who lived at Gamewell Lodge, hard by Nottingham town ; the other was Marian Fitzwalter, only child of the Earl of Huntingdon. The castle of Huntingdon could be seen from the top of one of the tall trees in Sherwood, and on more than one bright day Rob's white

18

*muscle

How Robin Hood Became an Outlaw

signal from this tree told Marian that he awaited her there; for you must know that Rob did not visit her at the castle. His father and her father were enemies. Some people whispered that Hugh Fitzooth was the rightful Earl of Huntingdon, but that he had been defrauded of his lands by Fitzwalter, who had won the King's favour by a Crusade to the Holy Land. But little cared Rob or Marian for this enmity, however it had arisen. They knew that the great greenwood was open to them, and that the wide, wide world was full of the scent of flowers and the song of birds.

Days of youth speed all too swiftly, and troubled skies come all too soon. Rob's father had two other enemies besides Fitzwalter in the persons of the lean Sheriff of Nottingham and the fat Bishop of Hereford. These three enemies one day got possession of the King's ear, and whispered therein to such good—or evil—purpose that Hugh Fitzooth was removed from his post of King's Forester. He and his wife and Rob, then a youth of nineteen, were descended upon during a cold winter's evening, and dispossessed without warning. The Sheriff arrested the Forester for treason—of which, poor man, he was as guiltless as you or I—and carried him to Nottingham jail. Rob and his mother were sheltered overnight in the jail also, but next morning were roughly bade to go about their business. Thereupon they turned for succour to their only kinsman, Squire George of Gamewell, who sheltered them in all kindness.

But the shock and the winter night's journey proved too

much for Dame Fitzooth. She had not been strong for some time before leaving the forest. In less than two months she was no more. Rob felt as though his heart were broken at this loss. But scarcely had the first spring flowers begun to blossom upon her grave when he met another crushing blow in the loss of his father. That stern man had died in prison before his accusers could agree upon the charges on which he was to be brought to trial.

Two years passed by. Rob's cousin Will was away at school ; and Marian's father, who had learned of her friendship with Rob, had sent his daughter to the Court of Queen Eleanor. So these years were lonely ones to the orphaned lad. The bluff old Squire was kind to him, but secretly could make nothing of one who went about brooding and as though seeking for something he had lost. The truth is that Rob missed his old life in the forest no less than his mother's gentleness and his father's companionship. Every time he twanged the string of the long bow against his shoulder and heard the grey goose shaft sing it told him of happy days that he could not recall.

One morning as Rob came in to breakfast his uncle greeted him with : " I have news for you, Rob, my lad ! " and the hearty old Squire finished his draught of ale, and set his pewter tankard down with a crash.

" What may that be, Uncle Gamewell ? " asked the young man.

" Here is a chance to exercise your good long bow and win

How Robin Hood Became an Outlaw

a pretty prize. The Fair is on at Nottingham, and the Sheriff proclaims an archers' tournament. The best fellows are to have places with the King's Foresters, and the one who shoots straightest of all will win for prize a golden arrow—a useless bauble enough, but just the thing for your lady love, eh, Rob, my boy?" Here the Squire laughed, and whacked the table again with his tankard.

Rob's eyes sparkled. " 'Twere indeed worth shooting for, uncle mine," he said. " I should dearly love to let arrow fly alongside another man. And a place among the Foresters is what I have long desired. Will you let me try?"

" To be sure," rejoined his uncle. " Well I know that your good mother would have had me make a clerk of you; but well I see that the greenwood is where you will pass your days, so here's luck to you in the bout!" And the huge tankard came a third time into play.

The young man thanked his uncle for his good wishes, and set about making preparations for the journey. He travelled lightly; but his yew bow must needs have a new string, and his cloth-yard arrows must be of the straightest and soundest.

One fine morning, a few days after, Rob might have been seen passing by way of Lockesley through Sherwood Forest to Nottingham town. In his hand he gripped his trusty staff, and over his shoulder carried his bow of yew, whilst at his side swung a quiver full of arrows. He was a stalwart young man and clad from top to toe in cloth of Lincoln green. Briskly walked he and gaily, for his hopes were high, and never an enemy had he in the wide world. But 'twas the very last morning in all his life when he was to lack an enemy, for as he went his way through Sherwood, whistling a blithe tune, he came suddenly upon a group of Foresters making merry beneath the spreading branches of an oak-tree. They had a huge meat pie before them, and were washing down prodigious slices of it with nut-brown ale.

One glance at the leader, and Rob knew at once that he had found an enemy. 'Twas the man who had usurped his father's place as Head Forester, and who had roughly turned his mother out in the snow. But never a word said he for good or bad, and would have passed on his way, had not this man, clearing his throat with a huge gulp, bellowed out : " By my troth, here is a pretty little archer! Where go you, my lad, with that tupenny bow and toy arrows ? Belike he would shoot at Nottingham Fair ! Ho ! ho ! "

A roar of laughter greeted this sally. Rob flushed, for he was mightily proud of his shooting.

" My bow is as good as yours," he retorted, " and my shafts will carry as straight and as far, so I'll not take lessons of any of ye ! "

They laughed again loudly at this, and the leader said, with a frown :

" Show us some of your skill, and if you can hit the mark here's twenty silver pennies for you, but if you hit it not you are in for a sound drubbing for your pertness."

How Robin Hood Became an Outlaw

" Pick your own target," quoth Rob in a fine rage. " I'll lay my head against that purse that I can hit it."

" It shall be as you say," retorted the Forester angrily ; " your head for your sauciness that you hit not my target."

Now, at a little rise in the wood a herd of deer came grazing by, distant full fivescore yards. They were King's deer, but at that distance seemed safe from any harm. The Head Forester pointed to them.

" If your young arm could speed a shaft for half that distance I'd shoot with you."

" Done ! " cried Rob. " My head against twenty pennies I'll cause yon fine fellow in the lead of them to breathe his last."

And without more ado he tried the string of his long bow, placed a shaft thereon, and drew it to his ear. A moment, and the quivering string sang death as the shaft whistled across the glade. Another moment, and the leader of the herd leaped high in his tracks, and fell prone, dyeing the sward with his heart's blood.

A murmur of amazement swept through the Foresters, and then a growl of rage ; he who had wagered was angriest of all.

" Know you what you have done, rash youth ? " he said. " You have killed the King's deer, and by the laws of King Harry your head remains forfeit. Talk not to me of pennies but get ye gone straight, and let me not look upon your face again."

Rob's blood boiled within him, and he uttered a rash speech.

Robin Hood & His Merry Outlaws

" I have looked upon your face once too often already, my fine Forester ; 'tis you who wear my father's shoes."

And with this he turned upon his heel, and strode away.

The Forester heard his parting thrust with an oath. Red with rage he seized his bow, strung an arrow, and without warning launched it full at Rob. Well was it for the latter that the Forester's foot turned on a twig at the critical instant, for as it was the arrow whizzed by his ear so close as to take a stray strand of his hair with it.

His pent-up passion could be restrained no longer. Rob turned upon his assailant, now twoscore yards away.

" Ha ! " said he, " you shoot not so straight as I, for all your bravado ; take this from the tupenny bow ! "

Straight flew his answering shaft. The Head Forester gave one cry, then fell face downward, and lay still. With angry shouts, the Foresters crowded rounded their chief, only to find he was past all aid. His life had avenged Rob's father, but the son was outlawed. Forward he ran through the forest, before the band could gather their scattered wits—still forward into the great greenwood ; the swaying trees seemed to open their arms to the wanderer, and to welcome him home.

Toward the close of that same day, Rob paused, hungry and weary, at the cottage of a poor widow who dwelt upon the outskirts of the forest. Now this widow had often greeted him kindly in his boyhood days, giving him to eat and drink, so he boldly entered her door. The old dame was right glad to see

How Robin Hood Became an Outlaw

him, and baked him cakes in the ashes, and had him rest and tell her his story. Then she shook her head.

" 'Tis an evil wind that blows through Sherwood," she said. " The poor are despoiled, and the rich ride over their bodies. My three sons have been outlawed for shooting King's deer to keep us from starving, and now hide in the wood, and they tell me that twoscore of as good men as ever drew bow are in hiding with them."

" Where are they, good mother ? " cried Rob. " By my faith, I will join them ! "

" Nay, nay," replied the old woman at first. But when she saw that there was no other way, she said : " My sons will visit me to-night ; stay you here, and see them if you must."

So Rob stayed willingly to see the widow's sons that night, for they were men after his own heart. And when they found that his mood was with them they made him swear an oath of fealty, and told him the haunt of the band—a place he knew right well. Finally, one of them said :

" But the band lacks a leader—one who can use his head as well as his hand—so we have agreed that he who has skill enough to go to Nottingham an outlaw, and win the prize at archery, shall be our chief."

Rob sprang to his feet. " Said in good time," cried he, " for I had started to that self-same Fair, and all the Foresters and all the Sheriff's men in Christendom shall not stand between me and the centre of their target ! "

Robin Hood & His Merry Outlaws

And though he was but barely grown he stood so straight and his eye flashed with such fire that the three brothers seized his hand, and shouted :

" A Lockesley ! a Lockesley ! If you win the golden arrow you shall be chief of outlaws in Sherwood Forest ! "

So Rob fell to planning how he could best disguise himself to go to Nottingham town, for he knew that the Foresters would even then have set a price on his head in the market-place.

Arriving at the crowded scene of the contest, Rob made his way to the great market-place. Hearing a trumpet, and seeing people flocking to a space before the old Moot Hall, he arrived just as an officer began to read the following proclamation by the Sheriff of Nottinghamshire :

" One Robert, nephew of Squire Gamewell of Gamewell Hall, having murdered the King's Head Forester, is hereby declared an outlaw. Furthermore, a reward of one hundred pounds will be paid for the capture of the said Robert alive or dead."

The trumpeters sounded a final flourish, the officer and his company departed, and laughter and merriment became general.

Yet the crowds thronging the streets upon that busy Fair day often paused to read the notice and talk together about the death of the Head Forester.

But what with wrestling bouts and bouts with quarter-staves and wandering minstrels there came up so many other things

26

How Robin Hood Became an Outlaw

to talk about that the reward was forgotten for the nonce, and only the Foresters and Sheriff's men watched the gates with diligence, the Sheriff indeed spurring them to effort by offers of largess. His hatred of the father had descended to the son.

The great event of the day came in the afternoon. It was the archers' contest for the golden arrow, and twenty men stepped forth to shoot. Among them was a beggar-man, a sorry-looking fellow, with leggings of different colours, and brown, scratched face and hands. Over a tawny shock of hair he had a hood drawn, much like that of a monk. Slowly he limped to his place in the line, while the mob shouted in derision. But the contest was open to all comers, so no man said him nay.

Side by side with Rob—for it was he—stood a muscular fellow of swarthy visage and with one eye hid by a green bandage. Him also the crowd jeered, but he passed them by with indifference while he tried his bow with practised hand.

A great crowd had assembled in the amphitheatre enclosing the lists. All the gentry and populace of the surrounding country were gathered there in eager expectancy. The central box contained the lean but pompous Sheriff, his bejewelled wife, and their daughter, who, it was openly hinted, was hoping to receive the golden arrow from the victor, and thus be crowned queen of the day.

Next to the Sheriff's box was one occupied by the fat Bishop of Hereford; while on the other side was a box wherein sat a girl whose dark hair, dark eyes, and fair features caused Rob's heart to leap. 'Twas Maid Marian! She had come up for a visit from the Queen's Court at London town, and now sat demurely by her father, the Earl of Huntingdon. If Rob had been grimly resolved to win the arrow before, the sight of her sweet face multiplied his determination a hundredfold. He felt his muscles tightening into bands of steel, tense and true. Yet withal his heart would throb, making him quake in a most unaccountable way.

Then the trumpet sounded, and the crowd became silent while the herald announced the terms of the contest. The lists were open to all comers. The first target was to be placed at thirty ells*distance, and all those who hit its centre were allowed to shoot at the second target, placed ten ells farther off. · The third target was to be removed yet farther, until the winner was proved. The winner was to receive the golden arrow and a place with the King's Foresters. He it was also who crowned the queen of the day.

The trumpet sounded again, and the archers prepared to shoot. Rob looked to his string, while the crowd smiled and whispered at the odd figure he cut, with his varicoloured legs and little cape. But as the first man shot they grew silent.

The target was not so far but that twelve out of the twenty contestants reached its inner circle. Rob shot sixth in the line, and landed fairly, being rewarded by an approving grunt from the man with the green blinder, who shot seventh, and with apparent carelessness, yet true to the bull's-eye.

28

*one ell is equal to 45 inches

How Robin Hood Became an Outlaw

The mob cheered and yelled themselves hoarse at this even marksmanship. The trumpet sounded again, and a new target was set up at forty ells.

The first three archers again struck true, amid the loud applause of the onlookers, for they were general favourites, and expected to win. Indeed 'twas whispered that each was backed by one of the three dignitaries of the day. The fourth and fifth archers barely grazed the centre. Rob fitted his arrow quietly, and with some confidence sped it unerringly toward the shining circle.

"The beggar! the beggar!" yelled the crowd. "Another bull for the beggar!"

In truth his shaft was nearer the centre than any of the others. But it was not so near that "Blinder," as the mob had promptly christened his neighbour, did not place his shaft just within the mark. Again the crowd cheered wildly. Such shooting as this was not seen every day in Nottingham town.

The other archers in this round were disconcerted by the preceding shots or unable to keep the pace. They missed one after another, and dropped moodily back, while the trumpet sounded for the third round, and the target was set up fifty ells distant.

"By my halidom* you draw a good bow, young master," said Rob's queer comrade to him in the interval allowed for rest. "Do you wish me to shoot first on this trial?"

"Nay," said Rob; "but you are a good fellow by this token, and if I win not I hope you may keep the prize from yon strutters."

29

*By what I hold sacred

Robin Hood & His Merry Outlaws

And he nodded scornfully to the three other archers, who were surrounded by their admirers, and were being made much of by retainers of the Sheriff, the Bishop, and the Earl. From them his eye wandered toward Maid Marian's booth. She had been watching him, it seemed, for their eyes met ; then hers were hastily averted.

" Blinder's " quick eye followed those of Rob. " A fair maid, that," he said smilingly, " and one more worthy the golden arrow than the Sheriff's haughty miss."

Rob looked at him swiftly, and saw naught but kindliness in his glance.

" You are a shrewd fellow, and I like you well," was his only comment.

Now the archers prepared to shoot again, each with some little care. The target seemed hardly larger than the inner ring had looked at the first trial. The first three sped their shafts, and while they were fair shots they did not more than graze the inner circle.

Rob took his stand with some misgiving. Some flecking clouds overhead made the light uncertain, and a handful of wind frolicked across the range in a way quite disturbing to a bowman's nerves. His eyes wandered for a brief moment to the box wherein sat the dark-eyed girl. His heart leaped ! She met his glance and smiled at him reassuringly. And in that moment he felt that she knew him despite his disguise and looked to him to keep the honour of old Sherwood. He drew his bow firmly,

How Robin Hood Became an Outlaw

and, taking advantage of a momentary lull in the breeze, launched the arrow straight and true—singing across the range to the centre of the target.

" The beggar ! the beggar ! A bull ! a bull ! " yelled the fickle mob, who from jeering him were now his warm friends. " Can you beat that, Blinder ? "

The last archer smiled scornfully, and made ready. He drew his bow with ease and grace, and, without seeming to study the course, released the winged arrow. Forward it leaped toward the target, and all eyes followed its flight. A loud uproar broke forth when it alighted, just without the centre, and grazing the shaft sent by Rob. The stranger made a gesture of surprise when his own eyes announced the result to him, but saw his error. He had not allowed for the fickle gust of wind, which seized the arrow, and carried it to one side. But for all that he was the first to congratulate the victor.

" I hope we may shoot again," quoth he. " In truth I care not for the golden bauble, and wished to win it in despite of the Sheriff, for whom I have no love. Now crown the lady of your choice." And, turning suddenly, he was lost in the crowd before Rob could utter what it was upon his lips to say—that he would shoot again with him.

And now the herald summoned Rob to the Sheriff's box to receive the prize.

" You are a curious fellow enough," said the Sheriff, biting his lip coldly, " yet you shoot well. What name go you by ? "

Robin Hood & His Merry Outlaws

Marian sat near, and was listening intently.

" I am called Rob the Stroller, my lord Sheriff," said the archer.

Marian leaned back and smiled.

" Well, Rob the Stroller, with a little attention to your skin and clothes you would not be so bad a man," said the Sheriff. " How like you the idea of entering my service ? "

" Rob the Stroller has ever been a free man, my lord, and desires no service."

The Sheriff's brow darkened, yet for the sake of his daughter and the golden arrow he dissembled.

" Rob the Stroller," said he, " here is the golden arrow which has been offered to the best of archers this day. You are awarded the prize ; see that you bestow it worthily."

At this point the herald nudged Rob, and half inclined his head toward the Sheriff's daughter, who sat with a thin smile upon her lips. But Rob heeded him not ; he took the arrow, and strode to the next box, where sat Maid Marian.

" Lady," he said, " pray accept this little pledge from a poor stroller who would devote the best shafts in his quiver to serve you."

" My thanks to you, Rob in the Hood," replied she, with a roguish twinkle in her eye ; and she placed the gleaming arrow in her hair, while the people shouted : " The Queen ! the Queen ! "

The Sheriff glowered furiously upon this ragged archer

How Robin Hood Became an Outlaw

who had refused his service, taken his prize without a word of thanks, and snubbed his daughter. He would have spoken, but his proud daughter restrained him. He called to his guard, and bade them watch the beggar. But Rob had already turned swiftly, lost himself in the throng, and headed straight for the town gate.

That same evening within a forest glade a group of men— some twoscore, clad in Lincoln green—sat round a fire roasting venison and making merry. Suddenly a twig crackled, and they sprang to their feet, and seized their weapons.

" I look for the widow's sons," a clear voice said, " and I come alone."

Instantly the three men stepped forward.

" 'Tis Rob ! " they cried. " Welcome to Sherwood Forest, Rob ! " And all the men came and greeted him, for they had heard his story.

Then one of the widow's sons, Stout Will, stepped forth, and said :

" Comrades all, ye know that our band has sadly lacked a leader—one of birth, breeding, and skill. Belike we have found that leader in this young man. And I and my brothers have told him that you would choose that one who would bring the Sheriff to shame this day and capture his golden arrow. Is it not so ? "

The band assented, and Will turned to Rob. " What news bring you from Nottingham town ? " asked he.

Robin Hood & His Merry Outlaws

Rob laughed. " In truth I brought the Sheriff to shame for mine own pleasure, and won his golden arrow to boot. But as to the prize, ye must e'en take my word, for I bestowed it upon a maid."

And seeing the men stood in doubt at this, he continued : " But I'll gladly join your band, an you take me, as a common archer. For there are others older and mayhap more skilled than I."

Then stepped one forward from the rest, a tall swarthy man, and Rob recognized him as the man with the green blinder ; only this was now removed, and his freed eye gleamed as stoutly as the other one.

" Rob in the Hood—for such the lady called you," said he, " I can vouch for your tale. You shamed the Sheriff e'en as I had hoped to do ; and we can forgo the golden arrow since it is in such fair hands. As to your shooting and mine, we must let future days decide. But here I, Will Stutely, declare that I will serve none other chief save only you."

Then good Will Stutely told the outlaws of Rob's deeds, and gave him his hand of fealty. And the widow's sons did likewise, and the other members, every one, right gladly, because Will Stutely had heretofore been the truest bow in all the company. And they toasted him in nut-brown ale, and hailed him as their leader by the name of Robin Hood. And he accepted that name because Maid Marian had said it.

By the light of the camp-fire the band exchanged signs and

How Robin Hood Became an Outlaw

passwords. They gave Robin Hood a horn, upon which he was to blow to summon them. They swore, also, that while they might take money and goods from the unjust rich, they would aid and befriend the poor and the helpless, and that they would harm no woman, be she maid, wife, or widow. They swore all this with solemn oaths, while they feasted about the ruddy blaze, under the greenwood tree.

And that is how Robin Hood became an outlaw.

CHAPTER II

HOW ROBIN HOOD MET LITTLE JOHN

"O here is my hand," the stranger reply'd,
"I'll serve you with all my whole heart:
My name is John Little, a man of good mettle;
Ne'er doubt me for I'll play my part."

"His name shall be altered," quoth William Stutely,
"And I will his godfather be:
Prepare then a feast, and none of the least,
For we will be merry," quoth he.

ALL that summer Robin Hood and his merry men roamed in Sherwood Forest, and the fame of their deeds ran abroad in the land. The Sheriff of Nottingham waxed wroth at the report, but all his traps and excursions failed to catch the outlaws. The poor people began by fearing them, but when they found that the men in Lincoln green who answered Robin Hood's horn meant them no harm, but despoiled the oppressor to relieve the oppressed, they 'gan to have great liking for them. And the band increased by other stout hearts, till by the end of the summer fourscore good men and true had sworn fealty.

But the days of quiet which came on grew irksome to Robin's adventurous spirit. Up rose he, one gay morn, and slung his quiver over his shoulder.

"This fresh breeze stirs the blood, my lads," quoth he,

Robin Hood · meeteth · the · tall
Stranger · on · the · Bridge

CHAPTER II

The Shooting-Match:
Young Robin Goes to

CHAPTER I

How Robin Hood Met Little John

" and I would be seeing what the gay world looks like in the direction of Nottingham town. But tarry ye behind in the borders of the forest, within earshot of my bugle call."

Thus saying he strode merrily forward to the edge of the wood, and paused there a moment, his agile form erect, his brown locks flowing, and his brown eyes watching the road ; and a goodly sight he made as the wind blew the ruddy colour into his cheeks.

The highway led clear in the direction of the town, and thither he boldly directed his steps. But at a bend in the road he knew of a by-path leading across a brook, which made the way nearer and less open, into which he turned. As he approached the stream he saw that it had become swollen by recent rains into quite a pretty torrent. The log footbridge was still there, but at this end of it a puddle intervened, which could be crossed only with a leap if you would not get your feet wet.

But Robin cared little for such a handicap. Taking a running start his nimble legs carried him easily over, and balanced neatly upon the end of the broad log. But he was no sooner started across than he saw a huge ungainly giant, over six feet in height, approaching from the other side. For a staff he carried a young oak sapling. Robin quickened his pace, and the stranger did likewise, each thinking to cross first. Midway they met, and neither would yield an inch.

" Give way, fellow ! " roared Robin, whose leadership of a band, I am afraid, had not tended to mend his manners.

The stranger smiled. He was almost a head taller than the other.

" Nay," he retorted, " fair and softly ! I give way only to a better man than myself."

" Give way, I say," retorted Robin hotly, " or I shall have to show you a better man. Give way, or I'll pitch you into the stream, big as you are."

His opponent budged not an inch.

" Ho ! ho ! " he laughed good-naturedly. " Now by my halidom ! I would not move after hearing that speech, even if minded to it before ; for this better man I have sought my life long. Therefore show him to me, an it please you."

" That will I right soon," quoth Robin. " Stay you here a little while, thou huge oaf, till I cut me a cudgel like unto that you have been twiddling in your fingers." So saying he sought his own bank again with a leap, laid aside his long bow and arrows, and cut him a stout staff of oak, straight, knotless, and a good six feet in length. But still it was a full foot shorter than his opponent's. Then back came he boldly.

" I mind not telling you, fellow," said he, " that a bout with archery would have been an easier way with me. But there are other tunes in England besides that the arrow sings." Here he whirred the staff about his head by way of practice. " So

How Robin Hood Met Little John

make you ready for the tune I am about to play upon your ribs. Have at you!   One, two —— "

" Three! " roared the giant, smiting at him instantly.

Well was it for Robin that he was quick and nimble of foot, for the blow that grazed a hair's-breadth from his shoulder would have felled an ox.   Nevertheless, while swerving to avoid this stroke, Robin was poising for his own, and back came he forthwith—whack!

Whack! parried the other.

Whack! whack! whack! whack!

The fight waxed fast and furious.   It was strength pitted against subtlety, and the match was a merry one.   Hard blows were exchanged, and a stifled exclamation from one or the other, a grunt or a sharp cry of pain only sent the staves swinging swifter than before.   The mighty blows of the stranger went whistling around Robin's ducking head, while his own swift undercuts were fain to give the other an attack of indigestion. Yet each stood firmly in his place, not moving backward or forward a foot for a good half-hour, nor thinking of crying " Enough! " though some chance blow seemed likely to knock one or the other off the narrow footbridge.   The giant, who dearly loved a tussle of this kind, still smiled happily, and Robin smiled also, for a fight was meat and drink to him.   But at length the giant's face began to get red, and his breath came snorting forth like a bull's.   He stepped forward with a furious onslaught to finish this audacious fellow.   Robin dodged his blows lightly, then sprang in swiftly and unexpectedly, and dealt the stranger such a blow upon the short ribs that you would have sworn the tanner was trimming down his hides for market.

The stranger reeled, and came within an ace of falling, but regained his footing right quickly.

"By my life, you can hit hard ! " he gasped forth, giving back a blow almost while he was yet staggering.

The blow was a lucky one. It caught Robin off his guard. His stick had rested a moment while he looked to see the giant topple into the water, when down came the other upon his head, whack ! Robin saw more stars in that one moment than all the astronomers have since discovered, and forthwith he dropped neatly into the stream.

The cool, rushing current quickly brought him to his senses ; howbeit he was still so dazed that he groped blindly for the swaying reeds to pull himself up on the bank. His assailant could not forbear laughing heartily at his plight, but was also quick to lend his aid.

" Ho ! my fine friend," panted the giant as he rubbed his aching ribs, " where are you now ? Let me fish you out ! "

He thrust down his long staff to Robin, saying : " Lay hold of that, an your fists whirl not so much as your head ! "

Robin laid hold, and was hauled to dry land for all the world like a fish, except that the fish would never have come

How Robin Hood Met Little John

forth so wet and dripping. He lay upon the warm bank for a space to regain his senses; then he sat up, and gravely rubbed his pate.

"By all the saints!" said he, "you hit full stoutly; my head hums like a hive of bees on a summer morning."

Then he seized his horn, which lay near, and blew thereon three shrill notes that echoed against the trees. A moment of silence ensued, and then was heard the rustling of leaves and crackling of twigs like the coming of many men, and forth from the glade burst a score or two of stalwart yeomen, all clad in Lincoln green, like Robin, with good Will Stutely and the widow's three sons at their head.

"Good master," cried Will Stutely, "how is this? In sooth there is not a dry thread on your body."

"Why, marry," replied Robin, "this fellow would not let me pass the footbridge, and when I tickled him in the ribs he must needs answer by a pat on the head which landed me overboard."

"Then shall he taste some of his own porridge," quoth Will. "Seize him, lads!"

They laid firm and not too gentle hands upon the giant, and proceeded to take their own revenge. Holding him so tight that he could not move a limb, the party carried him to the edge of the water and with a "One, two, three," and a mighty swing, they hove him right into mid-stream, where he disappeared from view. Quickly Robin jumped upon the bridge and in mockingly smooth tones inquired : " Prithee, my fine comrade, and where are *you* now ? "

A vigorous splashing was the only answer, and in a trice the giant set foot upon ground and had Will Stutely bowled over before that astonished youth could lift his arm. Three others were treated in the same manner, and then the remaining archers flung themselves on him in a body and dragged him down. Yet still he breathed defiance, and offered to fight them all, three at a time.

" No more ! " cried Robin. " You are the likeliest man that ever I have met, and we'll fight no more."

" I am content," said the other, " for verily you now have the best end of the cudgel. Wherefore, I like you well, and would fain know your name."

" Why," said Robin, " my men, and even the Sheriff of Nottingham, know me as Robin Hood, the outlaw."

" Then am I right sorry that I beat you," exclaimed the man, " for I was on my way to seek you, and to try to join your merry company. But after my unmannerly use of the cudgel I fear we are still strangers."

" Nay, never say it ! " cried Robin. " I am glad you fell in with me ; though, sooth to say, I did all the falling ! "

And amid a general laugh the two men clasped hands, and in that clasp the strong friendship of a lifetime was begun.

" But you have not yet told us your name," said Robin, bethinking himself.

How Robin Hood Met Little John

" Whence I came, men call me John Little."

" Enter our company, then, John Little ; enter, and welcome. The rites are few, the fee is large. We ask your whole mind and body and heart even unto death."

" I give the bond, upon my life," said the tall man.

Thereupon Will Stutely, who loved a good jest, spoke up, and said : " The infant in our household must be christened, and I'll stand godfather. This fair little stranger is so small of bone and sinew that his old name is not to the purpose." Here he paused long enough to fill a horn in the stream. " Hark ye, my son "—standing on tiptoe to splash the water on the giant— " take your new name on entering the forest. I christen you Little John."

At this jest the men roared long and loud.

" Give him a bow, and find a full sheath of arrows for Little John," said Robin joyfully. " Can you shoot as well as fence with the staff, my friend ? "

" I have hit an ash twig at forty yards," said Little John.

Thus chatting pleasantly the band turned back into the woodland, and sought their secluded dell, where the trees were the thickest, the moss was the softest, and a secret path led to a cave, at once a retreat and a stronghold. Here under a mighty oak they found the rest of the band, some of whom had come in with a brace of fat does. And here they built a ruddy fire, and sat down to the meat and ale, Robin Hood in the centre, with

Robin Hood & His Merry Outlaws

Will Stutely on the one hand and Little John on the other. And Robin was right well pleased with the day's adventure, even though he had got a drubbing ; for sore ribs and heads will heal, and 'tis not every day that one can find a recruit as stout of bone and true of soul as Little John.

CHAPTER III

HOW ROBIN HOOD TURNED BUTCHER AND ENTERED THE SHERIFF'S SERVICE

The butcher he answered jolly Robin,
" No matter where I do dwell,
For a butcher am I, and to Nottingham
Am I going, my flesh to sell."

THE next morning the weather had turned ill, and Robin Hood's band stayed close to their dry and friendly cave. The third day brought a diversion in the shape of a trap by a roving party of the Sheriff's men. A fine stag had been struck down by one of Will Stutely's fellows, and he and others had stepped forth from the covert to seize it, when twenty bowmen from Nottingham appeared at the end of the glade. Down dropped Will's men on all fours, barely in time to hear a shower of arrows whistle above their heads. Then from behind the friendly trees they sent back such a welcome that the Sheriff's men deemed it prudent not to tarry in their steps. Two of them, in sooth, bore back unpleasant wounds in their shoulders from the encounter.

When they returned to town the Sheriff waxed red with rage.

" What," he gasped, " do my men fear to fight this Robin Hood face to face ? Would that *I* could get him within my reach once. We should see then ; we should see ! "

Robin Hood & His Merry Outlaws

What it was the Sheriff would see he did not state. But he was to have his wish granted in short space, and you and I will see how he profited by it.

The fourth day and the one following this friendly bout Little John was missing. One of his men said that he saw him talking with a beggar, but did not know whither they had gone. Two more days passed. Robin grew uneasy. He did not doubt the faith of Little John, but he was fearful lest a roving band of Foresters had captured him.

At last Robin could not remain quiet. Up sprang he, with bow and arrows, and a short sword at his side.

" I must away to Nottingham town, my men," he cried. " The goodly Sheriff has long desired to see me ; and mayhap he can tell me tidings of the best quarter-staff in the shire "— meaning Little John.

Others of the band besought him to let them go with him, but he would not.

" Nay," he said smilingly ; " the Sheriff and I are too good friends to put doubt upon our meeting. But tarry ye in the edge of the wood opposite the west gate of the town, and ye may be of service ere to-morrow night."

So saying he strode forward to the road leading to Nottingham, and stood as before, looking up and down to see if the way were clear. Back at a bend in the road he heard a rumbling and a lumbering, when up drove a stout butcher, whistling gaily, and driving a mare that sped slowly

How Robin Turned Butcher

enough because of the weight of meat with which the cart was loaded.

" A good morrow to you, friend," hailed Robin. " Whence come you and where go you with your load of meat ? "

" A good morrow to you," returned the butcher civilly enough. " No matter where I dwell ; I am but a simple butcher, and to Nottingham am I going, my flesh to sell. 'Tis Fair week, and my beef and mutton would fetch a fair penny," and he laughed loudly at his jest. " But whence come you ? "

" A yeoman am I, from Lockesley town ; men call me Robin Hood."

" The saints forfend that you should treat me ill ! " said the butcher in terror. " Oft have I heard of you, and how you lighten the purses of the fat priests and knights. But I am naught but a poor butcher, selling this load of meat, perchance, for enough to pay my quarter's rent."

" Rest you, my friend, rest you," quoth Robin ; " not so much as a silver penny would I take from you, for I love an honest Saxon face and a fair name with my neighbours. But I would strike a bargain with you."

Here he took from his girdle a well-filled purse, and continued : " I would fain be a butcher this day, and sell meat at Nottingham town. Could you sell me your meat, your cart, your mare, and your good-will, without loss, for five marks ? "

" Heaven bless ye, good Robin," cried the butcher right joyfully ; " that can I ! " And he leaped down forthwith from the cart, and handed Robin the reins in exchange for the purse.

"One moment more," laughed Robin; "we must e'en change garments for the nonce. Take mine, and scurry home quickly, lest the King's Foresters try to put a hole through this Lincoln green."

So saying he donned the butcher's blouse and apron, and, climbing into the cart, drove merrily down the road to the town.

When he came to Nottingham he greeted the scowling gate-keeper blithely, and proceeded to the market-place. Boldly he lead his shuffling horse to the place where the butchers had their stalls. He had no notion of the price to ask for his meat, but put on a foolish and simple air as he called aloud his wares:

> "Hark ye, lasses and dames, hark ye,
> Good meat come buy, come buy;
> Three pen'orths go for one penny,
> And a kiss is good, say I!"

Now, when the folk found what a simple butcher he was they crowded round his cart, for he really did sell three times as much for one penny as was sold by the other butchers. And one or two serving-lasses with twinkling eyes liked his comely face so well that they willingly gave boot of a kiss.

But the other butchers were wroth when they found how he was taking their trade, and they accordingly put their heads together.

How Robin Turned Butcher

One said : " He is a prodigal, and has sold his father's land, and this is his first venture in trading."

Another said : " He is a thief who has murdered a butcher, and stolen his horse and meat."

Robin heard these sayings, but only laughed merrily and sang his song the louder. His good-humour made the people laugh also and crowd round his cart closely, shouting uproariously when some buxom lass submitted to be kissed.

Then the butchers saw that they must meet craft with craft, and they said to him : " Come, brother butcher, if you would sell meat with us you must e'en join our guild and stand by the rules of our trade."

" We dine at the Sheriff's mansion to-day," said another, " and you must make one of our party."

> " Accurst of his heart," said jolly Robin,
> " That a butcher will deny.
> I'll go with you, my brethren true,
> And as fast as I can hie."

Whereupon, having sold all his meat, he left his horse and cart in charge of a friendly hostler, and prepared to follow his mates to the Mansion House.

It was the Sheriff's custom to dine various guilds of the trade from time to time on Fair days, for he got a pretty profit out of the fees they paid him for the right to trade in the market-place. The Sheriff was already come with great pomp into the banqueting-room when Robin Hood and three or four butchers entered, and he greeted them all with great condescension, and presently the whole of a large company was seated at a table groaning beneath the good cheer of the feast.

Now, the Sheriff bade Robin sit by his right hand at the head of the board, for one or two butchers had whispered to the official : " That fellow is a right mad blade, who yet made us much sport to-day. He sold more meat for one penny than we could sell for three, and he gave extra weight to whatsoever lass would buss him." And others said : " He is some prodigal who knows not the value of goods, and may be plucked by a shrewd man right closely."

The Sheriff was willing to pluck a prodigal with the next man, and he was, moreover, glad to have a guest who promised to enliven the feast. So, as I have told you, he placed Robin by his side, and he made much of him, and laughed boisterously at his jests ; though, sooth to say, the laugh was come by easily, for Robin had never been in merrier mood, and his quips and jests soon put the whole table in a roar.

Then my lord Bishop of Hereford came in, last of all, to say a ponderous grace, and take his seat on the other side of the Sheriff—the prelate's fat body showing up in goodly contrast to the other's lean bones.

After grace was said, and while the servants clattered in with meat-platters, Robin stood up, and said :

" An amen say I to my lord Bishop's thanks ! How, now, my fine fellows, be merry, and drink deep, for the shot I'll pay

How Robin Turned Butcher

ere I go my way, though it cost me five pounds and more. So, my lords and gentlemen all, spare not the wine, but fall to lustily."

" Hear ! hear ! " shouted the butchers.

" Now are you a right jolly soul," quoth the Sheriff ; " but this feast is mine own. Howbeit, you must have many a head of horned beasts, and many an acre of broad land, to spend from your purse so freely."

" Ay, that have I," returned Robin, his eyes all a-twinkle ; " five hundred horned beasts have I and my brothers, and none of them have we been able to sell. That is why I have turned butcher. But I know not the trade, and would gladly sell the whole herd, an I could find a buyer."

At this the Sheriff's greed 'gan to rise. Since this fool *would* be plucked, thought he, why should not he do the plucking ?

" Five hundred beasts, say you ? " he queried sharply.

" Five hundred and ten fat beasts by actual count that I would sell for a just figure. Ay, to him who will pay me in right money would I sell them for twenty pieces of gold. Is that too much to ask, lording ? "

Was there ever such an idiot butcher ? thought the Sheriff ; and he so far forgot his dignity as to nudge the Bishop in his fat ribs.

" Nay, good fellow," quoth he, chuckling, " I am always ready to help any in my shire. An you cannot find a buyer for your herd at this just figure, I well e'en buy them myself."

At this generosity Robin was quite overcome, and fell to

praising the Sheriff to the skies, and telling him that he should not have cause to forget the kindness.

" Tut, tut," said the Sheriff, " 'tis naught but a trade. Drive in your herd to-morrow to the market-place, and you shall have money down."

" Nay, excellence," said Robin, " that can I not easily do, for they are grazing in scattered fashion. But they are over near Gamewell, not more than a mile therefrom at most. Will you not come and choose your own beasts to-morrow ? "

" Ay, that I will," said the Sheriff, his greediness casting caution to the winds. " Tarry with me over-night, and I will go with you in the morning."

This was a poser for Robin, since he liked not the idea of staying over-night at the Sheriff's house. He had hoped to appoint a meeting-place for the other, but now saw that this might excite doubt. He looked round at the company. By this time, you must know, the feast had progressed far, and the butchers were deep in their cups. The Sheriff and Robin had talked in a low voice, and my lord Bishop was almost asleep.

" Agreed," said Robin presently, and the words were no sooner out of his mouth than the door opened, and a serving-man entered bearing a tray of mulled wine. At sight of the fellow's face Robin gave an involuntary start of surprise, which was instantly checked. The other also saw him, stood still a moment, and, as if forgetting something, turned about, and left the hall.

It was Little John.

How Robin Turned Butcher

A dozen questions flashed across Robin's mind, and he could find answer for none of them. What was Little John doing in the Sheriff's house? Why had he not told the band? Was he true to them? Would he betray him?

But these questions of distrust were dismissed from Robin's open mind as soon as they had entered. He knew that Little John was faithful and true.

He recovered his spirits, and began again upon a vein of foolish banter, for the amusement of the Sheriff and his guests, all being now merry with wine.

" A song ! " one of them shouted, and the cry was taken up round the table. Robin mounted his chair, and trolled forth :

> " A lass and a butcher of Nottingham
> Agreed 'twixt them for to wed :
> Says he, ' I'll give ye the meat, fair dame,
> And ye will give me the bread.' "

Then they joined in the chorus amid a pounding of cups upon the board :

> " With a hey and a ho
> And a hey nonny no,
> A butcher of Nottingham ! "

While the song was at its height Little John reappeared with other servants, and refilled the cups. He came up to Robin, and, as if asking him if he would have more wine, said softly : " Meet me in the pantry to-night."

Robin nodded, and sang loudly. The day was already far spent, and presently the company broke up, with many

Robin Hood & His Merry Outlaws

hiccupy bows to the Sheriff and little notice of the drowsy Bishop.

When the company was dispersed, the Sheriff bade a servant show Robin to his room, and promised to see him at breakfast the next day.

Robin kept his word, and met Little John that night and the Sheriff next day ; but Little John has been doing so much in the meantime that he must be allowed a chapter to himself.

So let us turn to another story that was sung of in the ballads of olden time, and find out how Little John entered the Sheriff's service.

CHAPTER IV

HOW LITTLE JOHN ENTERED THE SHERIFF'S SERVICE

List and hearken, gentlemen,
All ye that now be here,
Of Little John, that was Knight's-man,
Good mirth ye now shall hear.

I T had come round to another Fair day at Nottingham town, and folk crowded there by all the gates. Goods of many kinds were displayed in gaily coloured booths, and at every cross-street a free show was in progress. Here and there, stages had been erected for the play at quarter-staff, a highly popular sport.

There was a fellow, one Eric of Lincoln, who was thought to be the finest man with the staff for miles around. His feats were sung about in ballads through all the shire. A great boaster was he withal, and to-day he strutted about on one of these corner stages, and vaunted of his prowess, and offered to crack any man's crown for a shilling. Several had tried their skill with Eric, but he had soon sent them spinning in no gentle manner, amid the jeers and laughter of the onlookers.

A beggar-man sat over against Eric's stage, and grinned every time a pate was cracked. He was an uncouth fellow, ragged and dirty and unshaven. Eric caught sight of his leering face at one of his boasts—for there was a lull in the game, because no man else wanted to come within reach of Eric's blows. Eric, I say, noticed the beggar-man grinning at him rather impudently, and turned toward him sharply.

" How now, you dirty villain ! " quoth he. " Mend your manners to your betters, or, by our Lady, I'll dust your rags for you ! "

The beggar-man still grinned. " I am but a poor beggar, yet I am always ready to mend my manners to my *betters*," said he, " but I am afraid *you* cannot teach me any better than you can dust my jacket."

" Come up ! Come up ! " roared the other, flourishing his staff.

" That will I," said the beggar, getting up slowly and with difficulty. " It will pleasure me hugely to take a braggart down a notch, an some good man will lend me a stout quarter-staff."

At this a score of idlers reached him their staves—being ready enough to see another man have his head cracked, even if they wished to save their own—and he took the stoutest and heaviest of all. He made a sorry enough figure as he climbed awkwardly upon the stage, but when he had gained it he towered full half a head above the other, for all his awkwardness. Nathless, he held his stick so clumsily that the crowd laughed in great glee.

" Strike a blow for Nottingham, lad ! " shouted many voices.

Then each man took his place, and looked the other up and

How Little John Entered Service

down, watching warily for an opening. Only a moment stood they thus, for Eric, intent on teaching this rash beggar a lesson and sweeping him speedily off the stage, launched forth boldly, and gave the other a sounding crack on the shoulder. The beggar danced about, and made as though he would drop his staff from very pain, while the crowd roared, and Eric raised himself for another crushing blow. But just then the awkward beggar came to life. Straightening himself like a flash he dealt Eric a back-handed blow, the like of which he had never before felt. Down went the boaster to the floor with a sounding thump, and the fickle people yelled and laughed themselves purple, for it was a new sight to see Eric of Lincoln eating dust.

But he was up again almost as soon as he had fallen, and right quickly retreated to his own ringside to gather his wits and watch for an opening. He saw instantly that he had no easy antagonist, and he came in cautiously this time.

And now those who stood around saw the merriest game of quarter-staff that was ever played inside the walls of Nottingham town. Both men were on their guard, and fenced with fine skill, being well matched in prowess. Again and again did Eric seek to force an opening under the other's guard, and just as often were his blows parried. The beggar stood sturdily in his tracks, contenting himself with beating off the attack. For a long time their blows met like the steady crackling of some huge forest fire, and Eric strove to be wary, for he now knew that the other had no mean wits or mettle. But he grew right mad at last, and began to send down blows so fierce and fast that you would have sworn a great hail-storm was pounding on the roof over your head. Yet he never so much as entered the tall beggar's guard.

Then at last the stranger saw his chance, and changed his tune of fighting. With one upward stroke he sent Eric's staff whirling through the air ; with another he tapped Eric on the head ; and with a third broad swing, ere the other could recover himself, he swept him clear off the stage, much as you would brush a fly off the window-pane.

The champion of Lincoln rolled over and lay very still.

" Go brag in Lincoln of how you met a Nottingham man ! " laughed the victor.

Now the people danced and shouted and made so much ado that the shopkeepers left their stalls, and others came running from every direction. The victory of the queer beggar made him immensely popular. Eric had been a great bully, and many had suffered defeat and insult at his hands. So the ragged stranger found money and food and drink everywhere at his disposal, and he feasted right comfortably till the afternoon.

Then a long-bow contest came on, and to it the beggar went with some of his new friends. It was held in the same arena that Robin had formerly entered ; and again the Sheriff and lords and ladies graced the scene with their presence, while the people crowded to their places.

How Little John Entered Service

When the archers had stepped forward the herald rose, and proclaimed the rules of the game : how that each man should shoot three shots, and to him who shot best the prize of a yoke of fat steers should belong. A dozen keen-eyed bowmen were there, and among them some of the best fellows in the Foresters' and Sheriff's companies. Down at the end of the line towered the tall beggar-man, who must needs twang a bowstring with the best of them.

The Sheriff noted his queer figure, and asked : " Who is that ragged fellow ? "

" 'Tis he that hath but now so soundly cracked the crown of Eric of Lincoln," was the reply.

The shooting presently began, and the targets soon showed a fine reckoning. Last of all came the beggar's turn.

" By your leave," he said loudly, " I'd like it well to shoot with any other man here present at a mark of my own placing." And he strode down the lists with a slender peeled sapling, which he stuck upright in the ground, one hundred yards beyond the target. " There," said he, " is a right good mark, a *man's* mark. Will any man try it ? "

A Forester stepped forward and made careful preparations to shoot first and, taking a long and steady aim, amid a perfect silence, he shot. Instantly tongues wagged, but above all a long and scornful laugh rang out, for the arrow had whistled by the wand and buried itself in earth a few yards behind. The Forester turned aside that none might see his deep annoyance, while the beggar, fitting his arrow with careful preciseness, lightly loosed his shaft.

This time the silence was broken by a ringing cheer, for the wand was split down the centre.

" Long live the beggar ! " yelled the bystanders.

The Sheriff swore a full great oath, and said : " This man is the best archer that ever yet I saw." And he beckoned to him, and asked him : " How now, good fellow, what is your name, and in what country were you born ? "

" In Holderness I was born," the man replied ; " men call me Reynold Greenleaf, and I go wandering round, seeking to improve my fortune."

" You are a sturdy fellow, Reynold Greenleaf, and deserve better apparel than that you wear at present. Will you enter my service ? I will give you twenty marks a year, above your living, and three good suits of clothes."

" Three good suits, say you ? Then right gladly will I enter your service, for my back has been bare this many a long day."

Then Reynold turned him about to the crowd, and shouted : " Hark ye, good people, I have entered the Sheriff's service, and need not the yoke of steers for prize, so take them for your-selves to feast withal."

At this the crowd shouted more merrily than ever, and threw their caps high into the air. And none so popular a man

Little·John·overcomes·Eric· o'·Lincoln

CHAPTER IV

The·Mighty·Fight·betwixt:
Little·John·and·the·Cook:

CHAPTER IV

How Little John Entered Service

had come to Nottingham town in many a long day as this same Reynold Greenleaf.

Now, you may have guessed, by this time, who Reynold Greenleaf really was; so I need hardly tell you that he was none other than Little John. And forth went he to the Sheriff's house, and entered his service. But it was a sorry day for the Sheriff when he got his new man. For Little John winked his shrewd eye and said softly to himself: "By my faith, I shall be the worst servant to him that ever yet had he!"

Two days passed by. Little John, it must be confessed, did not make a good servant. He insisted upon eating the Sheriff's best bread and drinking his best wine, so that the steward waxed wroth. Nathless, not only because of his skill as an archer, but because of his prowess as a wrestler in several notable bouts with some of his own jealous retainers, the Sheriff held him in high esteem, and made great talk of taking him along on the next hunting trip.

It was now the day of the banquet to the butchers, about which we have already heard. The banquet-hall, you must know, was not in the main house, but connected with it by a corridor. All the servants were bustling about making preparations for the feast, save only Little John, who must needs lie abed the greater part of the day. But he presented himself at last, when the dinner was half over; and being desirous of seeing the guests for himself he went into the hall with the other servants to pass the wine. First, however, I am afraid that some of the wine passed his own lips while he went down the corridor.

When he entered the banqueting-hall, whom should he see but Robin Hood himself? We can imagine the start of surprise felt by each of these bold fellows upon seeing the other in such strange company. But they kept their secrets, as we have seen, and arranged to meet each other that same night. Meanwhile, the proud Sheriff little knew that he harboured the two chief outlaws of the whole countryside beneath his roof.

After the feast was over and night was beginning to advance, Little John felt faint of stomach, and remembered him that he had eaten nothing all that day. Back went he to the pantry to see what eatables were laid by. But there, locking up the stores for the night, stood the fat steward.

" Good Sir Steward," said Little John, " give me to dine, for it is long for Greenleaf to be fasting."

The steward looked grimly at him, and rattled the keys at his girdle.

" Sirrah Lie-a-bed," quoth he, " 'tis late in the day to be talking of eating. You lazy villain—no meat till you have worked for it. Since you have waited thus long to be hungry, you can e'en take your appetite back to bed again."

" Now, by mine appetite, that will I not do!" cried Little John. " Your own paunch of fat would be enough for any

How Little John Entered Service

bear to sleep on through the winter. But my stomach craves food, and food it shall have!"

Saying this he brushed past the steward, and tried the door, but it was locked fast; whereat the fat steward chuckled, and jangled his keys again.

Then was Little John right mad, and he brought down his huge fist on the door-panel with a sledge-hammer blow that shivered an opening you could thrust your hand into. Little John stooped, and peered through the hole to see what food lay within reach, when crack went the steward's keys upon his crown, and that worthy danced around him, playing a tattoo that made Little John's ears ring. At this he turned upon the steward and gave him such a rap that his back went nigh in two, and over went the fat fellow rolling on the floor.

"Lie there," quoth Little John, "till ye find strength to go to bed. Meanwhile, I must be about my dinner." And he kicked open the buttery door without ceremony, and brought to light a venison pasty and cold roast pheasant—goodly sights to a hungry man. Placing these down on a convenient shelf, he fell to with right good will, and ate and drank as much as he would.

Now, the Sheriff had in his kitchen a cook, a stout man and bold, who heard the rumpus, and came in to see how the land lay. There sat Little John, eating away for dear life, while the fat steward was rolled under the table like a bundle of rags.

"Oh, ho!" blustered the cook. "What do you here?"

Robin Hood & His Merry Outlaws

" Hast eyes ? " curtly inquired Little John. " I am dining. Wilt join me ? Come ! drink the Sheriff's health in his best red wine ! "

" I make my vow," said the cook, " you are an impudent hind to dwell thus in a household, and ask thus to dine." So saying, he suddenly darted at Little John and crashed a pile of plates upon his head ; but Little John returned the blow with interest. The twain fought with anything that came to hand— plates, dishes, pots, pans—even spoons, till all was confusion. But at length, in a fury, the cook drew a good sword that hung at his side.

" I make my vow," said Little John, " you are a bold man and hardy to come thus between me and my meat. So defend yourself, and see that you prove the better man." And he drew his own sword, and crossed weapons with the cook.

Then back and forth they clashed with sullen sound. The old ballad which tells of their fight says that they thought nothing for to flee, but stiffly for to stand. There they fought sore together, but neither might the other harm for the space of a full hour.

" I make my vow," cried Little John, " you are the best swordsman that ever yet I saw. What say you to resting a space, and eating and drinking good health with me ? Then we may fall to again with the swords."

" Agreed ! " said the cook, who loved good fare as well as a good fight, and they both laid by their swords, and fell

How Little John Entered Service

to the food with hearty will. The venison pasty soon disappeared, and the roast pheasant flew at as lively a rate as ever the bird itself had sped. Then the warriors rested a space, and patted their stomachs, and smiled across at each other like bosom friends ; for a man when he has dined looks out pleasantly upon the world.

" And now, good Reynold Greenleaf," said the cook, " we may as well settle this brave fight we have in hand."

" A true saying," rejoined the other ; " but first tell me, friend—for I protest you are my friend henceforth—what is the score we have to settle ? "

" Naught save who can handle the sword best," said the cook. " By my troth, I had thought to carve you like a capon ere now."

" And I had long since thought to shave your ears," replied Little John. " This bout we can settle in right good time, but just now I and my master have need of you, and you can turn your stout blade to better service than that of the Sheriff."

" Whose service would that be ? " asked the cook.

" Mine," answered the would-be butcher, entering the room, " and I am Robin Hood."

CHAPTER V

HOW THE SHERIFF LOST THREE GOOD SERVANTS
AND FOUND THEM AGAIN

" Make good cheer," said Robin Hood.
" Sheriff ! for charity !
And for the love of Little John
Thy life is granted thee ! "

THE cook gasped in amazement. This Robin Hood, and under the Sheriff's very roof !

" Now, by my troth, you are a brave fellow," he said. " I have heard great tales of your prowess, and the half has not been told. But who might this tall slasher be ? "

" Men do call me Little John, good fellow."

" Then Little John, or Reynold Greenleaf, I like you well, on my honour as Much, the miller's son ; and you too, bold Robin Hood. An you take me, I will enter your service right gladly. Oft have I longed for a change."

" Spoken like a stout man ! " said Robin, seizing him by the hand. " But I must back to my own bed, lest some sleepy warden stumble upon me, and I be forced to run him through. Lucky for you twain that wine flowed so freely in this house to-day, else the noise of your combat would have brought other onlookers besides Robin Hood. Now, if ye would

66

Three Good Servants

flee the house to-night, I will join you in the good greenwood to-morrow."

"But, good master," said the cook, "you would not stay here over-night! Verily, it is running your head into a noose. Come with us. The Sheriff has set strict watch on all the gates, since 'tis Fair week, but I know the warden at the west gate, and could bring us through safely; to-morrow you will be stayed."

"Nay; that will I not," laughed Robin, "for I shall go through with no less escort than the Sheriff himself. Now do you, Little John, and do you, Much, the miller's son, go right speedily. In the borders of the wood you will find my merry men. Tell them to kill two fine harts against to-morrow eve, for we shall have great company and lordly sport."

And Robin left them as suddenly as he had come.

"Comrade," then said Little John, "we may as well bid the Sheriff's roof farewell. But, ere we go, it would seem a true pity to fail to take such of the Sheriff's silver plate as will cause us to remember him, and also grace our special feasts."

"'Tis well said indeed," quoth the cook.

Thereupon they got a great sack, and, with much chuckling, filled it with silver plate from the shelves where it would not at once be missed, and they swung the sack between them, and away they went, out of the house, out of the town, and into the friendly shelter of Sherwood Forest.

Robin Hood & His Merry Outlaws

The next morning the servants were late astir in the Sheriff's house. The steward awoke from a heavy sleep, but his cracked head was still in such a whirl that he could not have sworn whether the Sheriff had ever owned so much as one silver dish, so the theft went undiscovered for the nonce.

Robin Hood met the Sheriff at breakfast, when his host soon spoke of what was uppermost in his heart—the purchase of that fine herd of cattle near Gamewell. 'Twas clear that a vision of them, purchased for twenty paltry gold pieces, had been with him all through the night in his dreams. And Robin again appeared such a silly fellow that the Sheriff saw no need of dissembling, but said that he was ready to start at once to look at the herd.

Accordingly they set forth, Robin in his little butcher's cart, behind the lean mare, and the Sheriff mounted on a horse. Out of Nottingham town, through gates open wide they proceeded, and took the hill road leading through Sherwood Forest. And as they went on, and plunged deeper among the trees, Robin whistled blithely and sang snatches of tunes.

" Why are you so gay, fellow ? " said the Sheriff, for, sooth to say, the silence of the woods was making him uneasy.

" I am whistling to keep my courage up ! " replied Robin.

" What is there to fear when you have the Sheriff of Nottingham beside you ? " quoth the other pompously.

Robin scratched his head.

Three Good Servants

"They do say that Robin Hood and his men care little for the Sheriff," he said.

"Pooh!" said the Sheriff. "I would not give *that* for their lives if I could once lay hands upon them." And he snapped his fingers angrily.

"But Robin Hood himself was on this very road the last time I came to town," said the other.

The Sheriff started at the crackling of a twig under his horse's feet, and looked around.

"Did you see him?" he asked.

"Aye, that did I! He wanted the use of this mare and cart to drive to Nottingham. He said he would fain turn butcher. But see!"

As he spoke he came to a turn in the road, and there before them stood a herd of the King's deer, feeding. Robin pointed to them, and continued:

"There is my herd of cattle, good Master Sheriff! How do you like them? Are they not fat and fair to see?"

The Sheriff drew rein quickly. "Now, fellow," quoth he, "I would I were well out of this forest, for I care not to see such herds as these or such faces as yours. Choose your own way, therefore, whoever you be, and let me go mine."

"Nay," laughed Robin, seizing the Sheriff's bridle; "I have been at too much pains to cultivate your company to forgo it now so easily. Besides, I wish you to meet some of my friends and dine with me, since you have so lately entertained me at your board."

So saying he clapped a horn to his lips, and winded three merry notes. The deer bounded away, and before the last of them was seen there came a running and a rustling, and out from behind covert and tree came full twoscore of men, clad in Lincoln green, and bearing good yew bows in their hands and short swords at their sides. Up they ran to Robin Hood, and doffed their caps to him respectfully, while the Sheriff sat still from very amazement.

"Welcome to the greenwood!" said one of the leaders, bending the knee with mock reverence before the Sheriff.

The Sheriff glared. It was Little John.

"Woe the worth, Reynold Greenleaf," he said; "you have betrayed me!"

"I make my vow," said Little John, "that you are to blame, master. I was misserved of my dinner when I was at your house. But we shall set you down to a feast we hope you will enjoy."

"Well spoken, Little John," said Robin Hood. "Take you his bridle, and let us do honour to the guest who has come to feast with us."

Then, turning abruptly, the whole company plunged into the heart of the forest.

After twisting and turning till the Sheriff's bewildered head sat dizzily upon his shoulders, the greenwood men passed

Three Good Servants

through a narrow alley amid the trees which led to a goodly open space flanked by wide-spreading oaks. Under the largest of these a pleasant fire was crackling, and near it two fine harts lay ready for cooking. Around the blaze were gathered another company of yeomen quite as large as that which came with Robin Hood. Up sprang they as the latter advanced, and saluted their leader with deference, but with hearty gladness to see him back again.

That merry wag Will Stutely was in command, and when he saw the pale-faced Sheriff being led in like any culprit he took his cloak, and laid it humbly upon the ground, and besought the Sheriff to alight upon it, as the ground of Sherwood was unused to such dignitaries.

" Bestir yourselves, good fellows ! " cried Robin Hood ; " and while our new cook, whom I see with us, is preparing a feast worthy of our high guest let us have a few games to do him honour ! "

Then, while the whole glade was filled with the savoury smell of roasting venison and fat capons, and brown pasties warmed beside the blaze, and mulled wine sent forth a cordial fragrance, Robin Hood placed the Sheriff upon a knoll beneath the largest oak, and sat himself down by him.

First stepped forward several pairs of men armed with the quarter-staff, the widow's sons among them, and so skilfully did they thrust and parry and beat down guards that the Sheriff, who loved a good game as well as any man, clapped his hands, forgetting where he was, and shouted : " Well struck ! well struck ! Never have I seen such blows at all the Fairs of Nottingham ! "

Then the best archers of the band set up a small wand at eightscore paces distant, and thereon they affixed a wreath of green. And the archers began to shoot, and he who shot not through the garland without disturbing its leaves and tendrils was fain to submit to a good sound buffet from Little John. But right cunning was the shooting, for the men had spent a certain time in daily practice, and many were the shafts which sped daintily through the circle. Nathless, now and again some luckless fellow would shoot awry, and would be sent spinning from a long-arm blow from the tall lieutenant, while the glade echoed with laughter. And none more hearty a guffaw was given than came from the Sheriff's own throat, for the spirit of the greenwood was upon him.

But presently his high mood was dashed. The company sat down to meat, and the guest was treated to two more disturbing surprises. The cook came forward to serve the food, when the Sheriff beheld in him his own former servant, and one whom he supposed was at that moment in the scullery at Nottingham.

Much, the miller's son, grinned by way of answer to the Sheriff's amazement, and served the plates, and placed them before the party. Then did the Sheriff gasp and fairly choke

Three Good Servants

with rage. The service was his own silver ware from the Mansion House !

" You rascals ! you rogues ! " he spluttered. " Was it not enough to defraud me out of three of my servants that you must also rob me of my best silver service ? Nay ; by my life, but I will not touch your food ! "

But Robin Hood bade him pause.

" Grammercy ! " quoth he, " servants come and go in Merry England, and so does service. The platters are but used to do your worship honour. And as for your life, it is forfeit to your eagerness to buy my herd of cattle so cheaply. Now, sit you down again, and make good cheer, Sheriff, for charity ! And for the love of Little John your life is granted you ! "

So the Sheriff sat him down again with the best face he could assume, and soon the cook's viands were disappearing down his gullet as rapidly as the next man's. And they feasted royally, and clinked each other's cups, until the sun had ceased to print the pattern of the leaves upon the forest carpet.

Then the Sheriff arose, and said : " I thank you, Robin Hood, one-time butcher, and you, Little John, one-time beggar, and you, Much, one-time cook, and all you good men who have entertained me in Sherwood so well. Promises I make not as to how I shall requite you when next you come to Nottingham, for I am in the King's service, so for the present the score rests with you. But the shadows grow long, and I must away, if you will be pleased to pilot me to the road."

Then Robin Hood and all his men arose, and drank the Sheriff's health, and Robin said : " If you must needs go at once we will not detain you—except that you have forgotten two things."

" What may they be ? " asked the Sheriff, while his heart sank within him.

" You forget that you came with me to-day to buy a herd of horned beasts ; likewise that he who dines at the Greenwood Inn must pay the landlord."

The Sheriff fidgeted like a small boy who has forgotten his lesson.

" Nay; I have but a small sum with me," he began apologetically.

" What is that sum, gossip ? " questioned Little John. " For my own wage should also come out of it ! "

" And mine ! " said Much.

" And mine ! " smiled Robin.

The Sheriff caught his breath. " By my troth, are all these silver dishes worth anything ? "

The outlaws roared heartily at this.

" I'll tell you what it is, worship," said Robin; " we three rascally servants will compound our back wages for those plates. And we will keep the herd of cattle free for our own use—and the King's. But this little tavern

Three Good Servants

bill should be settled! Now, what sum have you about you?"

"I have only these twenty pieces of gold, and twenty others," said the Sheriff; and well it was that he told the truth for once, for Robin said:

"Count it, Little John."

Little John turned the Sheriff's wallet inside out. "'Tis true enough," he said.

"Then you shall pay no more than twenty pieces for your entertainment, excellence," decreed Robin. "Speak I soothly, men of the greenwood?"

"Good!" echoed the others.

"The Sheriff should swear by his patron saint that he will not molest us," said Will Stutely, and this addition was carried unanimously.

"So be it, then," cried Little John, approaching the Sheriff. "Now, swear by your life and your patron saint——"

"I will swear it by St George, who is patron of us all," said the Sheriff vigorously, "that I will never disturb or distress the outlaws in Sherwood."

"But let me catch any of you *out* of Sherwood!" thought he to himself.

Then the twenty pieces of gold were paid over, and the Sheriff once more prepared to depart.

"Never had we so worshipful a guest before," said Robin; "and as the new moon is beginning to silver the leaves, I shall

Robin Hood & His Merry Outlaws

bear you company myself for part of the way—'twas I who brought you into the wood."

" Nay, I protest against your going needlessly far," said the Sheriff.

" But I protest that I am loth to lose your company," replied Robin ; " the next time I may not be so pleased."

And he took the Sheriff's horse by the bridle rein, and led him through the lane and by many a thicket till the main road was reached.

" Now, fare you well, good Sheriff," he said, " and when next you think to despoil a poor prodigal, remember the herd you would have bought over against Gamewell. And when next you employ a servant, make certain that he is not employing you."

So saying he smote the nag's haunch, and off went the Sheriff upon the road to Nottingham.

And that is how—you will find from many ballads that came to be sung at the Sheriff's expense, and which are known even to the present day—that, I say, is how the Sheriff lost three good servants and found them again.

CHAPTER VI

HOW ROBIN HOOD MET WILL SCARLET

The youngster was clothed in scarlet red,
In scarlet fine and gay ;
And he did frisk it o'er the plain,
And chanted a roundelay.

ONE fine morning, soon after the proud Sheriff had been brought to grief, Robin Hood and Little John went strolling down a path through the wood. It was not far from the footbridge where they had fought their memorable battle, and by common impulse they directed their steps to the brook to quench their thirst and rest them in the cool bushes. The morning gave promise of a hot day. The road even by the brook was dusty, so the cooling stream was very pleasing and grateful to their senses.

On each side of them, beyond the dusty highway, stretched out broad fields of tender young corn. On the yon side of the fields uprose the sturdy oaks and beeches and ashes of the forest ; while at their feet modest violets peeped out shyly, and greeted the loiterers with an odour which made the heart glad. Over on the far side of the brook, in a tiny bay, floated three lily-pads, and from amid some clover-blossoms on a bank an industrious bee rose with the hum of busy contentment. It was a day so brimful of quiet joy that the two friends lay

77

flat on their backs, gazing up at the scurrying clouds, and neither caring to break the silence.

Presently they heard someone coming up the road whistling gaily, as though he owned the whole world, and 'twas but made to whistle in ; anon he chanted a roundelay with a merry note.

" By my troth, a gay bird ! " quoth Robin, raising up on his elbow. " Let us lie still, and trust that his purse is not as light as his heart."

So they lay still, and in a minute more up came a smart stranger dressed in scarlet and silk, and wearing a jaunty hat with a curling cock feather in it. His whole costume was of scarlet, from the feather to the silk hosen on his legs. A goodly sword hung at his side, its scabbard all embossed with tilting knights and weeping ladies. His hair was long and yellow, and hung clustering about his shoulders for all the world like a schoolgirl's, and he bore himself with as mincing a gait as the pertest of them.

Little John clucked his teeth drolly at this sight. " By my troth, a gay bird ! " he said, echoing the other's words—then added : " But not so bad a build for all his prettiness. Look you, those calves and thighs are well rounded and straight. The arms, for all that gold-wrought cloak, hang stoutly from full shoulders. I warrant you the fop can use his dainty sword right well on occasion."

" Nay," retorted Robin ; " he is naught but a ladies' man from Court. My long bow 'gainst a plugged shilling that he

How Robin Met Will Scarlet

would run and bellow lustily at sight of a quarter-staff. Stay you behind this bush, and I will soon get some rare sport out of him. Belike his silk purse may contain more pennies than the law allows to one man in Sherwood or Barnesdale."

So saying Robin Hood stepped forth briskly from the covert, and planted himself in the way of the scarlet stranger. The latter had walked so slowly that he was scarce come to their resting-place; and now on beholding Robin he neither slackened nor quickened his pace, but sauntered idly straight ahead, looking to the right and to the left, with the finest air in the world, but never once at Robin.

"Hold!" quoth the outlaw. "What mean ye by running thus over a wayfarer, rough shod?"

"Wherefore should I hold, good fellow?" said the stranger in a smooth voice, and looking at Robin for the first time.

"Because I bid you to," replied Robin.

"And who may you be?" asked the other as coolly as you please.

"What my name is matters not," said Robin; "but know that I am a public tax-gatherer and equalizer of shillings. If your purse have more than a just number of shillings or pence, I must e'en lighten it somewhat, for there are many worthy people round about these borders who have less than the just amount. Wherefore, sweet gentleman, I pray you hand over your purse without more ado, that I may judge of its weight in proper fashion."

Robin Hood & His Merry Outlaws

The other smiled as sweetly as though a lady were paying him a compliment.

"You are a droll fellow," he said calmly. "Your speech amuses me mightily. Pray continue, if you have not done, for I am in no hurry this morning."

"I have said all with my tongue that is needful," retorted Robin, beginning to grow red under the collar. "Nathless, I have other arguments which may not be so pleasing to your dainty skin. Prithee, stand and deliver; I promise to deal fairly with the purse."

"Alack-a-day!" said the stranger, with a little shrug of his shoulders; "I am deeply sorrowful that I cannot show my purse to every rough lout that asks to see it. But I really could not, as I have further need of it myself and every farthing it contains. Wherefore, pray stand aside."

"Nay, that will I not! and 'twill go the harder with you if you do not yield at once."

"Good fellow," said the other gently, "have I not heard all your speech with patience? Now, that is all I promised to do. My conscience is salved, and I must go on my way. 'To-rol-o-rol-e-loo!'" he carolled, making as though to depart.

"Hold, I say!" quoth Robin hotly, for he knew how Little John must be chuckling at this from behind the bushes. "Hold, I say, else I shall have to bloody those fair locks of yours!" And he swung his quarter-staff threateningly.

"Alas!" moaned the stranger, shaking his head. "The

How Robin Met Will Scarlet

pity of it all! Now I shall have to run this fellow through with my sword! And I had hoped to be a peaceable man henceforth!" And sighing deeply he drew his shining blade, and stood on guard.

"Put by your weapon," said Robin; "it is too pretty a piece of steel to get cracked with a common oak cudgel—and that is what would happen on the first pass I made at you. Get you a stick like mine out of yon undergrowth, and we will fight fairly, man to man."

The stranger thought a moment with his usual slowness, and eyed Robin from head to foot. Then he unbuckled his scabbard, laid it and the sword aside, and walked deliberately over to the oak thicket. Choosing from among the shoots and saplings he found a stout little tree to his liking, when he laid hold of it, without stopping to cut it, and gave a tug. Up it came, root and all, as though it were a stalk of corn, and the stranger walked back, trimming it as quietly as though pulling up trees were the easiest thing in the world.

Little John from his hiding-place saw the feat, and could hardly restrain a long whistle. "By our Lady," he muttered to himself, "I would not be in Master Robin's boots!"

Whatever Robin thought upon seeing the stranger's strength, he uttered not a word and budged not an inch. He only put his oak staff at parry as the other took his stand.

There was a threefold surprise that day by the brookside. The stranger and Robin, and Little John in the bushes, all found a combat that upset all reckoning. The stranger, for all his easy strength and cool nerve, found an antagonist who met his blows with the skill of a woodman. Robin found the stranger as hard to hit as though fenced in by an oak hedge ; while Little John rolled over and over in silent joy.

Back and forth swayed the fighters, their cudgels pounding this way and that, knocking off splinters and bark, and threatening direst damage to bone and muscle and skin. Back and forth they pranced, kicking up a cloud of dust, and gasping for fresh air. From a little way off you would have vowed that these two men were trying to put out a fire, so thickly hung the cloud of battle over them. Thrice did Robin smite the scarlet man—with such blows that a less stout fellow must have bowled over. Only twice did the scarlet man smite Robin, but the second blow was like to finish him. The first had been delivered over the knuckles, and though 'twas a glancing stroke it well-nigh broke Robin's fingers, so that he could not easily raise his staff again. And while he was dancing about in pain and muttering a dust-covered oath the other's staff came swinging through the cloud at one side—zip !—and struck him under the arm. Down went Robin as though he were a nine-pin— flat down into the dust of the road. But despite the pain he was bounding up again like an india-rubber man to renew the attack, when Little John interfered.

" Hold ! " said he, bursting out of the bushes, and seizing the stranger's weapons. " Hold, I say ! "

How Robin Met Will Scarlet

" Nay," retorted the stranger quietly ; " I was not offering to smite him while he was down. But if there be a whole nest of you hatching here by the waterside, cluck out the other chicks, and I'll make shift to fight them all."

" Not for all the deer in Sherwood ! " cried Robin. " You are a good fellow and a gentleman. I'll fight no more with you, for verily I feel sore in wrist and body, nor shall any of mine molest you henceforth."

Sooth to say, Robin did not look in good fighting trim. His clothes were coated with dirt, one of his hosen had slipped half-way down from his knee, the sleeve of his jerkin was split, and his face was streaked with sweat and dirt. Little John eyed him drolly.

" How now, good master," quoth he, " the sport you were to kick up has left you in sorry plight. Let me dust your coat for you."

" Marry, it has been dusted enough already," replied Robin ; " and I now believe the Scripture saying that all men are but dust, for it has sifted me through and through and lined my gullet an inch deep. By your leave," and he went to the brookside, and drank deep, and laved his face and hands.

All this while the stranger had been eyeing Robin attentively, and listening to his voice, as though striving to recall it.

" If I mistake not," he said slowly at last, " you are that famous outlaw Robin Hood of Barnesdale."

Robin Hood & His Merry Outlaws

" You say right," replied Robin ; " but my fame has been tumbling sadly about in the dust to-day."

" Now, why did I not know you at once ? " continued the stranger. " This battle need not have happened, for I came abroad to find you to-day, and thought to have remembered your face and speech. Know you not me, Rob, my lad ? Hast ever been to Gamewell Lodge ? "

" Ha ! Will Gamewell ! my dear old chum Will Gamewell ! " shouted Robin, throwing his arms about the other in sheer affection. " What an ass I was not to recognize you ! But it has been years since we parted, and your gentle schooling has polished you off mightily."

Will embraced his cousin no less heartily. " We are quits on not knowing kinsmen," he said, " for you have changed and strengthened much from the stripling with whom I used to run races in old Sherwood."

" But why seek you me ? " asked Robin. " You know I am an outlaw and dangerous company. And how left you mine uncle ? and have you heard aught of late of—of Maid Marian ? "

" Your last question first," answered Will, laughing, " for I perceive that it lies nearest your heart. I saw Maid Marian not many weeks after the great shooting at Nottingham, when you won her the golden arrow. She prizes the bauble among her dearest possessions, though it has made her an enemy in the Sheriff's proud daughter. Maid Marian bade me tell you, if I ever saw you, that she must return to Queen Eleanor's Court,

but she could never forget the happy days in the greenwood. As
for the old Squire, he is still hale and hearty, though rheumatic
withal. He speaks of you as a sad young dog, but for all that
is secretly proud of your skill at the bow and of the way you are
pestering the Sheriff, whom he likes not. 'Twas for my father's
sake that I am now in the open, an outlaw like yourself. He
has had a steward, a surly fellow enough, who, while I was away
at school, boot-licked his way to favour until he lorded it over the
whole house. Then he grew right saucy and impudent, but my
father minded it not, deeming the fellow indispensable in manag-
ing the estate. But when I came back it irked me sorely to see
the fellow strut about as though he owned the place. He was
sly enough with me at first, and would browbeat the Squire only
while I was out of earshot. It chanced one day, however, that
I heard loud voices through an open window, and paused to
hearken. That vile servant called my father ' a meddling old
fool.' ' Fool and meddler art thou thyself, varlet,' I shouted,
springing through the window ; ' *that* for thy impudence ! ' and
in my heat I smote him a blow mightier than I intended, for I
have some strength in mine arm. The fellow rolled over, and
never breathed afterward. I think I broke his neck or something the like. Then I knew that the Sheriff would use this as
a pretext to hound my father if I tarried, so I bade the Squire
farewell, and told him I would seek you in Sherwood."

"Now, by my halidom ! " said Robin Hood, " for a man
escaping the law you took it about as coolly as one could wish.

Robin Hood & His Merry Outlaws

To see you come tripping along decked out in all your gay plumage, and trolling forth a roundelay, one would think you had not a care in all the world. Indeed, I remarked to Little John here that I hoped your purse was not as light as your heart."

" Belike you meant *head*," laughed Will. " And is this Little John the Great ? Shake hands with me, an you will, and promise me to cross a staff with me in friendly bout some day in the forest ! "

" That will I ! " quoth Little John heartily. " Here's my hand on it. What is your last name again, say you ? "

" 'Tis to be changed," interposed Robin ; " then shall the men armed with warrants go hang for all of us. Let me bethink myself. Ah !—I have it ! In scarlet he came to us, and that shall be his name henceforth. Welcome to the greenwood, Will Scarlet ! "

" Aye, welcome, Will Scarlet ! " said Little John, and they all clasped hands again, and swore to be true each to the other and to Robin Hood's men in Sherwood Forest.

Merry·Robin·stops·a·Stranger·
in·Scarlet :·

CHAPTER VI

The Merry Friar carrieth
Robin across the Water :

CHAPTER VII

CHAPTER VII

HOW ROBIN HOOD MET FRIAR TUCK

The friar took Robin Hood on his back,
Deep water he did bestride,
And spake neither good word nor bad,
Till he came at the other side.

I N summer-time, when leaves grow green and flowers are
fresh and gay, Robin Hood and his merry men were all
disposed to play. Thus runs a quaint old ballad which
begins the next adventure. Then some would leap and some
would run, and some try archery and some ply the quarter-staff,
and some fall to with the good broadsword. Some, again,
would try a round at buffet and fisticuff ; and thus by every
variety of sport and exercise they perfected themselves in skill,
and made the band and its prowess well known throughout all
England.

It had been a custom of Robin Hood's to pick out the best
men in all the countryside. Whenever he heard of one more
than usually skilled in any feat of arms he would seek the man,
and test him in personal encounter—which did not always end
happily for Robin. And when he had found a man to his
liking he offered him service with the bold fellows of Sherwood
Forest.

Thus it came about that one day, after a practice at shooting,

Robin Hood & His Merry Outlaws

in which Little John struck down a hart at five hundred feet distance, Robin Hood was fain to boast.

" God's blessing on your heart ! " he cried, clapping the burly fellow on the shoulder ; " a finer shot I never saw—I would travel an hundred miles to find one who could match you ! "

At this Will Scarlet laughed full roundly, for he was a little jealous of the praise bestowed upon his comrade.

" There lives a curtal friar in Fountains Abbey—Tuck, by name—who can beat both him and you," he said.

Robin pricked up his ears at this free speech.

" By our Lady," he said, " I'll neither eat nor drink till I see this same friar, and prove your words true or untrue ! "

With his usual impetuosity he at once set about arming himself for the adventure. On his head he placed a cap of steel, underneath his Lincoln green he wore a coat of chain metal, and with sword and buckler girded at his side he made a goodly show. He also took with him his stout yew bow and a sheaf of chosen arrows.

So he set forth upon his way with blithe heart, for it was a day when the whole face of the earth seemed glad and rejoicing in pulsing life. Steadily he pressed forward by winding ways till he came to a green, broad pastureland, at whose edge flowed a stream dipping in and out among the willows and rushes on the banks. A pleasant stream it was, but it flowed calmly, as though of some depth in the middle. Robin did not fancy

How Robin Met Friar Tuck

getting his feet wet or his fine suit of mail rusted, so he paused on the hither bank to rest and take his bearings.

As he sat down quietly under the shade of a drooping willow he heard snatches of a jovial song floating to him from the farther side ; then came a sound of two men's voices arguing. One was upholding the merits of hasty pudding and the other stood out stoutly for meat pie, " especially "—quoth this one—" when flavoured with young onions ! "

" Grammercy ! " muttered Robin to himself, " that is a tantalizing speech to a hungry man ! But, 'od's bodikins ! did ever two men talk more alike than those two fellows yonder ! "

In truth Robin could well marvel at the speech, for the voices were curiously alike.

Presently the willows parted on the other bank, and Robin could hardly forbear laughing outright. His mystery was explained. It was not two men who had done all this singing and talking, but one—and that one a stout curtal friar who wore a long cloak over his portly frame, tied with a cord in the middle. On his head was a knight's helmet, and in his hand was a no more warlike weapon than a huge pasty pie, with which he sat down by the water's edge. His twofold argument was finished. The meat pie had triumphed ; and no wonder, for it was the present witness, soon to give its own testimony.

But first the friar took off his helmet to cool his head, and a droll picture he made. His head was as round as an apple, and

eke as smooth in spots. A fringe of close, curling black hair
grew round the base of his skull, but his crown was bare and shiny
as an egg. His cheeks also were smooth and red and shiny,
and his little grey eyes danced about with the funniest air imagin-
able. You would not have blamed Robin Hood for wanting to
laugh had you heard this serious two-faced talk and then seen
this jovial one-faced man. Good humour and fat living stood
out all over him, yet for all that he looked stout enough, and
able to take care of himself with any man. His short neck was
thick like that of a Berkshire bull, his shoulders were set far back,
and his arms sprouted therefrom like two oak limbs. As he sat
him down the cloak fell apart, disclosing a sword and buckler as
stout as Robin's own.

Nathless, Robin was not dismayed at sight of the weapons.
Instead, his heart fell within him when he saw the meat pie,
which was now in fair way to be devoured before his very eyes,
for the friar lost no time in thrusting one hand deep into the pie,
while he crossed himself with the other.

Thereupon Robin seized his bow, and fitted a shaft.

"Hey, friar!" he sang out, "carry me over the water, or
else I cannot answer for your safety."

The other started at the unexpected greeting, and laid his
hand upon his sword. Then he looked up, and beheld Robin's
arrow pointing full upon him.

"Put down your bow, fellow," he shouted back, "and I
will bring you over the brook. 'Tis our duty in life to help

How Robin Met Friar Tuck

each other, and your keen shaft shows me that you are a man worthy of some attention."

So the friar-knight got him up gravely, though his eyes twinkled with a cunning light, and laid aside his beloved pie and his cloak and his sword and his buckler, and waded across the stream with waddling dignity.

After Robin had clambered upon the broad back offered him, the friar entered the water again, and spoke neither good word nor bad till he came to the other side.

Lightly leaped Robin off his back, and said : " I am much beholden to you, good Father."

" Beholden, say you ! " rejoined the other, drawing his sword. " Then, by my faith, you shall e'en repay your score. Now, mine own affairs, which are of a spiritual kind, and much more important than yours, which are carnal, lie on the other side of the stream. I see that you are a likely man and one, moreover, who would not refuse to serve the Church. I must, therefore, pray of you that, whatsoever I have done unto you, you will do also unto me. In short, my son, you must e'en carry me back again."

Courteously enough was this said, but so suddenly had the friar drawn his sword that Robin had no time to unsling his bow from his back, whither he had placed it to avoid getting it wet, or to unfasten his scabbard, so he was fain to temporize.

" Nay, good Father ; but I shall get my feet wet," he commenced.

Robin Hood & His Merry Outlaws

" Are your feet any better than mine ? " retorted the other. " I fear me now that I have already wetted myself so sadly as to lay in a store of rheumatic pains by way of penance."

" I am not so strong as you," continued Robin ; " that helmet and sword and buckler would be my undoing on the uncertain footing amid-stream, to say nothing of your holy flesh and bones."

" Then I will lighten up, somewhat," replied the other calmly. " Promise to carry me across and I will lay aside my war gear."

" Agreed," said Robin, and the friar thereupon stripped himself ; and Robin bent his stout back, and took him up even as he had promised.

Now, the stones at the bottom of the stream were round and slippery, and the current swept along strongly, waist-deep in the middle. Moreover, Robin had a heavier load than the other had borne, for the friar was extremely weighty, nor did he know the ford, so he went stumbling along, now stepping into a deep hole, now stumbling over a boulder in a manner that threatened to unseat his rider or plunge them both clear under current. But the fat friar hung on, and dug his heels into his steed's ribs in as gallant manner as if he were riding in a tournament ; while, as for poor Robin, the sweat ran down him in torrents, and he gasped like the winded horse he was. But at last he managed to stagger out on the bank, and deposit his unwieldy load.

How Robin Met Friar Tuck

No sooner had he set the friar down than he seized his own sword.

" Now, holy friar," quoth he, panting, and wiping the sweat from his brow, " what say the Scriptures that you quote so glibly ?—' Be not weary of well-doing.' You must carry me back again, or I swear that I will make a cheese-cloth out of your jacket ! "

The friar's grey eyes once more twinkled with a cunning gleam that boded no good to Robin, but his voice was as calm and courteous as ever.

" Your wits are keen, my son," he said, " and I see that the waters of the stream have not quenched your spirit. Once more will I bend my back to the oppressor and carry the weight of the haughty."

So Robin mounted again in high glee, and carried his sword in his hand, and went prepared to tarry upon the other side. But while he was bethinking himself what great words to use, when he should arrive thither, he felt himself slipping from the friar's broad back. He clutched frantically to save himself, but, with a forward heave, the friar pitched Robin into the deepest part of the stream and down he went with a loud splash.

" There ! " quoth the holy man ; " choose you, choose you, my fine fellow, whether you will sink or swim ! " And he gained his own bank without more ado ; while Robin thrashed and spluttered about until he made shift to grasp a willow wand, and thus haul himself ashore on the other side.

Robin Hood & His Merry Outlaws

Then Robin's rage waxed furious despite his wetting, and he took his bow and his arrows, and let fly one shaft after another at the worthy friar. But they rattled harmlessly off his steel buckler, while he laughed, and minded them no more than if they had been hailstones.

" Shoot on, shoot on, good fellow," he sang out ; " shoot as you have begun ; if you shoot here a summer's day your mark I will not shun ! "

So Robin shot, and passing well, till all his arrows were gone, when from very rage he began to revile him.

" You villain ! " shouted he. " You psalm-singing hypocrite ! You reviler of good hasty pudding ! Come but within reach of my sword arm, and, friar or no friar, I'll shave your tonsure closer than ever bald-pated monk was shaven before ! "

" Soft you and fair ! " said the friar unconcernedly ; " hard words are cheap, and you may need your wind presently. An you would like a bout with swords meet me half-way i' the stream."

And with this speech the friar waded into the brook, sword in hand, where he was met half-way by the impetuous outlaw.

Thereupon began a fierce and mighty battle. Up and down, in and out, back and forth they fought a long and equal fight. The swords flashed in the rays of the declining sun, and then met with a clash that would have shivered less sturdy weapons or disarmed less sturdy wielders. For a length of time they fought thus, equally matched and each on the look-out for a point of

94

How Robin Met Friar Tuck

vantage. Many a smart blow was landed, but each perceived that the other wore an undercoat of linked mail which might not be pierced. Nathless, their ribs ached at the force of the blows. Once and again they paused by mutual consent, and caught breath, and looked hard each at the other, for never had either met so stout a fellow.

Finally, in a furious onset of lunge and parry, Robin's foot stepped on a rolling stone, and he went down upon his knees. But his antagonist would not take this advantage ; he paused until Robin should get upon his feet.

" Now, by our Lady," cried the outlaw, using his favourite oath, " you are the fairest swordsman that I have met in many a long day ! I would beg a boon of you."

" What is it ? " shouted the friar.

" Give me leave to set my horn to my mouth and blow three blasts thereon."

" That will I do," said the curtal friar ; " blow till your breath fails, an it please you."

Then—says the old ballad—Robin Hood set his horn to his mouth and straightway spent his remaining breath upon three mighty blasts that filled the air and echoed faintly in the hills around. Ere the horn dropped from his fingers half a hundred yeomen, with bows bent, came racing over the lee.

" Whose men are these," said the friar, " that come so hastily ? "

Robin Hood & His Merry Outlaws

" These men are mine," said relieved and wearied Robin Hood, feeling that his time to laugh was come at last.

Then said the friar in his turn : " A boon, a boon, the like I gave to you. Give me leave to set my fist to my mouth and whistle three blasts thereon."

" That will I do," said Robin, " or else I were lacking in courtesy."

The friar set his fist to his mouth and put the horn to shame by the piercing whistles he blew ; whereupon half a hundred huge, fierce-looking hounds came running and leaping so swiftly that they had reached their bank as soon as Robin Hood's men had reached his side.

" A dog for every man of yours and I myself for you ! " exclaimed the friar, still eager for the fray.

Then followed a rare, foolish conflict. Stutely, Much, Little John, and the other outlaws began sending their arrows whizzing toward the opposite bank, but the dogs, which were taught of the friar, dodged the missiles cleverly, and ran and fetched them back again in their mouths, just as the dogs of to-day catch sticks.

" I have never seen the like of this in my days ! " cried Little John, amazed ; " 'tis rank sorcery and witchcraft."

" Take off your dogs, Friar Tuck ! " shouted Will Scarlet, who had but then run up, and who now stood laughing heartily at the scene.

" Friar Tuck ! " exclaimed Robin, astounded. " Are you

How Robin Met Friar Tuck

Friar Tuck ? Then am I your friend, for you are he I came to seek."

" I am but a poor anchorite, a curtal friar," said the other, whistling to his pack, " by name Friar Tuck of Fountains Dale. For seven years have I tended the Abbey here, preached o' Sundays, and married and christened and buried folk—aye, and fought too, if need were ; and, if it smacks not too much of boasting, I have not yet met the knight or trooper or yeoman that I would yield before. But yours is a stout blade ; I would fain know you."

" 'Tis Robin Hood, the outlaw, who has been assisting you at this christening," said Will Scarlet, glancing roguishly at the two opponents' dripping garments. And at this sally the whole band burst into a shout of laughter, in which Robin and Friar Tuck joined.

" Robin Hood ! " cried the good friar presently, holding his sides ; " are you indeed that famous yeoman ? Then I like you well ; many a time and oft have I heard of your merry doings ; and had I known you earlier I would have both carried you across and shared my pasty pie with you."

" To speak soothly," replied Robin gaily, " 'twas that same pie that led me to be rude. Now, therefore, bring it and your dogs, and repair with us to the greenwood. We have need of you —with this message came I to-day to seek you. We will build you a hermitage in Sherwood Forest, and you shall keep us from evil ways. Will you not join our band ? "

Robin Hood & His Merry Outlaws

" Marry, that will I, provided there be no fast days ! "
cried Friar Tuck jovially. " Once more will I cross this much
beforded stream, and go with you to the good greenwood, there
to serve faithfully as becomes a poor, meek friar ! " he ended, in
a tone hardly befitting the words.

Thus did Robin meet his match, and his band became the
richer by Friar Tuck, who turned out to be a skilled forester
and an excellent cook.

The Merry Friar sings a goodly song

CHAPTER VII

Allan·a·Dale·lieth·beside·the·Fountain·

CHAPTER VIII

CHAPTER VIII

HOW ALLAN-A-DALE'S WOOING WAS PROSPERED

" What is thy name ? " then said Robin Hood,
  " Come tell me, without any fail."
" By the faith o' my body," then said the young man,
  " My name it is Allan-a-Dale."

FRIAR TUCK and Much, the miller's son, soon became right good friends over the steaming stew they jointly prepared for the merry men that evening. Tuck was mightily pleased when he found a man in the forest who could make pasties and who had cooked for no less a person than the High Sheriff himself, while Much marvelled at the friar's knowledge of herbs and simples and woodland things which savoured a stew greatly ; so they gabbled together like two old gossips, and between them made such a tasty mess that Robin Hood and his stout followers were like never to leave off eating. And the friar said grace, too, with great unction over the food, and Robin said " Amen ! " and that henceforth they were always to have mass of Sundays.

So Robin walked forth into the wood that evening with his stomach full and his heart, therefore, in great contentment and love for other men. He did not stop the first passer-by, as his manner often was, and desire a fight. Instead he stepped behind a tree when he heard a man's voice in song, and waited

99

to behold the singer. Perhaps he remembered also the merry chanting of Will Scarlet, and how he had tried to give it pause a few days before.

Like Will, this fellow was clad in scarlet, though he did not look quite as fine a gentleman. Nathless, he was a sturdy yeoman of honest face, with a voice far sweeter than Will's. He seemed to be a strolling minstrel, for he bore a harp in his hand, which he thrummed, while his lusty tenor voice rang out with a merry love-song :

> " Hey down, and a down, and a down !
> I've a lassie back i' the town ;
>   Come day, come night,
>   Come dark or light,
> She will wed me, back i' the town ! "

Robin let the singer pass, carolling on his way.

" 'Tis not in me to disturb a light-hearted lover this night," he muttered, a memory of Marian coming back to him. " Pray Heaven she may be true to him, and the wedding be a gay one ' back i' the town ! ' "

So Robin went back to his camp, where he told of the minstrel.

" If any of ye set eyes on him after this," quoth he in ending, " bring him to me, for I would have speech with him."

The very next day his wish was gratified. Little John and Much, the miller's son, were out together on a foraging expedition when they espied the same young man—at least they thought it must be he, for he was clad in scarlet, and carried a harp in his hand. But now he came drooping along the way, his scarlet was all in tatters, and at every step he fetched a sigh : " Alack and a well-a-day ! " Then stepped forth Little John and Much, the miller's son.

" Ho ! do not wet the earth with your weeping," said Little John, " else we shall all have lumbago."

No sooner did the young man catch sight of them than he bent his bow, and held an arrow back to his ear.

" Stand off ! stand off ! " he said. " What is your will with me ? "

" Put by your weapon," said Much ; " we will not harm you, but you must come before our master straight, under yon greenwood tree."

So the minstrel put by his bow, and suffered himself to be led before Robin Hood.

" How now ! " quoth Robin, when he beheld his sorry countenance. " Are you not he whom I heard no longer ago than yesternight carolling so blithely about ' a lassie back i' the town ' ? "

" The same in body, good sir," replied the other sadly, " but my spirit is grievously changed."

" Tell me your tale," said Robin courteously ; " belike I can help you. What is your trouble ? If it be in my power to help, right willingly will I, or my name is not Robin Hood."

Robin Hood & His Merry Outlaws

" Nor mine Little John," came in husky tones from the tender-hearted giant.

" No man on earth can help me, I fear," said the stranger; " nathless, I'll tell you the tale. Yesterday I stood pledged to a maid, and thought soon to wed her. But she has been taken from me to a strong castle, and is to become an old knight's bride this very day; and as for me, I care not what ending comes to my days, or how soon, without her."

" Marry, come up!" said Robin, with an angry light in his eyes. " How got the old knight so sudden vantage?"

" Look you, worship, 'tis this way. The Normans overrun us, and are in such great favour that none may say them nay. This old returned Crusader coveted the land whereon my lady dwells. The estate is not large, but all in her own right; whereupon her brother says she shall wed a title, and he and the old knight have fixed it up for to-day."

" Nay; but surely——" began Robin.

" Hear me out, worship," said the other. " Belike you think me a sorry dog not to make fight of this. But the old knight, look you, is not come-at-able. Surely, I went to the castle and demanded my love, but the knight scoffed at me from the battlements and sent his men to beat me. I threw one of his varlets into a thorn hedge, and another into a water-butt, and a third landed head-first into a ditch. But I couldn't do any fighting at all. The rest beat me sorely and with many gibes drove me away."

Allan-a-Dale's Wooing

" 'Tis a pity ! " quoth Little John gravely. He had been sitting cross-legged, listening to this tale of woe. " What think you, Friar Tuck, doth not a bit of fighting ease a man's mind ? "

" Blood-letting is ofttimes recommended of the leeches," replied Tuck.

" Does the maid love you ? " asked Robin Hood.

" By our troth, she loved me right well," said the minstrel. " I have a little ring of hers by me which I have kept for seven long years."

" What is your name ? " then said Robin Hood.

" By the faith of my body," replied the young man, " my name is Allan-a-Dale."

" What will you give me, Allan-a-Dale," said Robin Hood, " in ready gold or fee, to help you to your true love again, and deliver her back unto you ? "

" I have no money, save only five shillings," quoth Allan ; " but—are you not Robin Hood ? "

Robin nodded.

" Then you, if anyone, can aid me ! " said Allan-a-Dale eagerly. " And if you give me back my love I swear upon a book that I will be your true servant for ever after."

" Now we know you for a true man," answered Robin, " and willingly will we help you. But where is this wedding to take place, and when ? "

" At Plympton Church, scarce five miles from here ; and at three o' the afternoon."

" Then to Plympton we will go ! " cried Robin, suddenly springing into action ; and he gave out orders like a general : " Will Stutely, do you have four and twenty good men over against Plympton Church 'gainst three o' the afternoon. Much, good fellow, do you cook up some porridge for this youth, for he must have a good round stomach—ay, and a better gear ! Will Scarlet, you will see to decking him out bravely for the nonce. And Friar Tuck, hold yourself in readiness, good book in hand, at the church—mayhap you had best go ahead of us all."

Then, turning to the downcast lover, he said : " Smile, Allan lad. See, the sun hath not yet reached its zenith, yet before it sets thy lady shall be restored to you, and as she thinks to be married by my lord Bishop, 'twere a shame to disappoint her," continued Robin cheerfully.

Placing his horn to his lips, the outlaw chief blew one loud blast that brought many fellows dressed in green from all directions, with their quivers slung over shoulders and their bows in hand.

" Who's for a wedding, lads ? " questioned Robin, smiling.

" All of us ! " responded the men as one voice, and even poor Allan-a-Dale was seen to smile at their enthusiasm.

" See, then, that you are all in good time," laughed Robin, " for we must not keep the Bishop of Hereford waiting."

Allan-a-Dale's Wooing

The fat Bishop of Hereford was full of pomp and importance that day at Plympton Church. He was to celebrate the marriage of an old knight—a returned Crusader—and a landed young woman ; and all the gentry thereabout were to grace the occasion with their presence. The church itself was gaily festooned with flowers for the ceremony, while out in the churchyard at one side brown ale flowed freely for all the servitors.

Already were the guests beginning to assemble, when the Bishop, back in the vestry, saw a minstrel clad in green walk boldly up to the door, and peer within. It was Robin Hood, who had borrowed Allan's beribboned harp for the time.

" Now, who are you, fellow," rapped out the Bishop, in angry tones, " and what do you here at the church door with your harp and saucy air ? "

" May it please your reverence," returned Robin, bowing very humbly, " I am but a strolling harper, yet likened the best in the whole North Countree, and I had hope that my thrumming might add zest to the wedding to-day."

" What tune can you harp ? " demanded the Bishop.

" I can harp a tune so merry that a forlorn lover will forget he is jilted," said Robin. " I can harp another tune that will make a bride forsake her lord at the altar. I can harp another tune that will bring loving souls together though they were up hill and down dale five good miles away from each other."

Robin Hood & His Merry Outlaws

" Then welcome, welcome, good minstrel," said the Bishop in conciliatory tones; "music pleases me right well, and if you can play up to your prattle 'twill indeed grace our ceremony. Let us have a sample of your wares."

" Nay; I must not put finger to string until the bride and groom have come. Such a thing would ill-fortune both us and them."

" Have it as you will," said the Bishop; "but here comes the party now."

Then up the lane to the church hobbled the old knight, preceded by ten archers liveried in scarlet and gold. A brave sight the archers made, but their master walked slowly, leaning upon a cane, and shaking as though in a palsy.

And after them came a sweet lass, leaning upon her brother's arm. Her hair did shine like glistering gold, and her eyes were like blue violets that peep out shyly at the sun. The colour came and went in her cheeks like the tinting of a sea-shell, and her face was flushed as though she had been weeping. But now she walked with a proud air, as though she defied the world to crush her spirit. She had but two maids with her, finikin lasses, with black eyes and broad bosoms, who set off their lady's more delicate beauty well. One held up the bride's gown from the ground; the other carried flowers in plenty.

" Now, by all the wedding bells that were ever rung," quoth

Allan-a-Dale's Wooing

Robin boldly, " this is the worst-matched pair that ever mine eyes beheld ! "

" Silence, miscreant ! " said a man who stood near.

The Bishop had hurriedly donned his gown, and now stood ready to meet the couple at the chancel.

But Robin paid no heed to him ; he let the knight and his ten archers pass by, then he strode up to the bride, and placed himself on the other side from her brother.

" Courage, lady ! " he whispered, " there is another minstrel near who, mayhap, may play more to your liking."

The lady glanced at him with a frightened air, but read such honesty and kindness in his glance that she brightened and gave him a grateful look.

" Stand aside, fool ! " cried the brother wrathfully.

" Nay ; but I am to bring good fortune to the bride by accompanying her through the church doors," said Robin, laughing.

Thereupon he was allowed to walk by her side unmolested up to the chancel with the party.

" Now strike up your music, fellow ! " ordered the Bishop.

" Right gladly will I," quoth Robin, " an you will let me choose my instrument, for sometimes I like the harp, and other times I think the horn makes the merriest music in all the world."

And he drew forth his bugle from underneath his green cloak, and blew three winding notes that made the church rafters ring again.

Robin Hood & His Merry Outlaws

"Seize him!" yelled the Bishop; "there's mischief afoot! These are the tricks of Robin Hood!"

The ten liveried archers rushed forward from the rear of the church, where they had been stationed. But their rush was blocked by the onlookers, who now rose from their pews in alarm, and crowded the aisles. Meanwhile Robin had leaped lightly over the chancel rail, and stationed himself in a nook by the altar.

"Stand where you are!" he shouted, drawing his bow; "the first man to pass the rail dies the death. And all ye who have come to witness a wedding stay in your seats. We shall e'en have one, since we are come into a church. But the bride shall chose her own swain!"

Then up rose another great commotion at the door, and four and twenty good bowmen came marching in, with Will Stutely at their head. And they seized the ten liveried archers and the bride's scowling brother and the other men on guard, and bound them prisoners.

Then in came Allan-a-Dale, decked out gaily, with Will Scarlet for best man. And they walked gravely down the aisle, and stood over against the chancel.

"Before a maiden weds she chooses—an the laws of good King Harry be just ones," said Robin. "Now, maiden, before this wedding continues, whom will you have to husband?"

The maiden answered not in words, but smiled with a glad

Allan-a-Dale's Wooing

light in her eyes, walked over to Allan, clasped her arms
about his neck, and sobbed happily there.

"That is her true love," said Robin: "young Allan instead
of the gouty knight. She has chosen well! And the true lovers
shall be married at this time before we depart away. Now, my
lord Bishop, proceed with the ceremony!"

"I know you—thief and robber!" screamed the Bishop.
"I'll not marry them either, for the banns must be cried three
times in the church—such is the law of our land. 'Three times
shall the banns be called from the altar.' You have overstepped
the mark this time."

After which he shut his book with a snap and sat upon it.

"Come here, Little John," called Robin impatiently, and he
plucked off the Bishop's frock from his back, and put it on the
yeoman. "What manner of bishop will you make, I wonder?"

Now, the Bishop was short and fat, and Little John was long
and lean. The gown hung loosely over Little John's shoulders,
and came only to his waist. He was a fine, comical sight, and
the people began to laugh consumedly at him.

"By the faith o' my body," said Robin, "this cloth makes
you a man. You're the finest bishop that ever I saw in my life.
Now, cry the banns."

So Little John clambered awkwardly into the choir, his short
gown fluttering gaily, and with mock dignity he called the banns
for the marriage of the maid and Allan-a-Dale once, twice,
and thrice.

Robin Hood & His Merry Outlaws

" That's not enough," said Robin ; " your gown is so short that you must talk longer."

Then Little John asked them in the church four, five, six, and seven times. Never before were banns called in such a voice and with such fervour.

" Good enough ! " said Robin. " You shall have double fees for this, I warrant you. Now, belike, I see a worthy friar in the back of this church who can say a better service than ever my lord Bishop of Hereford. My lord Bishop shall be witness, and seal the papers, but do you, good friar, bless this pair with book and candle."

So Friar Tuck, who all along had been back in one corner of the church, came forward ; and Allan and his maid kneeled before him, while the old knight, held an unwilling witness, gnashed his teeth in impotent rage ; and the friar began the ceremony.

When he asked : " Who giveth this maid ? " Robin stepped up, and answered in a hearty voice :

" I do !—I, Robin Hood of Barnesdale and Sherwood ! And he who takes her from Allan-a-Dale shall buy her full dearly."

So the twain were declared man and wife, and duly blessed, and the bride was kissed by each sturdy yeoman, beginning with Robin Hood.

Now, I cannot end this jolly tale better than in the words of the ballad which came out of the happening, and

Allan-a-Dale's Wooing

which has been sung in the villages and countryside ever
since :

> And thus having end of this merry wedding,
>   The bride lookt like a queen ;
> And so they returned to the merry greenwood,
>   Amongst the leaves so green.

CHAPTER IX

HOW THE WIDOW'S THREE SONS WERE RESCUED

Now Robin Hood is to Nottingham gone,
  With a link a down and a down,
And there he met with the proud Sheriff,
  Was walking along the town.

THE wedding party was a merry one that left Plympton Church, I ween ; but not so merry were the ones left behind. My lord Bishop of Hereford was stuck up in the organ loft, and left, gownless and fuming. The ten liveried archers were variously disposed about the church to keep him company ; two of them being locked in a tiny crypt, three in the belfry—" to ring us a wedding peal," as Robin said—and the others under choir seats or in the vestry. The bride's brother at her entreaty was released, but bidden not to return to the church that day or interfere with his sister again on pain of death ; while the rusty old knight was forced to climb a high tree, where he sat insecurely perched among the branches, feebly cursing the party as it departed.

It was then approaching sundown, but none of the retainers or villagers dared rescue the imprisoned ones that night for fear of Robin Hood's men, so it was not until sunrise the next day that they were released. The Bishop and the old knight, stiff as they were, did not delay longer than for breakfast, but—so

The Widow's Three Sons

great was their rage and shame—made straight to Notting-ham, and levied the Sheriff's forces. The Sheriff himself was not anxious to try conclusions again with Robin in the open; perhaps he had some slight scruples regarding his oath. But the others swore that they would go straight to the King if he did not help them, so he was fain to consent.

A force of a hundred picked men from the Royal Foresters and swordsmen of the shire was gathered together, and marched straightway into the greenwood. There, as fortune would have it, they surprised some score of outlaws hunting, and instantly gave chase. But they could not surround the outlaws, who kept well in the lead, ever and anon dropping behind a log or boulder to speed back a shaft which meant mischief to the pursuers. One shaft, indeed, carried off the Sheriff's hat, and caused that worthy man to fall forward upon his horse's neck from sheer terror; while five other arrows landed in the fleshy parts of Foresters' arms.

But the attacking party was not wholly unsuccessful. One outlaw in his flight stumbled and fell, when two others instantly stopped, and helped to put him on his feet again. They were the widow's three sons, Stout Will, and Lester, and John. The pause was an unlucky one for them, as a party of Sheriff's men got above them, and cut them off from their fellows. Swordsmen came up in the rear, and they were soon hemmed in on every side. But they gave good account of themselves, and before they

Robin Hood & His Merry Outlaws

had been overborne by force of numbers they had killed two and disabled three more.

The infuriated attackers were almost on the point of hewing the stout outlaws to pieces when the Sheriff cried :

" Hold ! Bind the villains ! We will follow the law in this, and take them to the town jail. But I promise ye the biggest public hanging that has been seen in this shire for many changes of the moon ! "

So they bound the widow's three sons, and carried them back speedily to Nottingham.

Now, Robin Hood had not chanced to be near the scene of the fight or with his men, so for a time he heard nothing of the happening, but that evening, while returning to the camp, he was met by the widow herself, who came weeping along the way.

" What news, what news, good woman ? " said Robin hastily but courteously ; for he liked her well.

" God save ye, Master Robin ! " said the dame, brokenly. " God keep ye from the fate that has met my three sons ! The Sheriff has laid hands on them, and they are condemned to die, for the Sheriff is a hard man," wailed the wretched mother.

" Now, by our Lady, that cuts me to the heart ! Stout Will, and Lester, and Merry John ! The earliest friends I had in the band, and still among the bravest. It must not be ! When is this hanging set ? "

" Middle, the tinker, tells me that it is for to-morrow noon," replied the dame, between her sobs.

114

The Widow's Three Sons

" By the truth o' my body," quoth Robin, " you could not tell me in better time ! The memory of the old days when you freely bade me sup and dine would spur me on even if three of the bravest lads in all the shire were not imperilled. Trust to me, good woman ! "

The old widow threw herself on the ground, and embraced his knees.

" 'Tis dire danger I am asking ye to face," she said, with a fresh outburst of weeping, " and yet I knew your brave, true heart would answer me. Heaven help ye, good Master Robin, to answer a poor widow's prayers ! "

Robin comforted the woman and told her to go home and that he would save her three sons.

Then, having seen her drooping figure totter out of sight, Robin Hood sped straightway to the forest camp, where he heard the details of the skirmish : how that his men had been out-numbered five to one, but got off safely, as they thought, until a count of their numbers had shown the loss of the widow's three sons.

" We must rescue them, my men," quoth Robin, " even from out the shadow of the rope itself ! "

Whereupon the band set to work to devise ways and means.

Robin walked apart a little way with his head leaned thought-fully upon his breast—for he was sore troubled—when whom should he meet but an old begging palmer, one of the devout order which made pilgrimages and wandered from place to place, supported by charity.

This old fellow walked boldly up to Robin, and asked alms of him, since Robin had been wont to aid members of his order.

" What news, what news, thou foolish old man ? " said Robin. " What news, I do thee pray ? "

" Three squires in Nottingham town," quoth the palmer, " are condemned to die. Belike that is greater news than the shire has had in some Sundays."

Then Robin's long-sought idea came to him like a flash.

" Come, change thine apparel with me, old man," he said, " and I'll give thee forty shillings in good silver to spend in beer or wine."

" Oh, thine apparel is good," the palmer protested, " and mine is ragged and torn. Holy Church teaches that thou should'st ne'er laugh an old man to scorn."

" I am in simple earnest, I say. Come, change thine apparel with mine. Here are twenty pieces of good broad gold to feast thy brethren right royally."

So the palmer was persuaded ; and Robin put on the old man's hat, which stood full high in the crown ; and his cloak, patched with black and blue and red, like Joseph's coat of many colours in its old age ; and his breeches, which had been sewed over with so many patterns that the original was scarce discernible ; and his tattered hose ; and his shoes, cobbled above and below. And while as he made the change in dress he made

The Widow's Three Sons

so many whimsical comments also about a man's pride and the dress that makes a man that the palmer was like to choke with cackling laughter.

I warrant you, the two were comical sights when they parted company that day ; nathless, Robin's own mother would not have known him had she been living.

The next morning the whole town of Nottingham was early astir, and as soon as the gates were open country-folk began to pour in, for a triple hanging was not held there every day in the week, and the bustle almost equalled a Fair day.

Robin Hood in his palmer's disguise was one of the first to enter the gates, and he strolled up and down and around the town as though he had never been there before in all his life. Presently he came to the market-place, and beheld thereon three gallows erected.

" Who are these builded for, my son ? " asked he of a rough soldier standing by.

" For three of Robin Hood's men," answered the other. " An it were Robin himself, 'twould be thrice as high, I warrant ye. But Robin is too smart to get within the Sheriff's clutches again."

The palmer crossed himself.

" They say that he is a bold fellow," he whined.

" Ha ! " said the soldier, " he may be bold enough out

behind the stumps i' the forest, but the open market-place is another matter."

" Who is to hang these three poor wretches ? " asked the palmer.

" That hath the Sheriff not decided ; but here he comes now to answer his own questions." And the soldier came to stiff attention as the Sheriff and his bodyguard stalked pompously up to inspect the gallows.

" Oh, Heaven save you, worshipful Sheriff ! " said the palmer. " Heaven protect you ! What will you give a silly old man to-day to be your hangman ? "

" Who are you, fellow ? " asked the Sheriff sharply.

" Naught save a poor old palmer ; but I can shrive their souls and hang their bodies most devoutly."

" Very good," replied the other. " The fee to-day is thirteen pence, and I will add thereunto some suits of clothing for that ragged back of yours."

" God bless ye ! " said the palmer. And he went with the soldier to the jail to prepare his three men for execution.

Just before the stroke of noon the doors of the prison opened, and the procession of the condemned came forth. Down through the long lines of packed people they walked to the market-place, the palmer in the lead, and the widow's three sons marching firmly erect between soldiers.

At the gallows' foot they halted. The palmer whispered to them, as though offering last words of consolation ; and the three

118

The Widow's Three Sons

men, with arms bound tightly behind their backs, ascended the scaffold, followed by their confessor.

All was ready, and the hangman stood as if awaiting the Sheriff's word.

A moment or two of anxious expectation. The Sheriff raised his hand.

A great groan arose from the people, and most of them turned their heads away and shuddered violently. Those who were hardened, however, still kept their eyes riveted on the gallows.

Then Robin stepped to the edge of the scaffold, while the people grew still as death, for they desired to hear the last words uttered to the victims. But Robin's voice did not quaver forth weakly, as formerly, and his figure had stiffened bolt upright beneath the black robe that covered his rags.

" Hark ye, proud Sheriff ! " he cried, " I was ne'er a hangman in all my life, nor do I now intend to begin that trade. Accurst be he who first set the fashion of hanging ! I have but three more words to say. Listen to them ! "

And forth from his robe he drew his horn, and blew three loud blasts thereon. Then his keen hunting-knife flew forth, and in a trice Stout Will, Lester, and Merry John were free men and had sprung forward and seized the halberds from the nearest soldiers guarding the gallows.

" Seize them ! 'Tis Robin Hood ! " screamed the Sheriff. " An hundred pounds if ye hold them, dead or alive ! "

Robin Hood & His Merry Outlaws

" I make it two hundred ! " roared the fat Bishop.

But their voices were drowned in the uproar that ensued immediately after Robin blew his horn. He himself had drawn his sword, and leaped down the stairs from the scaffold, followed by his three men. The guard had closed around them in vain effort to disarm them, when " A rescue ! " shouted Will Stutely's clear voice on one side of them, and " A rescue ! " bellowed Little John's on the other, and down through the terror-stricken crowd rushed fourscore men in Lincoln green, their force seeming twice that number in the confusion. With swords drawn they fell upon the guard from every side at once. There was a brief clash of hot weapons, then the guard scattered wildly, and Robin Hood's men formed in a compact mass around their leader, and forced their way slowly down the market-place.

" Seize them, in the King's name ! " shrieked the Sheriff. " Close the gates ! "

In truth the peril would have been even greater had this last order been carried out. But Will Scarlet and Allan-a-Dale had foreseen that event, and had already overpowered the two warders, so the gates stood wide open, and toward them the band of outlaws headed.

The soldiers rallied a force of twice their number, and tried resolutely to pierce their centre. But the retreating force turned thrice, and sent such volleys of keen arrows from their good yew bows, that they kept a distance between the two forces.

And thus the gate was reached, and the long road leading up

The Widow's Three Sons

the hill, and at last the protecting greenwood itself. The soldiers dared come no farther.

Great was the widow's joy as she beheld her lads once more, and over and over again did she thank Robin, and with many tears did she bless him. And her three sons, I warrant you, supped more heartily that night than ever before in their whole lives.

CHAPTER X

HOW A BEGGAR FILLED THE PUBLIC EYE

Good Robin accost him in his way,
  To see what he might be ;
If any beggar had money,
  He thought some part had he.

ONE bright morning, soon after the stirring events told in the last chapter, Robin wandered forth alone down the road to Barnesdale to see if aught had come of the Sheriff's pursuit. But all was still and serene and peaceful. No one was in sight, save a solitary beggar who came sturdily along his way in Robin's direction. A queer-looking fellow he was, too, his garments being split and torn past all recognition. The beggar caught sight of Robin at the same moment as he emerged from the trees, but gave no sign of having seen him. He neither slackened nor quickened his pace, but jogged forward merrily, whistling as he came, and beating time by punching holes in the dusty road with the stout pike-staff in his hand.

The curious look of the fellow arrested Robin's attention, and he decided to stop, and talk with him. The fellow was bare-legged and bare-armed, and wore a long shift of a shirt, fastened with a belt. About his neck hung a stout, bulging bag, which was buckled by a good piece of leather thong.

How a Beggar Filled the Public Eye

He had three hats upon his head,
  Together stickèd fast ;
He cared neither for the wind nor wet,
  In lands where'er he past.

The fellow looked so fat and hearty, in spite of his rags, and the wallet on his shoulder seemed so well filled, that Robin thought within himself :

" Ha ! this is a lucky beggar for me ! If any of them have money this is the chap, and, marry, he should share it with us poorer bodies."

So he flourished his own stick, and planted himself in the traveller's path.

" Sirrah, fellow ! " quoth he, " whither away so fast ? Tarry, for I would have speech with ye ! "

The beggar made as though he heard him not, and kept straight on with his faring.

" Tarry, I say, fellow," said Robin again, " for there's a way to make folks obey ! "

" Nay, 'tis not so," answered the beggar, speaking for the first time ; " I obey no man in all England, not even the King himself. So let me pass on my way, for 'tis growing late, and I have still far to go before I can care for my stomach's good."

" Now, by my troth," said Robin, once more getting in front of the other, " I see well by your fat countenance that you lack not for good food, while I go hungry. Therefore you must lend me of your means till we meet again, so that I may hie to the nearest tavern."

" I have no money to lend," said the beggar crossly. " Methinks you are as young a man as I, and as well able to earn a supper, so go your way, and I'll go mine. If you fast till you get aught out of me you'll go hungry for the next twelvemonth."

" Not while I have a stout stick to thwack your saucy bones ! " cried Robin. " Stand and deliver, I say, or I'll dust your shirt for you ; and if that will not teach you manners, then we'll see what a broad arrow can do with a beggar's skin ! "

The beggar smiled, and answered boast with boast. " Come on with your staff, fellow ! I care no more for it than for a pudding stick. And as for your pretty bow—*that* for it ! "

And, with amazing quickness, he swung his pike-staff round, and knocked Robin's bow clean out of his hand, so that his fingers smarted with pain. Robin danced, and tried to bring his own staff into action, but the beggar never gave him a chance. Biff ! whack ! came the pike-staff, smiting him soundly, and beating down his guard. Robin was very sore, for the beggar's pike-staff, bound with iron, was a formidable weapon, and in spite of all his efforts he could not get in a blow with his own staff, and ever and again the beggar's came swinging against his ribs.

There were but two things to do ; either stand there and take a sound drubbing, or beat a hasty retreat. Robin chose the latter—as you or I would probably have done—and scurried back into the wood, blowing his horn as he went.

How a Beggar Filled the Public Eye

" Fie, for shame, man ! " jeered the bold beggar after him.
" What is your haste ? We had but just begun. Stay and take
your money, else you will never be able to pay your reckoning
at the tavern ! "

But Robin answered him never a word ; he fled up hill and
down dale till he met three of his men, who were running up in
answer to his summons.

" What is wrong ? " they asked.

" 'Tis a saucy beggar," said Robin, catching his breath.
" He is back there on the high road, with the hardest stick I've
met in a good many days ; he gave me no chance to reason with
him, the dirty scamp ! "

The men—Much and two of the widow's sons—could scarce
conceal their mirth at the thought of Robin Hood running from
a beggar ; nathless, they kept grave faces, and asked their leader
if he were hurt.

" Nay," he replied ; " but I shall speedily feel better if you
will fetch me that same beggar and let me have a fair chance at
him."

So the three yeomen made haste, and came out upon the high
road, and followed after the beggar, who was going smoothly
along his way again, as though he were at peace with all the
world.

" The easiest way to settle this beggar," said Much, " is to
surprise him. Let us cut through yon neck of woods, and come
upon him before he is aware."

Robin Hood & His Merry Outlaws

The others agreed to this, and the three were soon close upon their prey.

" Now ! " quoth Much, and the other two sprang quickly upon the beggar's back, and wrested his pike-staff from his hand. At the same moment Much drew his dagger, and flashed it before the fellow's breast.

" Yield you, my man ! " cried he, " for a friend of ours awaits you in the wood to teach you how to fight properly."

" Give me a fair chance," said the beggar valiantly, " and I'll fight you all at once."

But they would not listen to him. Instead, they turned him about, and began to march him toward the forest. Seeing that it was useless to struggle, the beggar began to parley.

" Good my masters," quoth he, " why use this violence ? I will go with ye safe and quietly if ye insist, but if you will set me free I'll make it worth your while. I've an hundred pounds in my bag here ; let me go my way, and ye shall have all that's in the bag."

The three outlaws took counsel together at this.

" What say you ? " asked Much of the others. " Our master will be more glad to see this beggar's wallet than his sorry face."

The other two agreed, and the little party came to a halt, and loosed hold of the beggar.

" Count out your gold speedily, friend," said Much.

How a Beggar Filled the Public Eye

There was a brisk wind blowing, and the beggar turned about to face it directly they had unhanded him.

" It shall be done, gossips," said he. " One of you lend me your cloak, and we will spread it upon the ground, and put the wealth upon it."

The cloak was handed him, and he placed his wallet upon it as though it were very heavy indeed. Then he crouched down, and fumbled with the leather fastenings. The outlaws also bent over, and watched the proceeding closely, lest he should hide some of the money on his person. Presently he got the bag unfastened, and plunged his hands into it. Forth from it he drew, not shining gold, but handfuls of fine meal, which he dashed into the eager faces of the men around him. The wind aided him in this, and soon there arose a blinding cloud, which filled the eyes, noses, and mouths of the three outlaws till they could scarcely see or breathe.

While they gasped and choked and sputtered and felt around wildly for that rogue of a beggar, he finished the job by picking up the cloak by its corners, and shaking it vigorously in the faces of his suffering victims. Then he seized a stick which lay conveniently near, and began to rain blows down upon their heads, shoulders, and sides, all the time dancing first on one leg, then on the other, and crying :

" Villains ! rascals ! here are the hundred pounds I promised. How do you like them ? I' faith, you'll get all that's in the bag."

Robin Hood & His Merry Outlaws

Whack! whack! whack! whack! went the stick, emphasizing each word. Howls of pain might have gone up from the sufferers, but they had too much meal in their throats for that. Their one thought was to flee, and they stumbled off blindly down the road, the beggar following them a little way to give them a few parting love-taps.

" Fare ye well, my masters," he said finally, turning the other way ; " and when next I come along the Barnesdale road I hope you will be able to tell gold from meal dust ! "

With this he departed, an easy victor, and again went whistling on his way, while the three outlaws rubbed the meal out of their eyes, and began to catch their breath again.

As soon as they could look around them clearly, they beheld Robin Hood leaning against a tree trunk and surveying them smilingly. He had recovered his own spirits in full measure on seeing their plight.

" God save ye, gossips ! " he said, " ye must, in sooth, have gone the wrong way, and been to the mill, from the look of your clothes."

Then, when they looked shamefaced, and answered never a word, he went on in a soft voice :

" Did ye see aught of that bold beggar I sent you for lately ? "

" In sooth, master," responded Much, the miller's son, " we heard more of him than we saw of him. He filled us so full of meal that I shall sweat meal for a week. I was born in a mill, and had the smell of meal in my nostrils from my very birth, you

How a Beggar Filled the Public Eye

might say, and yet never before did I see such a quantity of the stuff in so small space."

And he sneezed violently.

" How was that ? " asked Robin demurely.

" Why, we laid hold of the beggar as you did order, when he offered to pay for his release out of the bag he carried upon his back."

" The same I did covet," quoth Robin as if to himself.

" So we agreed to this," went on Much, " and spread a cloak down, and he opened his bag, and shook it thereon. Instantly a great cloud of meal filled the air, whereby we could neither see nor breathe, and in the midst of this cloud he vanished like a wizard."

" But not before he left certain black and blue spots to be remembered by, I see," commented Robin.

" He was in league with the Evil One," said one of the widow's sons, rubbing himself ruefully.

Then Robin laughed outright, and sat him down upon the gnarled root of a tree to finish his merriment.

" Four bold outlaws put to rout by a sorry beggar ! " cried he. " I can laugh at ye, my men, for I am in the same boat with ye. But 'twould never do to have this tale get abroad, even in the greenwood—how that we could not hold our own with the odds in our favour. So let us have this little laugh all to our-selves, and no one else need be the wiser ! "

The others saw the point of this, and felt better directly,

despite their itching desire to get hold of the beggar again. And none of the four ever told of the adventure.

But the beggar must have boasted of it at the next tavern, or a little bird perched among the branches of a neighbouring oak must have sung of it, for it got abroad, as such tales will, and was put into a right droll ballad, which was sung the country over and which, I warrant you, the four outlaws did not like to hear.

CHAPTER XI

HOW ROBIN HOOD FOUGHT GUY OF GISBORNE

"I dwell by dale and down," quoth he,
"And Robin to take I'm sworn;
And when I am called by my right name,
I am Guy of good Gisborne."

SOME weeks passed after the rescue of the widow's three sons—weeks spent by the Sheriff in the vain effort to entrap Robin Hood and his men. For Robin's name and deeds had come to the King's ears in London town, and he sent word to the Sheriff to capture the outlaw, under penalty of losing his office, so the Sheriff tried every manner of means to surprise Robin Hood in the forest, but always without success. And he increased the price put upon Robin's head, in the hope that the best men of the kingdom could be induced to try their skill at a capture.

Now, there was a certain Guy of Gisborne, a hireling knight of the King's army, who heard of Robin and of the price upon his head. Sir Guy was one of the best men at the bow and the sword in all the King's service, but his heart was black and treacherous. He obtained the King's leave forthwith to seek out the forester, and, armed with the King's scroll, he came before the Sheriff at Nottingham.

Robin Hood & His Merry Outlaws

" I have come to capture Robin Hood," quoth he, " and mean to have him, dead or alive."

" Right gladly would I aid you," answered the Sheriff, " even if the King's seal were not sufficient warrant. How many men need you ? "

" None," replied Sir Guy, " for I am convinced that forces of men can never come at the bold robber. I must needs go alone. But do you hold your men in readiness at Barnesdale, and when you hear a blast from this silver bugle, come quickly, for I shall have the sly Robin within my clutches."

" Very good," said the Sheriff. " Marry, it shall be done." And he set about giving orders, while Guy of Gisborne sallied forth disguised.

Now, as luck would have it, Will Scarlet and Little John had gone to Barnesdale that very day to buy suits of Lincoln green for certain of the yeomen who had come out at the knees and elbows. But not deeming it best for both of them to run their necks into a noose together they parted just outside the town, and Will went within the gates, while John tarried and watched at the brow of the hill on the outside.

Presently whom should he see but this same Will flying madly forth from the gates again, closely pursued by the Sheriff and threescore men ! Over the moat Will sprang, through the bushes and briers, across the swamp, over stocks and stones, up the woodland roads in long leaps like a scared jack rabbit. And after him puffed the Sheriff and his men, their force scattering

How Robin Fought Guy of Gisborne

out in the flight as one man would tumble head-first into a ditch, another sprawl into the mire, another trip over a rolling stone, and still others sit down on the roadside, and gasp for wind like fish out of water.

Little John could not forbear laughing heartily at the scene, though he knew that 'twould be anything but a laughing matter if Will should stumble. And in truth one man was like to come upon him. It was William-a-Trent, the best runner among the Sheriff's men. He had come within twenty feet of Scarlet, and was leaping upon him with long bounds like a greyhound, when John rose up quickly, drew his bow, and let fly one of his fatal shafts. It would have been better for William-a-Trent to have been abed with sorrow—says the ballad—than to be that day in the greenwood shade to meet with Little John's arrow. He had run his last race.

The others halted a moment in consternation when the shaft came hurtling down from the hill ; but looking up they beheld none save Little John, and with a cry of fierce joy they turned upon him. Meanwhile Will Scarlet had reached the brow of the hill, and sped down the other side.

" I'll just send one more little message of regret to the Sheriff," said Little John, " before I join Will."

But this foolhardy deed was his undoing, for just as the arrow left the string, the good yew bow that had never before failed him snapped in twain.

" Woe worth, woe worth thee, wicked wood, that e'er thou

grew on a tree!" cursed Little John, and planted his feet resolutely in the earth, resolved to sell the path dearly, for the soldiers were now so close upon him that he dared not turn.

And a right good account of himself he gave that day, dealing with each man as he came up according to his merit. And so winded were the pursuers when they reached the top of the hill that he laid out the first ten of them right and left with huge blows of his brawny fist.

But if five men can do more than three a score can overcome one. A body of archers stood off at a prudent distance, and covered Little John with their arrows.

"Now yield you!" panted the Sheriff. "Yield you, Little John, or Reynold Greenleaf, or whatever else name you carry this day! Yield you, or some few of these shafts will reach your heart!"

"Marry, my heart has been touched by your words ere now," said Little John, "and I yield me."

So the Sheriff's men laid hold of Little John, and bound him fast with many cords, so fearful were they lest he should escape. And the Sheriff laughed aloud in glee, and thought of how he should avenge his stolen plate, and determined to make a good day's work of it.

"By the saints!" he said, "you shall be drawn by dale and down, and hanged high on a hill in Barnesdale this very day."

"Hang and be hanged!" retorted the prisoner. "You may fail of your purpose if it be Heaven's will."

How Robin Fought Guy of Gisborne

Back down the hill and across the moor went the company speedily, for they feared a rescue. And as they went the stragglers joined them. Here a man got up feebly out of the ditch, rubbing his pate, and fell in. Yonder came hobbling a man with a lame ankle, or another with his shins torn by the briers, or another with his jacket all muddy from the marsh. So in truth it was a sorry crew that limped and straggled and wandered back into Barnesdale that day. Yet all were merry, for the Sheriff had promised them flagons of wine, and, moreover, they were to hang speedily the boldest outlaw in England next to Robin Hood himself.

The gallows was quickly put up, and a new rope provided.

" Now, up with you ! " commanded the Sheriff, " and let us see if your greenwood tricks will avail you to-morrow."

" I would that I had bold Robin's horn," muttered poor John ; " methinks 'tis all up with me, even as the Sheriff hath spoken."

In good sooth the need was dire and pressing. The rope was placed round the prisoner's neck, and the men prepared to haul away.

" Are you ready ? " called the Sheriff. " One, two——"

But before the " three " left his lips the faint sound of a silver bugle came floating over the hill.

" By my troth, that is Sir Guy of Gisborne's horn," quoth the Sheriff, " and he bade me not to delay answering his summons. He has caught Robin Hood."

" Pardon, Excellency," said one of his men, " but if he has

caught Robin Hood this is a merry day indeed. And let us save this fellow, and build another gallows, and hang them both together."

"That's a brave thought!" said the Sheriff, slapping his knee. "Take the rascal down, and bind him fast to the gallows-tree against our return."

So Little John was made fast to the gallows-tree, while the Sheriff and all his men who could march or hobble went out to get Robin Hood and bring him in for the double hanging.

Let us leave talking of Little John and the Sheriff and see what has become of Robin Hood.

In the first place, he and Little John had come near having a quarrel that selfsame morning because both had seen a curious-looking yeoman, and each wanted to challenge him singly. But Robin would not give way to his lieutenant, and that is why John, in a huff, had gone with Will to Barnesdale.

Meanwhile Robin approached the curious-looking stranger. He seemed to be a three-legged creature at first sight, but on coming nearer you would have seen that 'twas really naught but a poorly clad man, who for a freak had covered up his rags with a capul-hide, nothing more nor less than the sun-dried skin of a horse, complete with head, tail, and mane. The skin of the head made a helmet, while the tail gave the curious three-legged appearance.

"Good-morrow, good fellow," said Robin cheerily. "Me-

How Robin Fought Guy of Gisborne

thinks by the bow you bear in your hand that you should be a good archer."

"Indifferent good," said the other returning his greeting; "but 'tis not of archery that I am thinking this morning, for I have lost my way, and would fain find it again."

"By my faith, I could have believed 'twas your wits you'd lost!" thought Robin, smiling. Then aloud: "I'll lead you through the wood," quoth he, "an you will tell me your business, for belike your speech is much gentler than your attire."

"Who are you to ask me my business?" asked the other roughly.

"I am one of the King's Rangers," replied Robin, "set here to guard his deer 'gainst curious-looking strollers."

"Curious-looking I may be," returned the other, "but no stroller. Hark ye, since you are a Ranger, I must e'en demand your service. I am on the King's business, and seek an outlaw. Men call him Robin Hood. Are you one of his men?"—eyeing him keenly.

"Nay, God forbid!" said Robin; "but what want you with him?"

"That is another tale. But I'd rather meet with that proud outlaw than forty good pounds of the King's money."

Robin now saw how the land lay.

"Come with me, good yeoman," said he, "and belike a little later in the day I can show you Robin's haunts when he is at home. Meanwhile let us have some pastime under the green-wood tree ; let us try the mastery at shooting arrows."

The other agreed, and they cut down two willow wands of a summer's growth that grew beneath a brier, and set them up at a distance of threescore yards.

"Lead on, good fellow," quoth Robin. "The first shot to you."

"Nay ; by my faith," said the other, "I will follow your lead."

So Robin stepped forth, and bent his bow carelessly and sent his shaft whizzing toward the wand, missing it by a scant inch. He of the horse-hide followed with more care, yet was a good three fingers' breadth away.

On the second round the stranger led off, and landed cleverly within the small garland at the top of the wand, but Robin shot far better, and clave the wand itself clean at the middle.

"A blessing on your heart !" shouted Capul-hide ; "never saw I such shooting as that ! Belike you are better than Robin Hood himself. But you have not yet told me your name."

"Nay, by my faith," quoth Robin ; "I must keep it secret till you have told me your own."

"I do not disdain to tell it," said the other. "I dwell by dale and down, and to take bold Robin am I sworn. This would I tell him to his face, were he not so great a craven. When I am called by my right name I am Guy of Gisborne."

How Robin Fought Guy of Gisborne

This he said with a great show of pride, and he strutted back and forth, forgetful that he had just been beaten at archery.

Robin eyed him quietly. " Methinks I have heard of you elsewhere. Do you not bring men to the gallows for a living ? "

" Ay ; but only outlaws such as Robin Hood."

" But, pray, what harm has Robin Hood done you ? "

" He is a highway robber," said Sir Guy, evading the question.

" Has he ever taken from the rich that he did not give again to the poor ? Does he not protect the women and children and side with the weak and helpless ? Is not his greatest crime the shooting of a few King's deer ? "

" Have done with your sophistry," said Sir Guy impatiently. " I am more than ever of opinion that you are of Robin's men yourself."

" I have told you I am not," quoth Robin briefly. " But if I am to help you catch him, what is your plan ? "

" Do you see this silver bugle ? " said the other. " A long blast upon it will summon the Sheriff and all his men when once I have Robin within my grasp. And if you show him to me I'll give you the half of my forty pounds reward."

" I would not help hang a man for ten times forty pounds," said the outlaw. " Yet will I point out Robin to you for the reward I find at my sword's point. I myself am Robin Hood of Sherwood and Barnesdale."

" Then have at you ! " cried the other, springing swiftly into action. His sword leaped forth from beneath the horse's hide with the speed born of long practice, and before Robin had come to guard the other had smitten at him full and foul. Robin eluded the lunge, and drew his own weapon.

"A scurvy trick," quoth he grimly, "to strike at a man unprepared!"

Then neither spoke more, but fell sternly to work—lunge and thrust and ward and parry; for two full hours the weapons smote together sullenly, and neither Robin Hood nor Sir Guy would yield an inch. I promise you that, if you could have looked forth on the fight from behind the trunk of some friendly tree, you would have seen deadly sport, such as few men beheld in Sherwood Forest. For the fighters glared sullenly at each other, the fires of hatred burning in their eyes. One was fighting for his life; the other for a reward and the King's favour.

Still circled the bright blades swiftly in the air—now gleaming in the peaceful sunlight—again hissing like maddened serpents. Neither had yet touched the other, until Robin, in an unlucky moment, stumbled over the projecting root of a tree, when Sir Guy, instead of giving him the chance to recover himself, as any courteous knight would have done, struck quietly at the fallen man, and wounded him in the left side.

"Ah, dear Lady in Heaven," gasped Robin, uttering his favourite prayer, "shield me now! 'Twas never a man's destiny to die before his day,"

And adroitly he sprang up again, and came straight at the other with an awkward but unexpected stroke. The knight had

How Robin Fought Guy of Gisborne

raised his weapon high to give a final blow, when Robin reached beneath and across his guard. One swift lunge, and Sir Guy of Gisborne staggered backward with a deep groan, Robin's sword through his throat.

Robin looked at the slain man regretfully.

"You did bring it upon yourself," said he; "and, traitor and hireling though you were, I would not willingly have killed you."

He looked to his own wound. It was not serious, and he soon staunched the blood and bound up the cut. Then he dragged the dead body into the bushes, and took off the horse's hide and put it upon himself. He placed his own cloak upon Sir Guy, and marked his face so none might tell who had been slain. Robin's own figure and face were not unlike the other's.

Pulling the capul-hide well over himself, so that the helmet hid most of his face, Robin seized the silver bugle and blew a long blast. It was the blast that saved the life of Little John over in Barnesdale, for you and I have already seen how it caused the fond Sheriff to prick up his ears and stay the hanging, and go scurrying up over the hill and into the wood with his men in search of another victim.

In five-and-twenty minutes up came running a score of the Sheriff's best archers.

"Did you signal us, lording?" they asked, approaching Robin.

"Aye," said he, going to meet the puffing Sheriff.

Robin Hood & His Merry Outlaws

" What news, what news, Sir Guy ? " said that officer.

" Robin Hood and Guy of Gisborne had a fight, and he that wears Robin's cloak lies under the covert yonder."

" That's the best news I have heard in all my life ! " exclaimed the Sheriff, rubbing his hands. " I would that we could have saved him for the hanging—though I cannot now complain."

" The hanging ? " repeated Robin.

" Yes. This is our lucky day on the calendar. After you left me we narrowly missed running one of the fellows—I believe 'twas Will Scarlet—to earth, and another who came to his relief we were just about to hang when your bugle blew."

" Who was the other ? " asked the disguised outlaw, excitedly.

" Whom do you suppose ? " laughed the Sheriff. " The best man in the greenwood next to Robin Hood himself—Little John, Reynold Greenleaf ! " for the Sheriff could not forget the name Little John had borne under his own roof at Nottingham.

" Little John ! " thought Robin with a start. Verily that was a lucky blast of the bugle !

" But I see you have not escaped without a scratch," continued the Sheriff, becoming talkative through pure glee. " Here, one of you men ! Give Sir Guy of Gisborne your horse, while others of you bury that dog of an outlaw where he lies, and let us hasten back to Barnesdale and finish hanging the other."

So they put spurs to their horses, and as they rode Robin

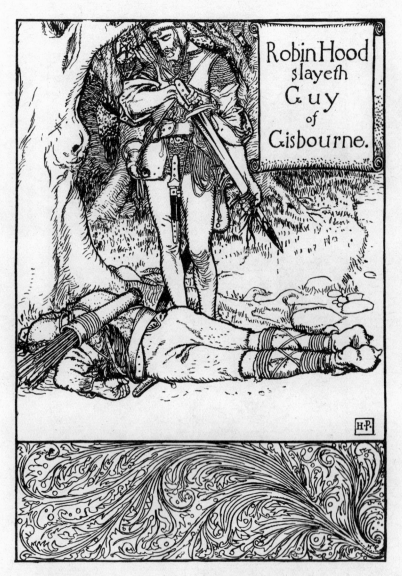

Robin Hood
slayeth
Guy
of
Gisbourne.

CHAPTER XI

"Villains! Rascals! Here are the hundred
pounds!" (CHAPTER X)

How Robin Fought Guy of Gisborne

forced himself to talk merrily, while all the time he was planning the best way to succour Little John.

" A boon, Sheriff," he said as they reached the gates of the town.

" What is it, worthy sir ? You have but to speak."

" I do not want any of your gold, for I have had a brave fight. But, now that I have slain the master, let me put an end to the man, so it shall be said that Guy of Gisborne despatched the two greatest outlaws of England in one day."

" Have it as you will," said the Sheriff ; " but you should have asked a knight's fee and double your reward, and it would have been yours ; it isn't every man that could have taken Robin Hood."

" No, Excellency," answered Robin. " I say it without boasting that no man took Robin Hood yesterday, and none shall take him to-morrow."

Then he approached Little John, who was still tied to the gallows-tree, and he said to the Sheriff's men : " Now stand you back here till I see if the prisoner has been shrived." And he stooped swiftly, and cut Little John's bonds, and thrust into his hands Sir Guy's bow and arrows, which he had been careful to take.

" 'Tis I, Robin ! " he whispered. But in truth Little John knew it already, and had decided there was to be no hanging that day.

Then Robin blew three loud blasts upon his own horn, and

drew forth his own bow, and before the astonished Sheriff and his men could come to arms the arrows were whistling in their midst in no uncertain fashion.

And look! Through the gates and over the walls came pouring another flight of arrows! Will Scarlet and Will Stutely had watched, and planned a rescue, ever since the Sheriff and Robin rode back down the hill. Now in good time they came, and the Sheriff's demoralized force turned tail and ran, while Robin and Little John stood under the harmless gallows, and sped swift arrows after them, and laughed to see them go.

Then they joined their comrades, and hasted back to the good greenwood, and there rested. They had had enough sport for one day.

CHAPTER XII

HOW MAID MARIAN CAME BACK TO SHERWOOD FOREST; ALSO, HOW ROBIN HOOD CAME BEFORE QUEEN ELEANOR

> But Robin Hood, he himself had disguis'd,
>   And Marian was strangely attir'd,
> That they proved foes, and so fell to blows,
>   Whose valour bold Robin admir'd.
>
> .   .   .   .
>
> And when he came at London's Court,
>   He fell down on his knee.
> " Thou art welcome, Lockesley," said the Queen,
>   " And all thy good yeomandree."

NOW, it fell out that one day not long thereafter Robin was minded to try his skill at hunting, and, not knowing whom he might meet in his rambles, he stained his face, and put on a sorry-looking jacket and a long cloak, before he sallied forth. As he walked, the peacefulness of the morning came upon him, and brought back to his memory the early days, so long ago, when he had roamed these same glades with Marian. How sweet they seemed to him now, and how far away ! Marian, too, the dainty friend of his youth—would he ever see her again ? He had thought of her very often of late, and each time with increasing desire to hear her clear voice and musical laugh, and see her eyes light up at his coming.

Perhaps the happiness of Allan-a-Dale and his lady had

Robin Hood & His Merry Outlaws

caused Robin's heart-strings to vibrate more strongly ; perhaps, too, the coming of Will Scarlet. But, certes, Robin was anything but a hunter this bright morning as he walked along, with head drooping in a most love-lorn way.

Presently a hart entered the glade in full view of him, grazing peacefully, and instantly the man of action awoke. His bow was drawn, and a shaft all but loosed, when the beast fell suddenly, pierced by a clever arrow from the far side of the glade.

Then a handsome little page, richly apparelled, sprang glee-fully from the covert and ran toward the dying animal. This was plainly the archer, for he flourished his bow aloft, and like-wise bore a sword at his side, though for all that he looked a mere lad.

Robin straightway approached the hart from the other side.

" Ho, stripling ! " he shouted in a severe tone, " how dare you shoot the King's deer ? "

" I have as much right to shoot them as the King himself," answered the page haughtily. " How dare you question me ? Away, fellow ! " commanded the youth.

The voice stirred Robin strongly. It seemed to chime into his memories of the old days. He looked at the page sharply, and the other returned the glance, straight and unafraid.

" Who might you be, my lad ? " Robin said, more civilly.

" No lad of yours, and my name's my own," retorted the other with spirit.

How Marian Came Back to Sherwood

" Softly ! Fair and softly, sweet page, or we of the forest will have to teach you manners ! " said Robin.

" Not if *you* stand for the forest ! " cried the page, whipping out his sword. " Come, draw, and defend yourself ! "

He swung his blade valiantly, and Robin, now angered, saw nothing for it but to draw likewise. The page thereupon engaged him quite fiercely, and Robin found that he had many pretty little tricks at fencing. Nathless, Robin contented himself with parrying, and was loth to exert all his superior strength upon the lad. So the fight lasted for above a quarter of an hour, at the end of which time the page was almost spent, and the hot blood flushed his cheeks in a most charming manner.

By this time Robin's good nature had returned, and the valiant nature of the slender youth in standing up to fight so tickled his fancy that as they fought he smiled.

Now the youth, seeing that smile, became suddenly enraged and tried to rain harder blows. Robin merely smiled more broadly, and the stripling, finding he could not penetrate the smiling man's guard, almost wept with rage and vexation.

The outlaw saw his distress, and, to end the fight, Robin made a feint and slipped and allowed himself to be pricked slightly on the wrist.

" Are you satisfied, fellow ? " asked the page, wincing a little at sight of the blood.

" Ay, honestly," replied Robin, dropping his sword ; " and

now, perhaps, you will grant me the honour of knowing to whom I owe this scratch ? "

" I am Richard Partington, page to her Majesty Queen Eleanor," answered the lad with dignity, and again the sound of his voice troubled Robin sorely.

" Why come you to the greenwood alone, Master Partington?"

The lad considered his answer while wiping his sword with a small lace kerchief. The action brought a dim, confused memory to Robin. The lad finally looked him again in the eye.

" Forester, whether or no you be a King's man, know that I seek Robin Hood, an outlaw, to whom I bring amnesty from the Queen. Can you tell me aught of him and where I may find him ? " And while waiting his answer he replaced the kerchief in his shirt ; as he did so, the gleam of a golden trophy caught the outlaw's eye.

Robin started forward with a joyful cry.

" Ah ! I know you now ! By the sight of yon golden arrow won at the Sheriff's tourney, you are she on whom I bestowed it, and none other than Maid Marian ! "

" You—are—— ? " gasped Marian, for it was she ; " not Robin ! "

" Robin's self ! " said he gaily, and forthwith, clad as he was in rags, and stained of face, he clasped the dainty page close to his breast, and she forsooth yielded right willingly, and much sweet talk had they together.

148

How Marian Came Back to Sherwood

"But Robin!" she exclaimed presently, greatly distressed, "I knew you not, and was rude, and wounded you!"

"'Twas nothing," he replied laughingly; "so long as it brought me you, I shall ever cherish the scar."

But she made more ado over the sore wrist than Robin had received for all his former hurts put together. And she bound it with a little kerchief, and said: "Now 'twill get well!" and Robin was convinced she spoke the truth, for he never felt better in all his life. The whole woods seemed tinged with a roseate hue since Marian had come again.

But she, while happy also, was ill at ease; and Robin, with a man's slow discernment, at last saw that it was because of her boy's attire. He thought bluntly that there was naught to be ashamed of, yet smilingly handed her his tattered long cloak, which she blushingly wrapped about her, and forthwith recovered her spirits directly.

Then they began to talk of each other's varied fortunes and of the many things which had parted them, and so much did they find to tell that the sun had begun to decline well into the afternoon before they realized how the hours sped.

"I am but a sorry host!" exclaimed Robin, springing to his feet. "I have not once invited you to my wild roof."

"And I am but a sorry page," replied Marian, "for I had clean forgot that I was Richard Partington, and really did bring you a message from Queen Eleanor!"

"Tell me on our way home, and there you shall be entrusted

149

to Mistress Dale, while the first of my men we meet will I send back for your deer."

So she told him, as they walked back through the glade, how that the fame of his prowess had reached Queen Eleanor's ears in London town. And the Queen had said : " Fain would I see this bold yeoman, and behold his skill at the long bow." And the Queen had promised him amnesty if he and four of his archers would repair to London against the next tournament the week following, there to shoot against King Henry's picked men, of whom the King was right vain. All this Marian told in detail, and added :

" When I heard her Majesty say she desired to see you I asked leave to go in search of you, saying I had known you once. And the Queen was right glad, and bade me go, and sent this gold ring to you from off her finger in token of her faith."

Then Robin took the ring, and bowed his head, and kissed it loyally. " By this token will I go to London town," quoth he, " and, ere I part with the Queen's pledge, may the hand that bears it be stricken off at the wrist ! "

By this time they were come to the grove before the outlaws' retreat, and as Robin blew a loud blast upon his horn the whole band assembled.

Will Scarlet at once recognized the sweet face beneath the drooping plumes, and, jumping forward, he took Marian in both arms and kissed her heartily upon both cheeks. Then, whispering

How Marian Came Back to Sherwood

aside with Robin, he turned to the band and announced, with a very important air :

"Merry men all! to-day the band welcomes its mistress—Maid Marian, who is to wed our master, Robin Hood!"

Amid deafening cheers from the delighted outlaws the blushing and happy Marian was given into the tender care of the sweet wife of Allan-a-Dale, and later in the evening, attired once more in bodice and kirtle, and looking more winsome than ever, she took her seat at Robin's right hand at a great feast of welcome, at which every outlaw was present.

After they had supped royally upon the very hart that Marian had slain, Allan sang sweet songs of Northern minstrelsy to the fair guest as she sat by Robin's side, the golden arrow gleaming in her dark hair. The others all joined in the chorus, from Will Scarlet's baritone to Friar Tuck's heavy bass. Even Little John essayed to sing, although looked at threateningly by Much, the miller's son.

Then Robin bade Marian repeat her message from the Queen, which Marian did in a way befitting the dignity of her royal mistress. After which the yeomen gave three cheers for the Queen, and three more for her page, and drank toasts to them both, rising to their feet.

"Ye have heard," quoth Robin, standing forth, "how that her Majesty—whom God preserve!—wishes but four men to go with me. Wherefore, I choose Little John and Will Stutely, my two lieutenants, Will Scarlet, my cousin, and Allan-a-Dale, my minstrel. Mistress Dale, also, can go with her husband, and be company for the Queen's page. We will depart with early morning, decked in our finest. So stir ye, my lads! and see that not only your tunics are fresh, but your swords bright and your bows and arrows fit. For we must be a credit to the Queen as well as to the good greenwood. You, Much, with Stout Will, Lester, and John, the widow's three sons, shall have command of the band while we are away, and Friar Tuck shall preside over the needs of your souls and stomachs."

The orders were received with shouts of approval, and toasts all round were drunk again in nut-brown ale ere the company dispersed to rest after making ready for the journey.

The next morning was as fine a summer's day as ever you want to see, and the green leaves of the forest made a pleasing background for the gay picture of the yeomen setting forth. Says the old ballad, it was a seemly sight to see how Robin Hood himself had dressed, and all his yeomanry. He clothed his men in Lincoln green and himself in scarlet red, with hats of black and feathers white to bravely deck each head; nor were the two ladies behindhand, I ween, at the bedecking.

Thus the chosen party of seven sallied forth, being accompanied to the edge of the wood by the whole band, who gave them a merry parting and Godspeed!

The journey to London town was made without incident. The party proceeded boldly along the King's high road, and no

How Robin Came before the Queen

man met them who was disposed to say them nay. Besides, the good Queen's warrant and ring would have answered for them, as, indeed, it did at the gates of London. So on they sped, and in due course came to the palace itself, and awaited audience with the Queen.

Apartments for Robin and his men were found within the palace itself, yet so well was the secret kept that no man knew of the Queen's guests.

Now, the King had gone that day to Finsbury Field, where the tourney was soon to be held, in order to look over the lists and see some of his picked men, whom he expected to win against all comers. So much had he boasted of these men that the Queen had secretly resolved to win a wager of him. She had heard of the fame of Robin Hood and his yeomen, as Marian had said ; and Marian, on her part, had been overjoyed to be able to add a word in their favour and to set out in search of them.

To-day the Queen sat in her private audience-room, chatting pleasantly with her ladies, when in came Mistress Marian Fitzwalter, attired again as befitted her rank of lady-in-waiting. She curtsied low to the Queen, and awaited permission to speak.

" How now ! " said the Queen, smiling ; " is this my lady Marian, or the page, Richard Partington ! "

" Both, an it please your Majesty. Richard found the man you sought, while Marian brought him to you."

" Where is he ? " asked Queen Eleanor eagerly.

" Awaiting your audience—he and four of his men, likewise

a lady, of whose wooing and wedding I can tell you a pretty story at another time."

" Have them admitted."

So Marian gave orders to an attendant, and presently Robin Hood and his little party entered the room.

Now, the Queen had half expected the men to be rude and uncouth in appearance because of their wild life in the forest, but she was delightfully disappointed. Indeed, she started back in surprise, and almost clapped her hands. For, sooth to say, the yeomen made a brave sight, and in all the Court no more gallant men could be found. Marian felt her cheeks glow with pride at sight of the half-hidden looks of admiration sent forth by the other ladies-in-waiting.

Robin had not forgot the gentle arts taught by his mother, and he wore his fine red velvet tunic and breeches with the grace of a courtier. We have seen before what a dandified gentleman Will Scarlet could be ; and Allan-a-Dale, the minstrel, was scarcely less goodly to look upon ; while the giant Little John and broad-shouldered Will Stutely made up in stature what little they lacked in outward polish. Mistress Dale, on her part, looked even more charming, if possible, than on the momentous day when she went to Plympton Church to marry one man and found another.

Thus came the people of the greenwood before Queen Eleanor in her own private audience-room. And Robin advanced and knelt down before her, and said :

How Robin Came before the Queen

" Here I am, Robin Hood—I and my chosen men ! At your Majesty's bidding am I come, bearing the ring of amnesty, which I will protect—as I would protect your Majesty's honour—with my life ! "

" Thou art welcome, Lockesley," said the Queen, smiling graciously. " Thou art come in good time, thou and all thy brave yeomanry."

Then Robin presented each of his men in turn, and each fell on his knee, and was greeted with most kindly words. And the Queen kissed fair Mistress Dale upon the cheek, and bade her remain in the palace with her ladies while she was in the city. And she made all the party be seated to rest themselves after their long journey. Fine wines were brought, and cake, and rich food, for their refreshment. And as they ate and drank, the Queen told them further of the tourney to be held at Finsbury Field, and of how she desired them to wear her colours and shoot for her. Meantime, she concluded, they were to lie by quietly, and be known of no man.

To do all this Robin and his men pledged themselves full heartily. The Queen took a great liking to all the outlaws, and at her request they related to her and her ladies some of their merry adventures ; whereat the listeners were vastly entertained and laughed heartily. But the story she liked best, and one she never tired of hearing, was that one which told of the exploit of the Bishop of Hereford. For Marian, who had heard of the wedding at Plympton Church, told of the event so drolly that tears stood in the Queen's eyes from merriment.

"My lord Bishop of Hereford!" she laughed. "'Twas, indeed, a comical business for him! I shall keep that to twit his bones, I promise you! So this is our minstrel?" she added presently, turning to Allan-a-Dale. "Methinks I have already heard of him. Will he not harp awhile for us to-day?"

Allan bowed low, and took a harp which was brought to him, and he thrummed the strings, and sang full sweetly the border songs of the North Countree. And the Queen and all her ladies listened in rapt silence till all the songs were ended.

ALLAN·A·DALE·SINGETH·BEFORE·OVR·GOOD·QVEEN·ELEANOR· ⊬Þ⊦ ·MDCCCXXCIII·

CHAPTER XII

With one blow of his fist the knight sent the friar
spinning to the ground. (CHAPTER XII)

CHAPTER XIII

HOW THE OUTLAWS SHOT IN KING HARRY'S TOURNEY

The King is into Finsbury Field
Marching in battle 'ray ;
And after follows bold Robin Hood,
And all his yeomen gay.

THE morning of the great archery contest dawned fair and bright, bringing with it a fever of impatience to every citizen of London town, from the proudest courtier to the lowest kitchen wench. Ay ; and all the surrounding country folk were early awake too, and began to wend their way to Finsbury Field, a fine broad stretch of practice ground near Moorfields. Around three sides of the Field were erected tier upon tier of seats for the spectators, with the royal boxes and booths for the nobility and gentry in the centre. Down along one end were pitched gaily coloured tents for the different bands of King's archers. There were ten of these bands, each containing a score of men, headed by a captain of great renown ; so to-day there were ten of the pavilions, each bearing aloft the royal arms and varicoloured pennants which fluttered lightly in the fresh morning breeze.

Each captain's flag was of peculiar colour and device. First came the royal purple streamer of Tepus, own bowbearer to the

King, and esteemed the finest archer in all the land. Then came the yellow of Clifton of Buckinghamshire ; and the blue of Gilbert of the White Hand—he who was renowned in Nottinghamshire ; and the green of Elwyn, the Welshman ; and the white of Robert of Cloudesdale ; and, after them, five other captains of bands, each a man of proved prowess. As the Queen had said aforetime, the King was mightily proud of his archers, and now held this tourney to show their skill and, mayhap, to recruit their forces.

The uprising tiers of seats filled early, upon this summer morning, and the merry chatter of the people went abroad like the hum of bees in a hive. The royal party had not yet put in an appearance, nor were any of the King's archers visible. So the crowd was content to hide its impatience by laughing gibes passed from one section to another, and crying the colours of its favourite archers. In and out among the seats went hawkers, their arms laden with small pennants to correspond with the rival tents. Other vendors of pies and small cakes and cider also did a thrifty business, for so eager had some of the people been to get good seats, that they had rushed away from home without their breakfast.

Whilst the common people waited and discussed the chances of their favourite archers, the lords and ladies slowly strolled into the grounds and took their seats, and soon after the blare of trumpets announced the approach of their Majesties.

Suddenly the gates at the far end, next the tents, opened wide,

King Harry's Tourney

and a courier in scarlet and gold, mounted upon a white horse, rode in blowing lustily upon the trumpet at his lips, and behind him came six standard-bearers riding abreast. The populace arose with a mighty cheer. King Harry had entered the arena. He bestrode a fine white charger, and was clad in a rich dark suit of slashed velvet with satin and gold facings. His hat bore a long curling ostrich plume of pure white, and he doffed it graciously in answer to the shouts of the people. By his side rode Queen Eleanor, looking regal and charming in her long brocade riding-habit ; while immediately behind them came Prince Richard and Prince John, each attired in knightly coats of mail and helmets. Lords and ladies of the realm followed ; and, finally, the ten companies of archers, whose progress round the field was greeted with hardly less applause than that given the King himself.

The King and Queen dismounted from their steeds, ascended the steps of the royal box, and seated themselves upon two thrones, decked with purple and gold trappings, upon a dais sheltered by striped canvas. In the booths at each side the members of the Court took their places ; while comely pages ran hither and thither bearing the royal commands. 'Twas a lordly sight, I ween, this shifting of proud courtiers, flashing of jewelled fans, and commingling of bright colours with costly gems !

Now the herald arose to command peace, and the clear note of his trumpet rose above the roar of the crowd, and hushed it to silence. The tenscore archers ranged themselves in two long rows on each side of the lists—a gallant array—while their captains, as a special mark of favour, stood near the royal box.

"Come hither, Tepus," said the King to his bowbearer. "Come, measure me out this line, how long our mark must be."

"What is the reward ? " then asked the Queen.

"That will the herald presently proclaim," answered the King. "For first prize we have offered a purse containing twoscore golden pounds ; for second, a purse containing twoscore silver pennies ; and for third, a silver bugle inlaid with gold. Moreover, if the King's companies keep these prizes, the winning companies shall have—first, two tuns of Rhenish wine ; second, two tuns of English beer ; and, third, five of the fattest harts that run on Dallom Lea ; methinks that is a princely wager," added King Harry laughingly.

Up spake bold Clifton, secure in the King's favour. "Measure no mark for us, most sovereign liege," quoth he ; "for such largess as that we'll shoot at the sun and the moon."

" 'Twill not be so far as that," said the King. "But get a line of good length, Tepus, and set up the targets at tenscore paces."

Forthwith Tepus bowed low, and set up ten targets, each bearing the pennant of a different company, while the herald stood forth again, and proclaimed the rules and prizes. The entries were open to all comers. Each man, also, of the King's archers should shoot three arrows at the target bearing the colours of his band, until the best bowman in each band should be chosen.

King Harry's Tourney

These ten chosen archers should then enter a contest for an open target—three shots apiece—and here any other bowman whatsoever was asked to try his skill. The result at the open targets should decide the tourney.

Then all the people shouted again, in token that the terms of the contest pleased them ; and the archers waved their bows aloft, and wheeled into position, facing their respective targets.

The shooting now began upon all the targets at once, and the multitude had so much ado to watch them that they forgot to shout. Besides, silence was commanded during the shooting. Of all the fine shooting that morning I have not now space to tell you. The full score of men shot three times at each target, and then three times again to decide a tie—for, more than once, the arrow shot by one man would be split wide open by his successor. Every man's shaft bore his number to ease the counting, and so close would they stick at the end of a round that the target looked like a big bristle hair-brush. Then must the spectators relieve their tense spirits by great cheering, while the King looked mighty proud of his skilled bowmen.

At last the company targets were decided, and Tepus, as was expected, led the score, having made six exact centres in succession. Gilbert of the White Hand followed with five, and Clifton with four. Two other captains had touched their centre four times, but not roundly ; while in the other companies it so chanced that the captains had been outshot by some of the men under them.

Robin Hood & His Merry Outlaws

The winners then saluted the King and Queen, and withdrew for a space to rest and renew their bowstrings for the keenest contest of all ; while the lists were cleared, and a new target— the open one—was set up at twelvescore paces. At the bidding of the King the herald announced that the open target was to be shot at to decide the title of the best archer in all England, and any man there present was privileged to try for it. But so keen had been the previous shooting that many yeomen who had come to enter the lists now would not do so, and only a dozen men stepped forth to give in their names.

" By my halidom ! " said the King, " these must be hardy men to pit themselves against my archers ! "

" Think you that your ten chosen fellows are the best bowmen in all England ? " asked the Queen.

" Ay ; and in all the world beside," answered the King, " and thereunto I would stake five hundred pounds."

" I am minded to take your wager," said the Queen musingly, " and will e'en do so if you grant me a boon."

" What is it ? " asked the King.

" If I produce five archers who can outshoot your ten will you grant my men full grace and amnesty ? "

" Assuredly ! " quoth the King in right good-humour. " Nathless, I tell you now your wager is in jeopardy, for there never were such bowmen as Tepus and Clifton and Gilbert ! "

" Hum ! " said the Queen, puckering her brow, still as though lost in thought, " I must see if there be none present to aid me

King Harry's Tourney

in my wager. Boy, call hither Sir Richard of the Lea and my lord Bishop of Hereford ! "

The two summoned ones, who had been witnessing the sport, came forward.

" Sir Richard," said she, " thou art a full knight and a good. Wouldst advise me to meet a wager of the King's that I can produce other archers as good as Tepus and Gilbert and Clifton ? "

" Nay, your Majesty," he said, bending his knee ; " there be none present that can match them. Howbeit "—he added, dropping his voice—" I have heard of some who lie hid in Sherwood Forest who could show them strange targets."

The Queen smiled, and dismissed him.

" Come hither, my lord Bishop of Hereford," quoth she. " Wouldst thou advance a sum to support my wager 'gainst the King ? "

" Nay, your Majesty," said the fat Bishop. " An you pardon me, I'd not lay down a penny on such a bet, for, by my silver mitre, the King's archers are men who have no peers."

" But suppose I found men whom *thou knewest* to be masters at the bow," she insisted roguishly, " wouldst thou not back them ? Belike, I have heard that there be men round about Nottingham and Plympton who carry such matters with a high hand ! "

The Bishop glanced nervously around, as if half expecting to see Robin Hood's men standing near, then turned to find the Queen looking at him with much amusement lurking in her eyes.

Robin Hood & His Merry Outlaws

" 'Od's bodikins ! the story of my misadventure must have preceded me ! " he thought ruefully.   Aloud he said, resolved to face it out :

" Your Majesty, such tales are idle and exaggerated.   An you pardon me, I would add to the King's wager that his men are invincible."

" As it pleases thee," replied the Queen imperturbably. " How much ? "

" Here is my purse," said the Bishop uneasily ; " it contains fifteen score nobles, or near an hundred pounds."

" I'll take it at even money," she said, dismissing him. " And, your Majesty "—turning to the King, who had been conversing with the two princes and certain of the nobles—" I accept your wager of five hundred pounds."

" Very good," said the King, laughing, as though it were a great jest.   " But what has minded you to take such interest in the sport of a sudden ? "

" It is as I have said.   I have found five men whom I will pit against any you may produce."

" Then we will try their skill speedily," quoth the King. " How say you if first we decide this open target and then match the five best thereat against your unknown champions ? "

" Agreed," said the Queen.   Thereupon she signed to Maid Marian to step forward, from a near-by booth where she sat with other ladies-in-waiting, and whispered something in her ear. Marian curtsied, and withdrew.

King Harry's Tourney

Now the ten chosen archers from the King's bands came forth again, and took their stand, and with them stood forth the twelve untried men from the open lists. Again the crowd was stilled, and every eye hung upon the speeding of the shafts. Slowly but skilfully each man shot, and as his shaft struck the inner ring a deep breath broke from the multitude like the sound of the wind upon the seashore. And now Gilbert of the White Hand led the shooting, and 'twas only by the space of a hair's-breadth upon the line that Tepus tied his score. Stout Elwyn, the Welshman, took third place ; one of the private archers, named Geoffrey, came fourth ; while Clifton must needs content himself with the fifth. The men from the open lists shot fairly true, but nervousness and fear of ridicule wrought their undoing.

The herald then came forward again, and, instead of announcing the prize-winners, proclaimed that there was to be a final contest. Two men had tied for first place, declared his Majesty the King, and the three others were entitled to honours. Now, all these five were to shoot again, and they were to be pitted against five others of the Queen's choosing—men who had not yet shot upon that day.

A thrill of astonishment and excitement swept around the arena. " Who were these men of the Queen's choosing ! " was upon every lip. The hubbub of eager voices grew intense, and in the midst of it all the gate at the far end of the field opened, and five men entered, and escorted a lady upon horseback across the arena to the royal box. The lady was instantly recognized as Mistress Marian of the Queen's household, but no one seemed to know the faces of her escort. Four were clad in Lincoln green, while the fifth, who seemed to be the leader, was dressed in a brave suit of scarlet red. Each man wore a close-fitting cap of black, decked with a curling white feather. For arms, he carried simply a stout bow, a sheaf of new arrows, and a short hunting-knife.

When the little party came before the dais on which the King and Queen sat, the yeomen doffed their caps humbly, while Maid Marian was assisted to dismount.

"Your gracious Majesty," she said, addressing the Queen, "these be the men for whom you sent me, and who are now come to wear your colours and serve you in the tourney."

The Queen leaned forward, and handed them each a scarf of green and gold.

"Lockesley," she said in a clear voice, "I thank thee and thy men for this service. Know that I have laid a wager with the King that ye can outshoot the best five whom he has found in all his bowmen."

The five men pressed the scarves to their lips in token of fealty.

The King turned to the Queen inquiringly.

"Who are these men you have brought before us?" asked he.

Up came the worthy Bishop of Hereford, growing red and pale by turns.

King Harry's Tourney

" Your pardon, my liege lord ! " cried he ; " but I must denounce these fellows as outlaws. Yon man in scarlet is none other than Robin Hood himself. The others are Little John and Will Stutely and Will Scarlet and Allan-a-Dale—all famous in the North Countree for their deeds of violence."

" As my lord Bishop personally knows ! " added the Queen significantly.

The King's brows grew dark. The name of Robin Hood was well known to him, as to every man there present.

" Is this true ? " he demanded sternly.

" Ay, my lord," responded the Queen demurely ; " but, bethink you—I have your royal promise of grace and amnesty."

" That will I keep," said the King, holding in check his ire by a mighty effort. " But, look you ! Only forty days do I grant of respite. When this time has elapsed let these bold outlaws look to their safety ! "

Then, turning to his five victorious archers, who had drawn near, he added : " Ye have heard, my men, how that I have a wager with the Queen upon your prowess. Now, here be men of her choosing—certain free shafts of Sherwood and Barnesdale. Wherefore look well to it, Gilbert and Tepus and Geoffrey and Elwyn and Clifton ! If ye outshoot these knaves I will fill your caps with silver pennies—ay, and knight the man who stands first. But if ye lose I give the prizes, for which ye have just striven, to Robin Hood and his men, according to my royal word."

Robin Hood & His Merry Outlaws

" Robin Hood and his men ! " The saying flew round the arena with the speed of wild-fire, and every neck craned forward to see the famous fellows who had dared to brave the King's anger for sake of the Queen.

Another target was now set up, at the same distance as the last, and it was decided that the ten archers should shoot three arrows in turn. Gilbert and Robin tossed up a penny for the lead, and it fell to the King's men, so Clifton was bidden to shoot first. Forth he stood, planting his feet firmly, and wetting his fingers before plucking the string, for he was resolved to better his losing score of that day. And in truth he did so, for the shaft he loosed sped true, and landed on the black bull's-eye, though not in the exact centre. Again he shot, and again he hit the black, on the opposite rim. The third shaft swerved downward, and came within the second ring, some two fingers'-breadths away. Nathless, a general cry went up, as this was the best shooting Clifton had done that day.

Will Scarlet was chosen to follow him, and now took his place, and carefully chose three round and full-feathered arrows.

" Careful, my sweet coz ! " quoth Robin in a low tone. " The knave has left wide space in the centre for all of your darts."

But Robin gave Will the wrong caution, for over-much care spoiled his aim. His first shaft flew wide, and lodged in the second ring, even farther away than the worst shot of Clifton.

168

King Harry's Tourney

"Your pardon, coz!" quoth Robin hastily. "Bid care go to the bottom of the sea, and do you loose your string before it sticks to your fingers!"

And Will profited by this hint, and loosed his next two shafts as freely as though they flew along a Sherwood glade. Each struck upon the bull's-eye, and one even nearer the centre than his rival's mark, yet the total score was adjudged in favour of Clifton. At this Will Scarlet bit his lip, but said no word, while the crowd shouted, and waved yellow flags, for very joy that the King's man had overcome the outlaw. They knew, also, that this demonstration would please the King.

The target was now cleared for the next two contestants— Geoffrey and Allan-a-Dale; whereat it was noticed that many ladies in the Queen's booths boldly flaunted Allan's colours, much to the honest pride which glowed in the cheeks of one who sat in their midst.

"In good truth," said more than one lady to Mistress Dale, "if thy husband can handle the long bow as skilfully as the harp, his rival has little show of winning!"

The saying augured well. Geoffrey had shot many good shafts that day—and, indeed, had risen from the ranks by virtue of them—but now each of his three shots, though well placed in triangular fashion around the rim of the bull's-eye, yet allowed an easy space for Allan to graze within. His shooting, more-over, was so prettily done that he was right heartily applauded —the ladies and their gallants leading in the hand-clapping.

Robin Hood & His Merry Outlaws

Now, you must know that there had long been a friendly rivalry in Robin Hood's band as to who was the best shot next after Robin himself. He and Will Stutely had lately decided their marksmanship, and Will had found that Robin's skill was now so great as to place the leader at the head of all good bowmen in the forest. But the second place lay between Little John and Stutely, and neither wished to yield to the other, so to-day they looked narrowly at their leader to see who should shoot third. Robin read their faces at a glance, and laughing merrily, broke off two straws, and held them out.

"The long straw goes next!" he decided—and it fell to Stutely.

Elwyn, the Welshman, was to precede him, and his score was no whit better than Geoffrey's. But Stutely failed to profit by it. His besetting sin at archery had ever been an undue haste and carelessness; to-day these were increased by a certain moodiness that Little John had outranked him. So his first two shafts flew swiftly, one after the other, to lodging-places outside the Welshman's mark.

"Man! man!" cried Robin entreatingly, "you do forget the honour of the Queen and the credit of Sherwood!"

"I ask your pardon, master!" quoth Will humbly enough, and loosing as he spoke his last shaft. It whistled down the course unerringly, and struck in the exact centre—the best shot yet made.

King Harry's Tourney

Now, some shouted for Stutely and some shouted for Elwyn, but Elwyn's total mark was declared the better. Whereupon the King turned to the Queen.

"What say you now ? " quoth he in some triumph. " Two out of the three first rounds have gone to my men. Your outlaws will have to shoot better than that in order to save your wager ! "

The Queen smiled gently.

" Yea, my lord," she said ; " but the twain who are left are able to do the shooting. You forget that I have still Little John and Robin Hood."

" And you forget, my lady, that I still have Tepus and Gilbert."

So each turned again to the lists, and awaited the next rounds in silent eagerness. I ween that King Harry had never watched the invasion of an enemy with more anxiety than he now felt.

Tepus was chosen to go next, and he fell into the same error as Will Scarlet. He held the string a moment too long, and both his first and second arrows came to grief. One of them, however, came within the black rim, and he followed it up by placing his third in the full centre, just as Stutely had done with his last. These two centres were the fairest shots that had been made that day, and loud was the applause which greeted this second one. But the shouting was as nothing to the uproar which followed Little John's shooting. That good-natured giant seemed determined to outdo Tepus by a tiny margin in each separate shot, for the first and the second shafts grazed his rival's on the inner side, while for the third Little John did the old trick of the forest: he shot his own arrow in a graceful curve, which descended from above upon Tepus's final centre shaft with a glancing blow that drove the other out and left the outlaw's in its place.

The King could scarce believe his eyes. " By my halidom ! " quoth he, " that fellow deserves either a dukedom or a hanging ! He must be in league with Satan himself ! Never saw I such shooting."

" The score is tied, my lord," said the Queen ; " we have still to see Gilbert and Robin Hood."

Gilbert now took his stand, and slowly shot his arrows, one after another, into the bull's-eye. 'Twas the best shooting he had yet done ; but there was still the smallest of spaces left— if you looked closely—at the very centre.

" Well done, Gilbert ! " spoke up Robin Hood. " You are a foeman worthy of being shot against." He took his own place as he spoke. " Now, if you had placed one of your shafts *there* " —loosing one of his own—" and another *there* "—out sped the second—" and another *there* "—the third was launched—" may-hap the King would have declared you the best bowman in all England ! "

But the last part of his merry speech was drowned in the wild tumult of applause which followed his exploit. His first two shafts had packed themselves into the small space left at the bull's-eye, while his third had split down between them, taking half of each, and making all three appear from a distance as one immense arrow.

Up rose the King in amazement and anger.

" Gilbert is not yet beaten ! " he cried. " Did he not shoot within the mark thrice ? And that is allowed a best in all the rules of archery."

Robin bowed low.

" As it please your Majesty ! " quoth he. " But may I be allowed to place the mark for the second shooting ? "

The King waved his hand sullenly. Thereupon Robin prepared another old trick of the greenwood, and got him a light, peeled willow wand, which he set in the ground in place of the target.

" There, friend Gilbert," called he gaily ; " belike you can hit that ! "

" I can scarce see it from here," said Gilbert, " much less hit it ; nathless, for the King's honour I will try."

But this final shot proved his undoing, and his shaft flew harmlessly by the thin white streak. Then came Robin to his stand again, and picked his arrow with exceeding care, and tried his string. Amid a breathless pause he drew the good yew bow back to his ear, glanced along the shaft, and let the feathered missile fly. Straight it sped, singing a keen note of triumph as it went. The willow wand was split in twain, as though it had met a hunter's knife.

" Verily, I think your bow is armed with witchcraft," cried Gilbert, " for I did not believe such shooting possible."

" You should come to see our merry lads in the greenwood," retorted Robin lightly, " for willow wands do not grow upon the cobble-stones of London town."

Meanwhile the King, in great wrath, had risen to depart, first signing to the judges to distribute the prizes. Never a word said he of good or ill to the Queen, but mounted his horse, and, followed by his sons and knights, rode off the field. The archers dropped upon one knee as he passed, but he gave them a single baleful look, and was gone.

Then the Queen beckoned the outlaws to approach, and they did so, and knelt at her feet.

" Right well have you served me," she said, " and sorry am I that the King's anger is aroused thereby. But fear ye not, his word and grace hold true. As to these prizes ye have gained, I add others of mine own—the wagers I have won from his Majesty the King and from the lord Bishop of Hereford. Buy with some of these moneys the best swords ye can find in London for all your band, and call them the swords of the Queen, and swear with them to protect all the poor and helpless and the womenkind who come your way."

" We swear," said the five yeomen solemnly.

Then the Queen gave each of them her hand to kiss, and

arose, and departed with all her ladies. And after they were gone the King's archers came crowding around Robin and his men, eager to get a glimpse of the fellows about whom they had heard so much. And behind them came a great crowd of the spectators, pushing and jostling in their efforts to come nearer.

" Verily ! " laughed Little John, " they must take us for a Merry Andrew show ! "

Now the judges came up, and announced to each man his prize, according to the King's command. To Robin was given the purse containing twoscore golden pounds ; to Little John the twoscore silver pennies ; and to Allan-a-Dale the fine inlaid bugle, much to his delight, for he was skilled at blowing sweet tunes upon the horn hardly less than touching the harp-strings ; but when the Rhenish wine and English beer and harts of Dallom Lea were spoken of, Robin said :

" Nay ; what need we of wine or beer so far from the greenwood ? And 'twould be like carrying coals to Newcastle to drive those harts to Sherwood ! Now, Gilbert and Tepus and their men have shot passing well—wherefore the meat and drink must go to them, an they will accept it of us."

" Right gladly," replied Gilbert, grasping his hand. " Ye are good men all, and we will toast you every one, in memory of the greatest day at archery that England has ever seen, or ever will see ! "

Thus said all the King's archers, and the hand of good-fellowship was given amid much shouting and clapping on the shoulder-blades.

And so ended King Harry's tourney, whose story has been handed down from sire to son even unto the present day.

CHAPTER XIV

HOW ROBIN HOOD WAS SOUGHT OF THE TINKER

> And while the tinker fell asleep,
> Robin made haste away,
> And left the tinker in the lurch,
> For the great shot to pay.

KING HARRY was as good as his word. Robin Hood and his party were suffered to depart from London—the parting bringing keen sorrow to Marian—and for forty days no hand was raised against them. But at the end of that time the royal word was sent to the worthy Sheriff at Nottingham that he must lay hold upon the outlaws without further delay, as he valued his office.

Indeed, the exploits of Robin and his band, ending with the great tourney in Finsbury Field, had made a mighty stir through all England, and many there were to laugh boldly at the Nottingham official for his failure to capture the outlaws.

The Sheriff thereupon planned three new expeditions into the greenwood, and was even brave enough to lead them, since he had fifteenscore men at his beck and call each time. But never the shadow of an outlaw did he see, for Robin's men lay close, and the Sheriff's men knew not how to come at their chief hiding-place in the cove before the cavern.

Now, the Sheriff's daughter had hated Robin Hood bitterly

in her heart ever since the day he refused to bestow upon her the golden arrow, and shamed her before all the company. His tricks, also, upon her father were not calculated to lessen her hatred, and so she sought about for means to aid the Sheriff in catching the enemy.

" There is no need to go against this man with force of arms," she said ; " we must meet his tricks with other tricks of our own."

" Would that we could," groaned the Sheriff ; " the fellow is becoming a nightmare unto me."

" Let me plan awhile," she replied ; " belike I can cook up some scheme for his undoing."

" Agreed," said the Sheriff ; " and if anything comes of your planning I will e'en give you an hundred silver pennies for a new gown, and a double reward to the man who catches the outlaw."

Now, upon that same day, while the Sheriff's daughter was racking her brains for a scheme, there came to the Mansion House a strolling tinker named Middle, a great gossip and braggart. And as he pounded away upon some pots and pans in the scullery he talked loudly about what *he* would do if he once came within reach of that rascal Robin Hood.

" It might be that this simple fellow could do something through his very simplicity," mused the Sheriff's daughter, overhearing his prattle. " 'Od's bodikins ! 'twill do no harm to try his service, while I bethink myself of some better plan."

And she called him to her, and looked him over—a big,

How Robin was Sought of the Tinker

brawny fellow enough, with an honest look about the eye, and a countenance so open that when he smiled his mouth seemed the only country on the map.

" I am minded to try your skill at outlaw-catching," she said, " and will add goodly measure to the stated reward if you succeed. Do you wish to make good your boasted prowess ? "

The tinker grinned broadly.

" Yes, your ladyship," he said.

" Then here is a warrant made out this morning by the Sheriff himself ; see that you keep it safely and use it to good advantage."

And she dismissed him.

Middle departed from the house mightily pleased with himself and proud of his commission. He swung his crab-tree staff recklessly in his glee—so recklessly that he imperilled the shins of more than one angry passer-by—and vowed he'd crack the ribs of Robin Hood with it though he were surrounded by every outlaw in the whole greenwood.

Spurred on by the thoughts of his own coming bravery he left the town, and proceeded toward Barnesdale. The day was hot and dusty, and at noon-time he paused at a wayside inn to refresh himself. He began by eating and drinking and dozing in turn, then sought to do all at once.

Mine host of the " Seven Does " stood by, discussing the eternal Robin with a drover.

" Folk do say that my lord Sheriff has sent into Lincoln for

Robin Hood & His Merry Outlaws

more men-at-arms and horses, and that when he has these behind him he'll soon rid the forest of these fellows."

" Of whom speak you ? " asked the tinker, sitting up.

" Of Robin Hood and his men," said the host. " But go to sleep again—you will never get the reward ! "

" And why not ? " asked the tinker, rising with great show of dignity.

" Where our Sheriff has failed, and the stout Guy of Gisborne, and many more beside, it behoves not a mere tinker to succeed."

The tinker laid a heavy hand upon the innkeeper's fat shoulder and tried to look impressive.

" There is your reckoning, host, upon the table. I must e'en go upon my way, because I have more important business than to stand here gossiping with you. But be not surprised if, the next time you see me, I shall have with me no less person than Robin Hood himself ! "

And he strode loftily out at the door, and walked up the hot white road toward Barnesdale.

He had not gone above a quarter of a mile when he met a young man with curling brown hair and merry eyes. The young man carried his light cloak over his arm because of the heat, and was unarmed save for a light sword at his side. The new-comer eyed the perspiring tinker in a friendly way, and, seeing he was a stout fellow, accosted him.

" Good-day to you ! " said he.

How Robin was Sought of the Tinker

" Good-day to you," said the tinker ; " and a morrow less heating."

" Ay," laughed the other. " Whence come you ? And know you the news ? "

" What is the news ? " said the gossipy tinker, pricking up his ears. " I am a tinker by trade, Middle by name, and come from over against Banbury."

" Why, as for the news," laughed the stranger, " I hear that two tinkers were set i' the stocks for drinking too much ale and beer."

" If that be all your news," retorted Middle, " I can beat you clear to the end of the lane."

" What news have you ? Seeing that you go from town to town I ween you can outdo a poor country yokel at tidings."

" All I have to tell," said the other, " is that I am especially commissioned "—he felt mightily proud of these big words— " especially commissioned to seek a bold outlaw which they call Robin Hood."

" So ? " said the other, arching his brows. " How ' especially commissioned ' ? "

" I have a warrant from the Sheriff, sealed with the King's own seal, to take him where I can, and if you can tell me where he is I will e'en make a man of you."

" Let me see the warrant," said the other, " to satisfy myself if it be right, and I will do the best I can to bring him to you."

" That will I not," replied the tinker ; " I will trust none with it. And if you'll not help me to come at him I must, forsooth, catch him by myself."

And he made his crab-tree staff whistle shrill circles in the air.

The other smiled at the tinker's simplicity, and said :

" The middle of the road on a hot July day is not a good place to talk things over. Now, if you're the man for me and I'm the man for you, let's go back to the inn, just beyond the bend of the road, and quench our thirst and cool our heads for thinking."

" Marry come up ! " quoth the tinker. " That will I ! For though I've just come from there, my thirst rises mightily at the sound of your voice."

So back he turned with the stranger, and proceeded to the " Seven Does."

The landlord arched his eyebrows silently when he saw the two come in, but served them willingly.

The tinker asked for wine, and the stranger for ale. The wine was not the most cooling drink in the cellars nor the clearest-headed. Nathless, the tinker asked for it, since it was expensive and the other man had invited him to drink. They lingered long over their cups, Master Middle emptying one after another, while the stranger expounded at great length on the best plans for coming at and capturing Robin Hood.

In the end the tinker fell sound asleep while in the act of trying to get a tankard to his lips. Then the stranger deftly

How Robin was Sought of the Tinker

opened the snoring man's pouch, took out the warrant, read it, and put it in his own wallet. Calling mine host to him, he winked at him with a half-smile, and told him that the tinker would pay the whole score when he awoke. Thus was Master Middle left in the lurch "for the great shot to pay."

Nathless, the stranger seemed in no great hurry. He had the whim to stay awhile and see what the droll tinker might do when he awoke. So he hid behind a window shutter, on the outside, and awaited events.

Presently the tinker came to himself with a prodigious yawn, and reached at once for another drink.

"What were you saying, friend, about the best plan (ya-a-a-ah !) for catching this fellow ? Hello ! where's the man gone ? "

He had looked round, and could see no one with him at the table.

"Host ! host ! " he shouted, "where is that fellow who was to pay my reckoning ? "

"I know not," answered the landlord sharply. "Mayhap he left the money in your purse."

"No ; he didn't ! " roared Middle, looking therein. "Help ! help ! I've been robbed ! Look you, host, you are liable to arrest for high treason ! I am here upon the King's business, as I told you earlier in the day. And yet while I did rest under your roof, thinking you were an honest man (hic !) and one loving of the King, my pouch has been opened, and many matters of State taken from it."

"Cease your bellowing!" said the landlord. "What did you lose?"

"Oh, many weighty matters, I do assure you. I had with me : Item, a warrant, granted under the hand of my lord High Sheriff of Nottingham, and sealed with the King's own seal, for the capture (hic !)—and arrest—and overcoming of a notorious rascal, one Robin Hood of Barnesdale. Item, one crust of bread. Item, one lump (hic !) of solder. Item, three pieces of twine. Item, six single keys (hic !), useful withal. Item, twelve silver pennies, the which I earned this week (hic !) in fair labour. Item——"

"Have done with your 'items'!" said the host. "And I marvel greatly to hear you speak in such fashion of your friend Robin Hood of Barnesdale. For was he not with you just now, and did he not drink with you in all good fellowship?"

"Wh-a-at? *That* Robin Hood?" gasped Middle, with staring eyes. "Why did you not tell me?"

"Faith, *I* saw no need o' telling you! Did you not tell me the first time you were here to-day that I need not be surprised if you came back with no less person than Robin Hood himself?"

"I see it all now," moaned the tinker. "He got me to drinking, and then took my warrant and my pennies and my crust——"

How Robin was Sought of the Tinker

" Yes, yes," interrupted the host. " I know all about that. But pay me the score for both of you."

" But I have no money, gossip. Let me go after that vile bag-o'-bones, and I'll soon get it out of him."

" Not so," replied the other. " If I waited for you to collect from Robin Hood I would soon close up shop."

" What is the account ? " asked Middle.

" Ten shillings, just."

" Then take here my working-bag and my good hammer too, and if I light upon that knave I will soon come back after them."

" Give me your leathern coat as well," said mine host ; " the hammer and bag of tools are as naught to me."

" Grammercy ! " cried Master Middle, losing what was left of his temper, " it seems that I have escaped one thief only to fall into the hands of another. If you will but walk with me out into the middle of the road I'll give you such a crack as shall drive some honesty into your thick skull."

" You are wasting your breath and my time," retorted the landlord. " Give me your things, and get you gone after your man speedily."

Middle thought this to be good advice, so he strode forth from the " Seven Does " in a black mood.

Ere he had gone half a mile he saw Robin Hood walking demurely among the trees a little in front of him.

" Ho, there, you villain ! " roared the tinker. " Stay your steps ! I am desperately in need of you this day ! "

Robin Hood & His Merry Outlaws

Robin turned about with a surprised face.

" What knave is this," he asked gently, " who comes shouting after me ? "

" No knave ! no knave at all ! " panted the other, rushing up, " but an honest man—who would have—that warrant—and the money for drink ! "

" Why, as I live, it is our honest tinker who was seeking Robin Hood ! Did you find him, gossip ? "

" Marry, that did I ! and I'm now going to pay him my respects ! "

And he plunged at him, making a sweeping stroke with his crab-tree cudgel.

Robin tried to draw his sword, but could not do it for a moment through dodging the other's furious blows. When he did get it in hand the tinker had reached him thrice with re-sounding thwacks. Then the tables were turned, for he dashed in right manfully with his shining blade, and made the tinker give back again.

The greenwood rang with the noise of the fray. 'Twas steel against wood, and they made a terrible clattering when they came together. Robin thought at first that he could hack the cudgel to pieces, for his blade was one of Toledo—finely tempered steel—which the Queen had given him. But the crab-tree staff had been fired and hardened and seasoned by the tinker's arts until it was like a bar of iron—no pleasant neighbour for one's ribs.

How Robin was Sought of the Tinker

Robin presently found this out to his sorrow. The long reach and long stick got to him when 'twas impossible for him to touch his antagonist, so his sides began to ache sorely.

" Hold your hand, tinker," he said at length ; " I cry a boon of you."

" Before I do it," said the tinker, " I'd hang you on this tree."

But even as he spoke, Robin found the moment's grace for which he longed ; and immediately grasped his horn, and blew the three well-known blasts of the greenwood.

" A murrain seize you ! " roared the tinker, commencing afresh. " Up to your old tricks again, are you ? Well, I'll have time to finish my job if I hurry."

But Robin was quite able to hold his own at a pinch, and they had not exchanged many lunges and passes when up came Little John and Will Scarlet and a score of yeomen at their heels. Middle was seized without ceremony, while Robin sat himself down to breathe.

" What is the matter," quoth Little John, " that you should sit so wearily upon the highway side ? "

" Faith, that rascally tinker yonder has paid his score well upon my hide," answered Robin ruefully.

" That tinker, then," said Little John, " must be itching for more work ; fain would I try if he can do as much for me."

" Or me," said Will Scarlet, who, like Little John, was always willing to swing a cudgel.

Robin Hood & His Merry Outlaws

" Nay," laughed Robin ; " belike I could have done better an he had given me time to pull a young tree up by the roots ; but I hated to spoil the Queen's blade upon his tough stick or no less tough hide. Besides, he had a good quarrel with me ; he had a warrant for my arrest, which I stole from him."

" Also : Item, twelve silver pennies," interposed the tinker, unsubdued. " Item, one crust of bread, 'gainst my supper. Item, one lump of solder. Item, three pieces of twine. Item, six single keys. Item——"

" Yes, I know," quoth the merry Robin ; " I stood outside the landlord's window, and heard you count over your losses. Here they are again, and the twelve silver pennies are turned by magic into gold. Here also, if you will, is my hand."

" I take it heartily, with the pence ! " cried Middle. " By my leathern coat and tools, which I shall presently have out of that sly host, I swear that I never yet met a man I liked as well as you ! An you and your men here will take me, I swear I'll serve you honestly. Do you want a tinker ? Nay ; but verily you must ! Who else can mend and grind your swords and patch your pannikins—and fight, too, when occasion serve ? Mend your pots ! mend your pa-a-ns ! "

And he ended his speech with the sonorous cry of his craft.

By this time the whole band was laughing uproariously at the tinker's talk.

" What say you, fellows ? " asked Robin. " Would not this tinker be a good recruit ? "

How Robin was Sought of the Tinker

" That he would," answered Will Scarlet, clapping the new man on the back ; " he will keep Friar Tuck and Much, the miller's son, from having the blues."

So amid great merriment and right good-fellowship the outlaws shook Middle by the hand, and he took oath of fealty, and thought no more of the Sheriff's daughter.

The words of the old ballad which tells of this adventure may interest you here at the last. Robin is ending his speech, after Master Middle has been sworn in :

" In manhood he's a mettled man
 And a metal-man by trade ;
Never thought I that any man
 Should have made me so afraid.

" And if he will be one of us,
 We will take all one fare ;
And whatsoever we do get,
 He shall have his rightful share."

So the tinker was content
 With them to go along,
And with them a part to take ;
 And so I end my song.

CHAPTER XV

HOW ROBIN HOOD WAS TANNED OF
THE TANNER

In Nottingham there lived a jolly tanner,
   With a hey down, down, a down down !
His name was Arthur-a-Bland ;
There was ne'er a squire in Nottinghamshire
Dare bid bold Arthur stand.

And as he went forth, in a summer's morning,
   With a hey down, down, a down down !
To the forest of merrie Sherwood,
To view the red deer, that range here and there
There met he with bold Robin Hood.

THE Sheriff's daughter bided for several days in the faint hope that she might hear tidings of the prattling tinker. But never a word heard she, and she was forced to the conclusion that her messenger had not so much as laid eyes upon the outlaw. Little recked she that he was even then grinding sword-points and sharpening arrows out in the good greenwood, while whistling blithely or chatting merrily with the good Friar Tuck.

Then she bethought herself of another good man, one Arthur-a-Bland, a tanner who dwelt in Nottingham town, and was far famed in the tourneys round about. He had done some pretty tricks at archery, but was strongest at wrestling and the quarter-staff. For three years he had cast all comers to the earth in

190

How Robin was Tanned of the Tanner

wrestling until the famous Eric of Lincoln broke a rib for him in a mighty tussle. Howsoever, at quarter-staff he had never yet met his match, so that there was never a squire in Nottingham-shire dare bid bold Arthur stand.

> With a long pike-staff on his shoulder,
> So well he could clear his way
> That by two and three he made men flee
> And none of them could stay.

Thus at least runs the old song which tells of his might.

"This is just the man for me!" thought the Sheriff's daughter to herself, and she forthwith summoned him to the Mansion House, and commissioned him to seek out Robin Hood.

The warrant was quite to Arthur's liking, for he was happiest when out in the forest taking a sly peep at the King's deer, and now he reckoned that he could look at them boldly instead of by the rays of the moon. He could say to any King's Forester who made bold to stop him: "I am here on the King's business!"

"Grammercy! no more oak-bark and ditch-water and the smell of half-tanned hides to-day!" quoth he gaily. "I shall e'en see what the free air of heaven tastes like when it sweeps through the open wood."

So the tanner departed joyfully upon his errand, but much more interested in the dun deer of the forest than in any two-legged rovers therein. This interest had, in fact, caused the

Robin Hood & His Merry Outlaws

Foresters to keep a shrewd eye upon him in the past, for his tannery was apt to have plenty of meat in it that was more like venison than the law allowed. As for the outlaws, Arthur bore them no ill-will; indeed, he felt a secret envy in his heart at their free life; but he was not afraid to meet any two men who might come against him. Nathless, the Sheriff's daughter did not choose a very good messenger, as you shall presently see.

Away sped the tanner, a piece of bread and some wine in his wallet, a good long-bow and arrows slung across his shoulders, his stout quarter-staff in his hand, and on his head a cap of trebled raw hide, so tough that it would turn the edge of a broadsword. He lost no time in getting out of the hot sun and into the welcome shade of the forest, where he stalked cautiously about, seeking some sign of the dun deer.

Now, it so chanced that upon that very morning Robin Hood had sent Little John to a neighbouring village to buy some cloth of Lincoln green for new suits for all the band. Some of the money recently won of the King was being spent in this fashion 'gainst the approach of winter. Will Scarlet had been sent on a similar errand to Barnesdale some time before, if you remember, only to be chased up the hill without his purchase. So to-day Little John was chosen, and for sweet company's sake Robin went with him a part of the way until they came to the " Seven Does," the inn where Robin had recently played his prank upon Middle, the tinker. Here they drank a glass

How Robin was Tanned of the Tanner

of ale to refresh themselves withal, and for good luck; and Robin tarried a bit while Little John went on his errand.

Presently Robin entered the edge of the wood, when whom should he see but Arthur-a-Bland, busily creeping after a graceful deer that browsed alone down the glade.

"Now by Saint George and the Dragon!" quoth Robin to himself, "I much fear that yon same fellow is a rascally poacher come after our own and the King's meat!"

For you must know, by a curious process of reasoning, Robin and his men had hunted in the royal preserves so long that they had come to consider themselves joint owners of every animal which roamed therein.

"Nay!" he added, "this must be looked into. That cow-skin cap, in sooth, must hide a scurvy varlet!"

And forthwith he crept behind a tree, and thence to another, stalking our friend Arthur as busily as Arthur was stalking the deer.

This went on for quite a space, until the tanner began to come upon the deer, and to draw his bow in order to tickle the victim's ribs with a cloth-yard shaft. But just at this moment Robin unluckily trod upon a twig, which snapped, and caused the tanner to turn suddenly.

Robin saw that he was discovered, so he determined to put a bold face on the matter, and went forward with some smart show of authority.

"Hold!" he cried. "Stay your hand! Why, who are

you, bold fellow, to range so boldly here? In sooth, to be brief, ye look like a thief that has come to steal the King's deer."

"Marry, it is scant concern of yours what I look like!" retorted Arthur-a-Bland. "Who are you, who speak so bravely?"

"You shall soon find out who I am!" quoth Robin, determining to find some sport in the matter. "I am a keeper of this forest. The King knows that I am looking after his deer for him, and, therefore, we must stay you."

"Have you any assistants, friend," asked the tanner calmly, "for it is not one man alone who can stop me?"

"Nay, truly, gossip," replied Robin; "I have a good yew bow, also a right sharp blade at my side. Nathless, I need no better assistant than a good oak-graff like unto yours. Give me a baker's dozen of minutes with it, and it shall pleasure me to crack that pate of yours for your sauciness!"

"Softly, my man! Fair and softly! Big words never killed so much as a mouse—least of all yon deer, which has got away while you were filling all the woods with your noisy breath. So choose your own playthings. For your sword and your bow I care not a straw, nor for all your arrows to boot. If I get but a knock at you 'twill be as much as you'll need."

"Now, by our Lady! will you listen to the braggart?" cried Robin in a fine rage. "Marry, but I'll teach ye to be more mannerly!"

How Robin was Tanned of the Tanner

So saying he unbuckled his belt, and, flinging his bow upon the ground, he seized hold of a young sapling that was growing near by. His hunting-knife soon had it severed and lopped into shape.

" Now come on, fellow ! " said Arthur-a-Bland, seeing that he was ready. " And if I do not tan your hide for you in better shape than ever calf-skin was turned into top-boots may a murrain seize me ! "

" Stay," said Robin, " methinks my cudgel is half a foot longer than yours. I would have them of even length before you begin your tanning."

" I pass not for length," bold Arthur replied ; " my staff is long enough, as you will shortly find out. Eight foot and a half, and 'twill knock down a calf "—here he made it whistle in the air—" and I hope it will knock down you."

Forthwith the two men spat on their hands, laid firm hold upon their cudgels, and began slowly circling round each other, looking for an opening.

Now, it so chanced that Little John had fared expeditiously with his errand. He had met the merchant from whom he was wont to buy Lincoln green coming along the road, and had made known his wants in few words. The merchant readily undertook to deliver the suits by a certain day in the following month. So Little John, glad to get back to the cool shelter of the greenwood, hastened along the road lately taken by Robin.

Robin Hood & His Merry Outlaws

Presently he heard the sound of angry voices, one of which he recognized as his captain's.

" Now, Heaven forfend," quoth he, " that Robin Hood has fallen into the clutches of a King's man ! I must take a peep at this fray."

So he cautiously made his way from tree to tree, as Robin had done, till he came to the little open space where Robin and Arthur were circling about each other, with angry looks, like two dogs at bay.

" Ha ! this looks interesting ! " muttered Little John to himself, for he loved a good quarter-staff bout above anything else in the world, and was the best man at it in all the greenwood. And he crawled quietly underneath a friendly bush—much as he had done when Robin undertook to teach Will Scarlet a lesson —and chuckled softly to himself, and slapped his thigh, and prepared to watch the fight at his ease.

Indeed, it was both exciting and laughable. You would have chuckled one moment and caught your breath the next, to see those two stout fellows swinging their sticks—each half as long again as the men were, and thick as their arms—and edging along sideways, neither wishing to strike the first blow.

At last Robin could no longer forbear, and his good right arm swung like a flash. Ping ! went the stick on the back of the other's head, raising such a welt that the blood came. But the tanner did not seem to mind it at all, for bing ! went his own

How Robin was Tanned of the Tanner

staff in return, giving Robin as good as he had sent. Then the battle was on, and furiously it waged. Fast fell the blows, but few save the first ones landed, being met in mid-air by a counter-blow, till the thwacking sticks sounded like the steady roll of a kettle-drum, and the oak-bark flew as fine as it had ever done in Arthur-a-Bland's tannery.

Round and round they fought, digging their heels into the ground to keep from slipping, so that you would have vowed there had been a yoke of oxen ploughing a potato-patch. Round and round, up and down, in and out, their arms working like threshing-machines, went the yeoman and the tanner for a full hour, each becoming more astonished every minute that the other was such a good fellow. While Little John, from underneath his bushy covert, had much ado to keep from roaring aloud in pure joy.

Finally Robin saw his chance, and brought a full-arm blow straight down upon the other's head with a force that would have felled a bullock. But Arthur's trebled cow-skin cap here stood him in good stead : the blow glanced off without doing more than stunning him. Nathless, he reeled, and had much ado to keep from falling ; seeing which Robin stayed his hand—to his own sorrow, for the tanner recovered his wits in a mar-vellous quick space, and sent back a sidelong blow which fairly lifted Robin off his feet, and sent him tumbling on to the grass.

" Hold your hand ! hold your hand ! " roared Robin with

what little breath he had left. "Hold, I say, and I will give you the freedom of the greenwood."

"Well, as to that," said Arthur, "I may thank my staff—not you."

"Well, well, gossip, let be as it may. But prithee tell me your name and trade. I like to know fellows who can hit a blow like that same last."

"I am a tanner," replied Arthur-a-Bland. "In Nottingham long have I wrought ; and if you'll come to me I swear I'll tan your hides for naught."

"'Od's bodikins ! " quoth Robin ruefully. "Mine own hide is tanned enough for the present. Howsoever, there be others in this wood I would fain see you tackle. Harkee, if you will leave your tan-pots and come with me, as sure as my name is Robin Hood you sha'n't want gold or fee."

"By the breath o' my body ! " said Arthur, " that will I do ! " and he gripped him gladly by the hand. " But I am minded that I clean forgot the errand that brought me to Sherwood. I was commissioned by some, under the Sheriff's roof, to capture you."

"So was a certain tinker now in our service," said Robin smilingly.

"Verily, 'tis a new way to recruit forces ! " said the tanner, laughing loudly. "But tell me, good Robin Hood, where is Little John ? I fain would see him, for he is a kinsman on my mother's side."

How Robin was Tanned of the Tanner

" Here am I, good Arthur-a-Bland ! " said a voice, and Little John literally rolled out from under the bush to the sward. His eyes were full of tears from much laughter, which had well-nigh left him powerless to get on his feet.

As soon as the astonished tanner saw who it was he gave Little John a mighty hug round the neck, and lifted him up on his feet, and the two pounded each other on the back soundly, so glad were they to meet again.

" Oh, man, man ! " said Little John as soon as he had got his breath. " Never saw I so fine a sight in all my born days. You did knock him over like as he were a ninepin ! "

" And you do joy to see me thwacked about on the ribs ? " asked Robin with some anger.

" Nay, not that, master ! " said Little John ; " but 'tis the second time I have had special view of a show from beneath the bushes, and I cannot forbear my delight. Howsoever, take no shame unto yourself, for this same Arthur-a-Bland is the best man at the quarter-staff in all Nottinghamshire. It commonly takes two or three men to hold him."

" Unless it be Eric o' Lincoln," said Arthur modestly ; " and I well know how you paid him out at the Fair."

" Say no more ! " said Robin, springing to his feet ; " for well I know that I have done good business this day, and a few bruises are easy payment for the stout cudgel I am getting into the band. Your hand again, good Arthur-a-

Bland! Come, let us after the deer of which I spoiled your stalking."

"Right gladly!" quoth Arthur. "Come, Cousin Little John! Away with vats and tan-bark and vile-smelling cowhides! I'll follow you two in the sweet open air to the very ends of the earth!"

Stout·Robin·hath·a·narrow·escape:

CHAPTER XIV

Merry·Robin·stops·a·Sorrowful·Knight:

HP

CHAPTER XVI

CHAPTER XVI

HOW ROBIN HOOD MET SIR RICHARD OF
THE LEA

Then answered him the gentle knight
With words both fair and free :
" God save thee, my good Robin,
And all thy company ! "

NOW, you must know that some months passed by.
The winter dragged its weary length through Sherwood Forest, and Robin Hood and his merry men
found what cheer they could in the big crackling fires before
their woodland cave.   Friar Tuck had built him a little hermitage
not far away, where he lived comfortably with his numerous
dogs.

The winter, I say, reached an end at last, and the blessed
spring came—and went.   Another summer passed on apace,
and still neither King nor Sheriff nor Bishop could catch the
outlaws, who, meanwhile, thrived and prospered mightily in
their outlawry.   The band had been increased from time to
time by picked men such as Arthur-a-Bland and David of Doncaster—he who was the jolliest cobbler for miles around—
until it now numbered a full sevenscore of men ; seven companies,
each with its stout lieutenant, serving under Robin Hood.   And
still they relieved the purses of the rich, and aided the poor, and

Robin Hood & His Merry Outlaws

feasted upon the King's deer, until the lank Sheriff of Nottingham was well-nigh distracted.

Indeed, that official would probably have lost his office
entirely had it not been for the fact of the King's death.
Henry passed away, as all kings will, in common with ordinary
men, and Richard of the Lion Heart was proclaimed as his
successor.

Then Robin and his men, after earnest debate, resolved to
throw themselves upon the mercy of the new King, swear
allegiance, and ask to be organized into Royal Foresters. So
Will Scarlet and Will Stutely and Little John were sent to London
with this message, which they were first to entrust privately
to Maid Marian. But they soon returned with bad tidings.
The new King had formerly set forth upon a crusade to the Holy
Land, and Prince John, his brother, was impossible to deal with
—being crafty, cruel, and treacherous. He was laying his hands
upon all the property which could easily be seized ; among
other estates that of the Earl of Huntingdon, Robin's old enemy
and Marian's father, who had lately died.

Marian herself was in sore straits. Not only had her estates
been taken away, and the maid been deprived of the former protection of the Queen, but the evil Prince John had persecuted
her with his attentions. He thought that, since the maid was
defenceless, he could carry her away to one of his castles and
none could gainsay him.

No word of this peril reached Robin's ears, although his

How Robin Met Sir Richard

men brought him word of the seizure of the Huntingdon lands. Nathless, he was greatly alarmed for the safety of Maid Marian, and his heart cried out for her strongly. She had been continually in his thoughts ever since the memorable shooting at London town.

One morning in early autumn, when the leaves were beginning to turn gold at the edges, the chestnut-pods to swell with promise of fatness, and the whole wide woodland was redolent of the ripe fragrance of fruit and flower, Robin was walking along the edge of a small open glade busy with his thoughts. The peace of the woods was upon him, despite his broodings of Marian, and he paid little heed to a group of does quietly feeding among the trees at the far edge of the glade.

But presently this sylvan picture was rudely disturbed for him. A stag, wild and furious, dashed suddenly forth from among the trees, scattering the does in swift alarm. The vicious beast eyed the green-and-gold tunic of Robin, and, lowering its head, charged at him impetuously. So sudden was its attack that Robin had no time to bend his bow. He sprang behind a tree while he seized his weapon.

A moment later the wild stag crashed blindly into the tree trunk with a shock which sent the beast reeling backward, while the dislodged leaves from the shivering tree fell in a small shower over Robin's head.

" By my halidom, I am glad it was not me you struck, my gentle friend ! " quoth Robin, fixing an arrow upon the string.

" Sorry indeed would be anyone's plight who should encounter you in this black humour."

Scarcely had he spoken when he saw the stag veer about and fix its glances rigidly on the bushes to the left side of the glade. These were parted by a delicate hand, and through the opening appeared the slight figure of a page. It was Maid Marian, come back again to the greenwood!

She advanced, unconscious alike of Robin's horrified gaze and the evil fury of the stag.

She was directly in line with the animal, so Robin dared not launch an arrow. Her own bow was slung across her shoulder, and her small sword would be useless against the beast's charge. But now, as she caught sight of the stag, she pursed her lips as though she would whistle to it.

" For the love of God, dear lady! " cried Robin, and then the words died in his throat.

With a savage snort of rage the beast rushed at this new and inviting target—rushed so swiftly and from so short a distance that she could not defend herself. She sprang to one side as it charged down upon her, but a side blow from its antlers stretched her upon the ground. The stag stopped, turned, and lowered its head, preparing to gore her to death.

Already its cruel horns were coming straight for her, while she, white of face and bewildered by the sudden attack, was struggling to rise and draw her sword. A moment more and

How Robin Met Sir Richard

the end would come. But the sharp voice of Robin had already spoken.

"Down, Marian!" he cried, and the girl instinctively obeyed, just as the shaft from Robin's bow went whizzing close above her head, and struck with terrific force full in the centre of the stag's forehead.

The beast stumbled in its charge, and fell dead across the body of the fainting maid.

Robin was quickly by her side, and dragged the beast from off the girl. Picking her up in his strong arms he bore her swiftly to the side of one of the brooks which watered the vale.

He dashed cool water upon her face, roughly almost, in his agony of fear that she was already dead, and he could have shed tears of joy to see those poor closed eyelids tremble. He redoubled his efforts, and presently she gave a little gasp.

"Where am I? What is't?"

"You are in Sherwood, dear maid, tho', i' faith, we gave you a rude reception!"

She opened her eyes, and sat up. "Methinks you have rescued me from sudden danger, sir," she said.

Then she recognized Robin for the first time, and a radiant smile came over her face, together with the rare blush of returned vitality, and her head sank upon his shoulder with a little tremble and sigh of relief.

"Oh, Robin, it is you!" she murmured.

"Ay; 'tis I. Thank Heaven, I was at hand to do you

service ! " Robin's tones were deep and full of feeling. " I swear, dear Marian, that I will not let you from my care henceforth."

Not another word was spoken for some moments, while her head still rested confidingly upon his breast. Then recollecting, he suddenly cried :

" Grammercy, I make but a poor nurse ! I have not even asked if any of your bones are broken."

" No ; not any," she answered, springing lightly to her feet to show him. " That foolish dizziness o'ercame me for the nonce, but we can now proceed on our way."

" Nay ; I meant not that," he protested. " Why should we haste ? First tell me of the news in London town and of yourself."

So she told him how that the Prince had seized upon her father's lands, and had promised to restore them to her if she would listen to his suit ; and how that she knew he meant her no good, for he was even then suing for a princess's hand.

" That is all, Robin," she ended simply ; " and that is why I donned again my page's costume and came to you in the greenwood."

Robin's brow had grown fiercely black at the recital of her wrongs, and he had laid stern hand upon the hilt of his sword.

" By this sword which Queen Eleanor gave me," he said impetuously, " and which was devoted to the service of all woman-

How Robin Met Sir Richard

kind, I take oath that Prince John and all his armies shall not harm you ! "

So that is how Maid Marian came to take up her abode in the greenwood, where the whole band of yeomen welcomed her gladly and swore fealty, and where the sweet lady of Allan-a-Dale made her fully at home.

But this was a day of deeds in Sherwood Forest, and we 'gan to tell you of another happening which led to later events.

While Robin and Marian were having their encounter with the stag, Little John, Much, the miller's son, and Will Scarlet had sallied forth to watch the high road leading to Barnesdale, if perchance they might find some haughty knight or fat priest whose wallet needed lightening.

They had scarcely watched the great road known as Watling Street—which runs from Dover in Kent to Chester town—for many minutes, when they espied a knight riding by in a very forlorn and careless manner.

" Now, what sorry scarecrow is this ? " asked Little John of the outlaws by his side. " ' Look not upon the outward appearance lest ye be deceived ' saith the proverb, and so our sorry friend upon a sorrier steed shall be our guest to-day."

The horseman was dressed as a knight, but his clothes, which were old and extremely shabby, hung loosely upon him. His visor was pulled down over his eyes and his head was sunk upon his breast. One foot held the stirrup limply, whilst the other hung dejectedly down.

Robin Hood & His Merry Outlaws

The poor lean beast on which he ambled was a picture of misery as it wearily shuffled along the road.

> All dreary was his semblance,
>   And little was his pride ;
> His one foot in the stirrup stood,
>   His other waved beside.
> His visor hung down o'er his eyes,
>   He rode in single array,
> A sorrier man than he was one
>   Rode never in summer's day.

Little John came up to the knight, and bade him stay ; for who can judge of a man's wealth by his looks ? The outlaw bent his knee in all courtesy, and prayed him to accept the hospitality of the forest.

" My master expects you to dine with him to-day," quoth he, " and, indeed, has been fasting while awaiting your coming, these three hours."

" Nay, good fellow," gently returned the knight, " I am full of trouble and in no mood for feasting. Yet would I thank your master for his courtesy to a broken man. Who is your master ? "

" None other than Robin Hood," replied Little John, laying his hand upon the knight's bridle.

Seeing the other two outlaws approaching the knight shrugged his shoulders, and replied indifferently.

" 'Tis clear that your invitation is too urgent to admit of refusal," quoth he, " and I go with you right willingly, my friends.

How Robin Met Sir Richard

My purpose was to have dined to-day at Blyth or Doncaster, but nothing matters greatly."

So in the same lackadaisical fashion which had marked all his actions that day, the knight suffered his horse to be led to the rendezvous of the band in the greenwood.

Marian had not yet had time to change her page's attire when the three escorts of the knight hove in sight. She recognized their captive as Sir Richard of the Lea, whom she had often seen at Court, and, fearing lest he might recognize her, she would have fled. But Robin asked her, with a twinkle, if she would not like to play page that day, and she in roguish mood consented to do so.

"Welcome, Sir Knight," said Robin courteously. "You are come in good time, for we were just preparing to sit down to meat."

"God save and thank you, good Master Robin," replied the knight, "and all your company. It likes me well to break the fast with you."

So while his horse was cared for, the knight laid aside his own heavy gear, and laved his face and hands, and sat down with Robin and all his men to a most plentiful repast of venison, swans, pheasants, various small birds, cakes, and ale. And Marian stood behind Robin, and filled his cup and that of the guest.

After eating right heartily of the good cheer, the knight brightened up greatly, and vowed that he had not enjoyed so good a dinner for nigh three weeks. He also said that if ever Robin and his fellows should come to his domains, he would strive to set them down to as good a dinner on his own behalf.

But this was not exactly the sort of payment which Robin had expected to receive. He thanked the knight, therefore, in set phrase, but reminded him that a yeoman like himself might hardly offer such a dinner to a knight as a gift of charity.

" I have no money, Master Robin," answered the knight frankly. " I have so little of the world's goods, in sooth, that I should be ashamed to offer you the whole of it."

" Money, however little, always jingles merrily in our pockets," said Robin, smiling. " Pray you, tell me what you deem a little sum."

" I have in this world but mine honour and ten silver pennies," said the knight, dejectedly. " Here they are, and I wish they were ten times as many."

He handed Little John his pouch, and Robin nodded carelessly.

" What say you to the total, Little John ? " he asked, as though in jest.

" 'Tis true enough, as the worthy knight hath said," responded the big fellow, gravely emptying the contents on his cloak.

Robin signed to Marian, who filled a bumper of wine for himself and his guest.

" Pledge me, Sir Knight ! " cried the merry outlaw, " and pledge me heartily, for these sorry times. I see that your armour

How Robin Met Sir Richard

is bent and that your clothes are torn. Yet methinks I saw you at Court, once upon a day, and in more prosperous guise. Tell me now, were you a yeoman and made a knight by force ? Or, have you been a bad steward to yourself, and wasted your property in lawsuits and the like ! Be not bashful with us. We shall not betray your secrets."

" I am a Saxon knight in my own right ; and I have always lived a sober and quiet life," the sorrowful guest replied. " 'Tis true you have seen me at Court, mayhap, for I was an excited witness at your shooting before King Harry—God rest his bones ! My name is Sir Richard of the Lea, and I dwell in a castle, not a league from one of the gates of Nottingham, which has belonged to my father, and his father, and his father's father before him. Within two or three years ago my neighbours might have told you that a matter of four hundred pounds one way or the other was as naught to me. But now I have only these ten pennies of silver, and my wife and son."

" In what manner have you lost your riches ! " asked Robin.

" Through folly and kindness," said the knight, sighing. " I went with King Richard upon a Crusade, from which I am but lately returned, in time to find my son—a goodly youth—grown up. He was but twenty, yet he had achieved a squire's training, and could play prettily in jousts and tournaments and other knightly games. But about this time he had the ill luck to push his sports too far, and did accidentally kill a knight in the open lists. To save the boy, I had to sell my lands and mortgage my ancestral castle, and this not being enough, in the end I have had to borrow money at a ruinous interest, from my lord of Hereford."

" A most worthy Bishop," said Robin ironically. " What is the sum of your debt ? "

" Four hundred pounds," said Sir Richard, " and the Bishop swears he will foreclose the mortgage if they are not paid promptly."

" Have you any friends who would become surety for you ? "

" Not one. If good King Richard were here, the tale might be otherwise."

" Fill your goblet again, Sir Knight," said Robin, and he turned to whisper a word in Marian's ear. She nodded, and drew Little John and Will Scarlet aside, and talked earnestly with them, in a low tone.

" Here is health and prosperity to you, gallant Robin," said Sir Richard, tilting his goblet. " I hope I may pay your cheer more worthily the next time I ride by."

Will Scarlet and Little John had meanwhile fallen in with Marian's idea, for they consulted the other outlaws, who nodded their heads. Thereupon Little John and Will Scarlet went into the cave near by, and presently returned bearing a bag of gold. This they counted out before the astonished knight, and there were four times one hundred gold pieces in it.

" Take this loan from us, Sir Knight, and pay your debt to the Bishop," then said Robin. " Nay, no thanks ; you are

How Robin Met Sir Richard

but exchanging creditors. Mayhap we shall not be so hard upon you as the Christian Bishop ; yet, again, we may be harder. Who can tell ? "

There were actual tears in Sir Richard's eyes as he essayed to thank the foresters. But, at this juncture, Much, the miller's son, came from the cave dragging a bale of cloth.

" The knight should have a suit worthy of his rank, master —think you not so ? "

" Measure him twenty ells of it," ordered Robin.

" Give him a good horse also," whispered Marian ; " 'tis a gift which will come back fourfold, for this is a worthy man. I know him well."

So the horse was given also, with gay trappings of leather and silver, and Robin bade Arthur-a-Bland ride as esquire with the knight as far as his castle.

The knight was sorrowful no longer ; yet could hardly voice his thanks through his broken utterance. And having spent the night in rest, after listening to Allan-a-Dale's singing, he mounted his new steed the following morning an altogether different man.

Before he turned to depart he wheeled round, and held his naked sword upright in the air.

" God save you, comrades, and keep you all ! " said he, with deep feeling in his tones ; " and give me a grateful heart ! Good Master Robin Hood, and you his merry men, sadness filled my heart when I rode through the forest, but you have turned it into joy and gladness, and from the fullness of my gratitude I thank you. Farewell! This day twelvemonth I will return and repay my debt. I swear it by my sword, and Sir Richard of the Lea never yet broke faith." So saying he raised the hilt and kissed it solemnly.

"We shall wait for you twelve months from to-day, here in this place," said Robin, shaking him by the hand, "and then you will repay us the loan if you have been prospered."

"I shall return it to you within the year, upon my honour as Sir Richard of the Lea. And for all time pray count me as a steadfast friend."

And then with a flourish and a clash as he clanked his sword into its sheath he put spurs to his horse and galloped off.

"Ho! Sir Knight, stop a moment," came in a deep round voice, and Friar Tuck, with his cooking apron all flying in the breeze, came running up at a break-neck speed and gave his steel helmet into the knight's hand. It was the envy of every man who saw it, being of finest metal with a delicate tracery of gold wrought upon the front. With a courteous acknowledgment the rider accepted the gift and set it upon his head, and, accompanied by his esquire, once more galloped off into the silent darkness of the forest.

CHAPTER XVII

HOW THE BISHOP WAS DINED

"O what is the matter?" then said the Bishop,
 "Or for whom do you make this a-do?
Or why do you kill the King's venison,
 When your company is so few?"

"We are shepherds," quoth bold Robin Hood,
 "And we keep sheep all the year,
And we are disposed to be merrie this day,
 And to kill of the King's fat deer."

NOT many days after Sir Richard of the Lea came to Sherwood Forest, word reached Robin Hood's ears that my lord Bishop of Hereford would be riding that way betimes on that morning. 'Twas Arthur-a-Bland who brought the tidings, and Robin's face brightened as he heard it.

"Now, by our Lady!" quoth he, "I have long desired to entertain my lord in the greenwood, and this is too fair a chance to let slip. Come, my men, kill me a venison; kill me a good fat deer. The Bishop of Hereford is to dine with me to-day, and he shall pay well for his cheer."

"Shall we dress it here as usual?" asked Much, the miller's son.

"Nay; we will play a droll game on the churchman. We

will dress it by the highway side, and watch for the Bishop narrowly, lest he should ride some other way."

So Robin gave his orders, and the main body of his men, each nudging his nearest neighbour, and all smiling and winking knowingly one at the other, dispersed to different parts of the forest, under Will Stutely and Little John, to watch other roads for the pompous Bishop of Hereford; while Robin Hood himself took six of his men, including Will Scarlet, and Much, and posted himself in full view of the main road. This little company appeared funny enough, I assure you, for they had disguised themselves as shepherds, wearing loose smocks and wide-brimmed hats. Robin had an old wool cap, with a tail to it, hanging over his ear, and a shock of hair stood straight up through a hole in the top. Besides, there was so much dirt on his face that you would never have known him. An old tattered cloak over his hunter's garb completed his make-up. The others were no less ragged and unkempt, even the foppish Will Scarlet being so badly run down at the heel that the Court ladies would hardly have had speech with him.

They quickly provided themselves with a deer, and made great preparations to cook it over a small fire, when a little dust was seen blowing along the highway, and out of it came the portly Bishop, cantering along, with ten men-at-arms at his heels. As soon as he saw the fancied shepherds he spurred up his horse, and came straight toward them.

How the Bishop was Dined

" Who are ye, fellows, who make so free with the King's deer ? " he asked sharply.

" We are shepherds," answered Robin Hood, pulling at his forelock awkwardly.

" Heaven have mercy ! Ye seem a sorry lot of shepherds. But who gave you leave to cease eating mutton ? "

" 'Tis one of our feast days, lording, and we were disposed to be merry this day, and make free with a deer, out here where they are so many."

" By my faith, the King shall hear of this. Who killed yon beast ? "

" Give me first your name, excellence, so that I may speak where 'tis fitting," replied Robin stubbornly.

" 'Tis my lord Bishop of Hereford, fellow ! " interposed one of the guards fiercely. " See that you keep a civil tongue in your head."

" If 'tis a churchman," retorted Will Scarlet, " he would do better to mind his own flocks rather than concern himself with ours."

" Ye are saucy fellows, in sooth," cried the Bishop, " and we will see if your heads will pay for your manners. Come ! quit your stolen roast and march along with me, for you shall be brought before the Sheriff of Nottingham forthwith."

" Pardon, excellence ! " said Robin, dropping on his knees. " Pardon, I pray you. It becomes not your lordship's coat to take so many lives away."

Robin Hood & His Merry Outlaws

"You rogues!" thundered the prelate. "Faith, I'll pardon you! I'll pardon you, when I see you hanged! Seize upon them, my men!"

But Robin had already sprung away, with his back against a tree. And from underneath his ragged cloak he drew his trusty horn, and winded the piercing notes which were wont to summon the band.

The Bishop no sooner saw this action than he knew his man, and that there was a trap set; and, being an arrant coward, he wheeled his horse sharply and would have made off down the road, but his own men, spurred on the charge, blocked his way. At almost the same instant the bushes round about seemed literally to become alive with outlaws. Little John's men came pouring from one side and Will Stutely's from the other. In less time than it takes to tell it the terrified Bishop found himself a prisoner, and began to crave mercy from the men he had so lately been ready to sentence.

"O pardon," said the Bishop,
"O pardon, I you pray,
For if I had known it had been you,
I'd have gone some other way."

"I owe you no pardon," retorted Robin, "but I will e'en treat you better than you would have treated me. Come, make haste, and go along with me. I have already planned that you shall dine with me this day."

So the unwilling prelate was dragged away, cheek by jowl

218

How the Bishop was Dined

with the half-cooked venison, upon the back of his own horse ; and Robin and his band took charge of the whole company, and led them through the forest glades till they came to an open space near Barnesdale.

Here they rested, and Robin gave the Bishop a seat full courteously. Much, the miller's son, fell to roasting the deer afresh, while another and fatter beast was set to frizzle on the other side of the fire. Presently the appetizing odour of the cooking reached the Bishop's nostrils, and he sniffed it eagerly. The morning's ride had made him hungry ; and he was nothing loath when they bade him come to the dinner. Robin gave him the best place, beside himself, and the Bishop prepared to fall to.

" Nay, my lord, craving your pardon, but we are accustomed to have grace before meat," said Robin decorously. "And as our own chaplain is not with us to-day, will you be good enough to say it for us ? "

The Bishop reddened, but pronounced grace in the Latin tongue hastily, and then settled himself to make the best of his lot. Red wines and ale were brought forth and poured out, each man having a horn tankard from which to drink.

Laughter bubbled among the diners, and the Bishop caught himself smiling at more than one jest. But who, in sooth, could resist a freshly broiled venison steak eaten out in the open air to the tune of jest and good fellowship ? Stutely filled the Bishop's beaker with wine each time he emptied it, and the Bishop got mellower and mellower as the afternoon shades lengthened on toward sunset. Then the approaching dusk warned him of his position.

" I wish, mine host," quoth he gravely to Robin, who had soberly drunk but one cup of ale, " that you would now call a reckoning. Right well have I enjoyed your excellent dinner. Tell me, therefore, what I owe and allow me to proceed on my way. 'Tis late, and I fear the cost of this entertainment may be more than my poor purse can stand."

For he bethought himself of his friend the Sheriff's former experience.

" Verily, your lordship," said Robin, scratching his head, " I have enjoyed your company so much that I scarce know how to charge for it."

" Lend me your purse, my lord," said Little John, interposing, " and I'll give you the reckoning by-and-by."

The Bishop shuddered. He had collected Sir Richard's debt only that morning, and was even then carrying it home.

" I have but a few silver pennies of my own," he whined ; " and as for the gold in my saddle-bags, 'tis for the Church. Ye surely would not levy upon the Church, good friends."

But Little John was already gone to the saddle-bags, and returning he laid the Bishop's cloak upon the ground, and poured out a matter of four hundred glittering gold pieces. 'Twas the identical money which Robin had lent Sir Richard a short while before !

" Ah ! " said Robin, as though an idea had but just then come

How the Bishop was Dined

to him. " The Church is always willing to aid in charity. And seeing this goodly sum reminds me that I have a friend who is indebted to a churchman for this exact amount. Now, we shall charge you nothing, on our own account, but suffer us to make use of this in aiding my good friend."

" Nay, nay," began the Bishop, with a wry face ; " this is requiting me ill indeed. Was this not the King's meat, after all, that we feasted upon ? Furthermore, I am a poor man."

" Poor, forsooth ! " answered Robin in scorn. " You are the Bishop of Hereford, and does not the whole countryside speak of your oppression ? Who does not know of your cruelty to the poor and ignorant—you who should use your great office to aid instead of oppress them ? Have you not been guilty of far greater robbery than this, even though less open ? Of my-self, and how you have pursued me, I say nothing, nor of your unjust enmity against my father. But on account of those you have despoiled and oppressed I take this money, and will use it far more worthily than you would. God be my witness in this ! There is an end of the matter, unless you will lead us in a song or dance to show that your body has a better spirit than your mind. Come, strike up the harp, Allan ! My heart misgives me that our honoured guest is sad. Which will your lordship give us— song or dance ? "

" Neither the one nor the other will I do," snarled the Bishop.

" Faith then, we must help you," said Little John, and he

and Arthur-a-Bland seized the fat, struggling churchman, and commenced to hop up and down to the lively tune played by Allan. The Bishop being shorter must perforce accompany them; while the whole company sat and rolled about over the ground, and roared to see my lord of Hereford's queer capers. At last he sank in a heap, fuddled with wine, and quite exhausted.

Little John picked him up as though he were a log of wood, and, carrying him to his horse, set him astride facing the animal's tail, and thus fastened him. Then, leading the animal toward the high road, he started the Bishop, more dead than alive, toward Nottingham.

CHAPTER XVIII

HOW THE BISHOP WENT OUTLAW-HUNTING

The Bishop he came to the old woman's house,
    And called with furious mood,
" Come let me soon see, and bring unto me
    That traitor, Robin Hood."

THE easy success with which they had got the better of the good Bishop led Robin to be a little careless. He thought that his guest was too great a coward to venture back into the greenwood for many a long day ; and so, after lying quiet for one day, the outlaw ventured boldly upon the highway, the morning of the second. But he had gone only half a mile when, turning a sharp bend in the road, he plunged full upon the prelate himself.

My lord of Hereford had been so deeply smitten in his pride that he had lost no time in summoning a considerable body of the Sheriff's men, offering to double the reward if Robin Hood could be come upon. This company was now at his heels, and, after the first shock of mutual surprise, the Bishop gave an exultant shout, and spurred upon the outlaw.

It was too late for Robin to retreat by the way he had come, but, quick as a flash, he sprang to one side of the road, dodged under some bushes, and disappeared so suddenly that his pursuers thought he had truly been swallowed up by magic.

Robin Hood & His Merry Outlaws

"After him!" yelled the Bishop; "some of you beat up the woods around him, while the rest of us will keep on the main road, and head him off on the other side!"

For, truth to tell, the Bishop did not care to trust his bones away from the high road.

About a mile away, on the other side of the neck of woods wherein Robin had been trapped, was a little tumbledown cottage. 'Twas where the widow lived, whose three sons had been rescued. Robin remembered the cottage, and saw his one chance to escape.

Doubling in and out among the underbrush and heather with the agility of a hare he soon came out of the wood in the rear of the cottage, and thrust his head through a tiny window.

The widow, who had been at her spinning-wheel, rose up with a cry of alarm.

"Quiet, good mother! 'Tis I, Robin Hood. Where are your three sons?"

"They should be with you, Robin. Well do you know that. Do they not owe their lives to you?"

"If that be so I come to seek payment of the debt," said Robin in a breath. "The Bishop is on my heels with many of his men."

"I'll cheat the Bishop and all!" cried the woman quickly. "Here, Robin, change your raiment with me, and we will see if my lord knows an old woman when he sees her."

"Good!" said Robin. "Pass your grey cloak out of the window, and also your spindle and twine, and I will give you my green mantle and everything else down to my bow and arrows."

While they were talking Robin had been nimbly changing clothes with the old woman through the window, and in a jiffy he stood forth complete, even to the spindle and twine.

Presently up dashed the Bishop and his men, and, at sight of the cottage and the old woman, gave pause. The crone was hobbling along with difficulty, leaning heavily upon a gnarled stick, and bearing the spindle on her other arm. She would have gone by the Bishop's company, while muttering to herself, but the Bishop ordered one of his men to question her. The soldier laid his hand upon her shoulder.

" Mind your business ! " croaked the woman, " or I'll curse ye ! "

" Come, come, my good woman," said the soldier, who really was afraid of her curses. " I'll not molest you. But my lord Bishop of Hereford wants to know if you have seen aught of the outlaw Robin Hood ? "

" And why shouldn't I see him ? " she whined. " Where's the King or law to prevent good Robin from coming to see me and bringing me food and raiment ? That's more than my lord Bishop will do, I warrant ye ! "

" Peace, woman ! " said the Bishop harshly. " We want none of your opinions. But we'll take you to Barnesdale and burn you for a witch if you do not instantly tell us when you last saw Robin Hood."

Robin Hood & His Merry Outlaws

" Mercy, good my lord ! " chattered the crone, falling on her knees. " Robin is there in my cottage now, but you'll never take him alive."

" We'll see about that," cried the Bishop triumphantly. " Enter the cottage, my men. Fire it, if need be. But I'll give a purse of gold pieces, above the reward, to the man who captures the outlaw alive."

The old woman, being released, went on her way slowly. But it might have been noticed that the farther she got away from the company and the nearer to the edge of the woods, the swifter and straighter grew her pace. Once inside the shelter of the forest she broke into a run of surprising swiftness.

" Gadzooks ! " exclaimed Little John, who presently spied her. " Who comes here ? Never saw I witch or woman run so fast. Methinks I'll send an arrow close over her head to see which it is."

" Oh, hold your hand ! hold your hand ! " panted the supposed woman. " 'Tis I, Robin Hood. Summon the yeomen, and return with me speedily. We have still another score to settle with my lord of Hereford."

When Little John could catch his breath from laughing he winded his horn.

" Now, Mistress Robin," quoth he, grinning, " lead on ! We'll be close to your heels."

Meanwhile, back at the widow's cottage, the Bishop was

growing more furious every moment. For all his bold words
he dared not fire the house, and the sturdy door had thus far
resisted all his men's efforts.

"Break it down! Break it down!" he shouted, "and
let me soon see who will fetch out that traitor Robin
Hood!"

At last the door crashed in, and the men stood guard on the
threshold. But not one dared enter for fear a sharp arrow
should meet him half-way.

"Here he is!" cried one keen-eyed fellow, peering in. "I
see him in the corner by the cupboard. Shall we slay him with
our pikes?"

"Nay," said the Bishop; "take him alive if you can. We'll
make the biggest public hanging of this that the shire ever
beheld."

But the joy of the Bishop over his capture was short-lived.
Down the road came striding the shabby figure of the old
woman who had helped him set the trap, and very wroth
was she when she saw that the cottage door had been
battered in.

"Stand by, you lazy rascals!" she called to the soldiers.
"A murrain seize ye for hurting an old woman's hut. Stand
by, I say!"

"Hold your tongue!" ordered the Bishop. "These are
my men and carrying out my orders."

"Well, to be sure," grumbled the beldame harshly, "things

have come to a pretty pass when our homes may be treated like common gaols. Couldn't all your men catch one poor forester without this ado ? Come ! clear out, you and your robbers, on the instant, or I'll curse every mother's son of ye, eating and drinking and sleeping ! "

" Seize on the hag ! " shouted the Bishop as soon as he could get in a word. " We'll see about a witch's cursing. Back to town she shall go, alongside of Robin Hood."

" Not so fast, your worship ! " she retorted, clapping her hands.

And at the signal a goodly array of greenwood men sprang forth from all sides of the cottage, with bows drawn back threateningly. The Bishop saw that his men were trapped again, for they dared not stir. Nathless, he determined to make a fight for it.

" If one of you budge an inch toward me, you rascals," he cried, " it shall sound the death of your master Robin Hood ! My men have him here under their pikes, and I shall command them to kill him without mercy."

" Faith, I should like to see the Robin you have caught," said a clear voice from under the widow's cape, and the outlaw chief stood forth with bared head, smilingly. " Here am I, my lord, in no wise imperilled by your men's fierce pikes. So let me see whom you have guarding so well."

The old woman, who, in the garb of Robin Hood, had been

lying quiet in the cottage through all the uproar, jumped up nimbly at this. In the bald absurdity of her disguise she came to the doorway, and bowed to the Bishop.

" Give you good-den, my lord Bishop," she piped in a shrill voice ; " and what does your grace at my humble door ? Do you come to bless me and give me alms ? "

" Ay, that does he," answered Robin. " We shall see if his saddle-bags contain enough to pay you for that battered door."

" Now, by all the saints——" began the Bishop.

" Take care ; they are all watching you," interrupted Robin ; " so name them not upon your unchurchly lips. But I will trouble you to hand over that purse of gold you had saved to pay for my head."

" I'll see you hanged first ! " raged the Bishop, stating no more than what would be so if he could do the ordering of things. " Have at them, my men, and hew them down in their tracks ! "

" Hold ! " retorted Robin. " See how we have you at our mercy." And aiming a sudden shaft he shot so close to the Bishop's head that it carried away both his hat and his skull-cap, which he always wore, leaving him quite bald.

The prelate turned as white as his shiny head, and clutched wildly at his ears. He thought himself dead almost.

" Help ! murder ! " he gasped. " Do not shoot again ! Here's your purse of gold ! "

And without waiting for further parley he fairly bolted down the road.

His men being left leaderless had nothing for it but to retreat after him, which they did in sullen order, covered by the bows of the yeomen. And thus ended the Bishop of Hereford's great outlaw-hunt in the forest.

CHAPTER XIX

HOW THE SHERIFF HELD ANOTHER
SHOOTING MATCH

> " To tell the truth, I'm well informed
>   Yon match it is a wile ;
> The Sheriff, I wis, devises this
>   Us archers to beguile."

NOW, the Sheriff was so greatly troubled in heart over the growing power of Robin Hood that he did a very foolish thing. He went to London town to lay his troubles before the King, and get another force of troops to cope with the outlaws. King Richard was not yet returned from the Holy Land ; but Prince John heard him with scorn.

" Pooh ! " said he, shrugging his shoulders. " What have I to do with all this ? Art thou not sheriff for me ? The law is in force to take thy course of them that injure thee. Go, get thee gone, and by thyself devise some tricking game to trap these rebels ; and never let me see thy face at Court again until thou hast a better tale to tell."

So away went the Sheriff in sorrier pass than ever, and cudgelled his brain on the way home for some plan of action.

His daughter met him on his return, and saw at once that he had been on a poor mission. She was minded to upbraid him when she learned what he had told the Prince. But the words of the latter started her to thinking afresh.

" I have it ! " she exclaimed at length. " Why should we not hold another shooting match ? 'Tis Fair year, as you know, and another tourney will be expected. Now, we will proclaim a general amnesty, as did King Harry himself, and say that the field is open and unmolested to all comers. Belike Robin Hood's men will be tempted to twang the bow, and then——"

" And then," said the Sheriff, jumping up with alacrity, " we shall see on which side of the gate they stop over-night ! "

So the Sheriff lost no time in proclaiming a tourney, to be held that same autumn at the Fair. It was open to all comers, said the proclamation, and none should be molested in their going and coming. Furthermore, an arrow with a golden head and shaft of silver-white should be given to the winner, who would be heralded abroad as the finest archer in all the North Countree. Also, many rich prizes were to be given to other clever archers.

These tidings came in due course to Robin Hood under the greenwood tree, and fired his impetuous spirit.

" Come, prepare ye, my merry men all," quoth he, " and we'll go to the Fair, and take some part in this sport."

With that stepped forth the merry cobbler, David of Don-caster.

" Master," quoth he, " be ruled by me, and stir not from the greenwood. To tell the truth, I'm well informed yon match is naught but a trap. I wis the Sheriff has devised it to beguile us archers into some treachery."

"That word savours of the coward," replied Robin, "and pleases me not. Let come what will, I'll try my skill at that same archery."

Then up spoke Little John, and said : "Come, listen to me how it shall be that we will not be discovered.

> "Our mantles all of Lincoln green
> Behind us we will leave ;
> We'll dress us all so several,
> They shall not us perceive.

> "One shall wear white, another red,
> One yellow, another blue ;
> Thus in disguise to the exercise
> We'll go, whate'er ensue."

This advice met with general favour from the adventurous fellows, and they lost no time in putting it into practice. Maid Marian and Mistress Dale, assisted by Friar Tuck, prepared some varicoloured costumes, and 'gainst the Fair day had fitted out the sevenscore men till you would never have taken them for other than villagers decked for the holiday.

And forth went they from the greenwood, with hearts all firm and stout, resolved to meet the Sheriff's men and have a merry bout. Along the highway they fell in with many other bold fellows from the countryside, going with their ruddy-cheeked lasses toward the wide-open gates of Nottingham.

So in through the gates trooped the whole gay company,

Robin Hood & His Merry Outlaws

Robin's men behaving as awkwardly and laughing and talking as noisily as the rest ; while the Sheriff's scowling men-at-arms stood round about, and sought to find one who looked like a forester, but without avail.

The herald now set forth the terms of the contest, as on former occasions, and the shooting presently began. Robin had chosen five of his men to shoot with him, and the rest were to mingle with the crowd and also watch the gates. These five were Little John, Will Scarlet, Will Stutely, Much, and Allan-a-Dale.

The other competitors made a brave showing on the first round, especially Gilbert of the White Hand, who was present, and never shot better. The contest later narrowed down until in the end Gilbert and Robin alone were left to shoot for the possession of the arrow with the golden head. But at the first lead, when the butts were struck so truly by various well-known archers, the Sheriff was in doubt whether to feel glad or sorry. He was glad to see such skill, but sorry that the outlaws were not in it.

Some said, " If Robin Hood were here,
    And all his men to boot,
Sure none of them could 'pass these men,
    So bravely do they shoot."

" Ay," quoth the Sheriff, and scratched his head,
    " I thought he would be here ;
I thought he would, but tho' he's bold,
    He durst not now appear."

This word was privately brought to Robin by David of Don-

Another Shooting Match

caster, and the saying vexed him sorely, but he bit his lip in silence.

" Ere long," he thought to himself, " we shall see whether Robin Hood be here or not ! "

Meantime the shooting had been going forward, and Robin's men had done so well that the air was filled with shouts.

> One cried, " Blue jacket ! " another cried, " Brown ! "
> And a third cried, " Brave Yellow ! "
> But the fourth man said, " Yon man in red
> In this place has no fellow."
>
> For that was Robin Hood himself,
> For he was clothed in red ;
> At every shot the prize he got,
> For he was both sure and dead.

Thus went the second round of the shooting, and thus the third and last, till even Gilbert of the White Hand was fairly beaten. During all this shooting Robin exchanged no word with his men, each treating the others as perfect strangers. Nathless, such great shooting could not pass without revealing the archers.

The Sheriff thought he discovered, in the winner of the golden arrow, the person of Robin Hood without peradventure, so he sent word privately for his men-at-arms to close round the group. But Robin's men also got wind of the plan.

To keep up appearances, the Sheriff summoned the crowd to form a circle, and after as much delay as possible the arrow was presented. The delay gave time enough for the soldiers to close in. As Robin received his prize, bowed awkwardly, and turned away, the Sheriff, letting his zeal get the better of his discretion, grasped him about the neck, and called upon his men to arrest the traitor.

But the moment the Sheriff touched Robin he received such a buffet on the side of his head that he let go instantly, and fell back several paces. Turning to see who had struck him he recognized Little John.

"Ah, rascal Greenleaf, I have you now!" he exclaimed, springing at him. Just then, however, he met a new check.

"This is from another of your devoted servants!" said a voice which he knew to be that of Much, the miller's son, and thwack! went his open palm upon the Sheriff's cheek, sending that worthy rolling over and over upon the ground.

By this time the conflict had become general, but the Sheriff's men suffered the disadvantage of being hampered by the crowd of innocent onlookers, whom they could not tell from the outlaws, and so dared not attack; while the other outlaws in the rear fell upon them, and put them in confusion.

For a moment a fierce rain of blows ensued; then the clear bugle-note from Robin ordered a retreat. The two warders at the nearest gate tried to close it, but were shot dead in their tracks. David of Doncaster threw a third soldier into the moat; and out through the gate went the foresters in good order, keeping a respectful distance between themselves and the advancing soldiery by means of their well-directed shafts.

Another Shooting Match

But the fight was not to go easily this day, for the soldiery, smarting from their recent discomfiture at the widow's cottage, and knowing that the eyes of the whole shire were upon them, fought well, and pressed closely after the retreating outlaws. More than one ugly wound was given and received. No less than five of the Sheriff's men were killed outright, and a dozen others injured ; while four of Robin's men were bleeding from severe flesh cuts.

Then Little John, who had fought by the side of his chief, suddenly fell forward with a slight moan. An arrow had pierced his knee. Robin seized the big fellow with almost superhuman strength.

> Up he took him on his back,
> And bare him well a mile ;
> Many a time he laid him down,
> And shot another while.

Meanwhile Little John grew weaker, and closed his eyes ; at last he sank to the ground, and feebly motioned Robin to let him lie.

" Master Robin," said he, " have I not served you well ever since we met upon the bridge ? "

" Truer servant never man had," answered Robin.

" Then if ever you loved me, and for the sake of that service, draw your bright brown sword and strike off my head ; never let me fall alive into the hands of the Sheriff of Nottingham."

" Not for all the gold in England would I do either of the things you suggest."

Robin Hood & His Merry Outlaws

" God forbid ! " cried Arthur-a-Bland, hurrying to the rescue. And, packing his wounded kinsman upon his own broad shoulders, he soon brought him within the shelter of the forest.

Once there the Sheriff's men did not follow ; and Robin caused litters of boughs to be made for Little John and the other four wounded men. Quickly were they carried through the wood until the hermitage of Friar Tuck was reached, where their wounds were dressed. Little John's hurt was pronounced to be the most serious of any, but he was assured that in two or three days' time he could get about again ; whereat the active giant was mightily relieved.

That evening consternation came into the hearts of the band. A careful roll-call was taken to see if all the yeomen had escaped, when it was found that Will Stutely was missing, and Maid Marian also was nowhere to be found. Robin was seized with dread. He knew that Marian had gone to the Fair, but felt that she would hardly come to grief. Her absence, however, portended some danger, and he feared that it was connected with Will Stutely. The Sheriff would hang him speedily, and without mercy, if he were captured.

The rest of the band shared their leader's uneasiness, though they said no word. They knew that, if Will were captured, the battle must be fought over again as early as possible, and Will must be saved at any cost. But no man flinched from the prospect.

238

Another Shooting Match

Several evenings later, while the Sheriff and his wife and daughter sat at meat in the Mansion House, the Sheriff boasted of how he would make an example of the captured outlaw, for Stutely had indeed fallen into his hands.

" He shall be strung high," he said in a loud voice, " and none shall dare lift a finger. I now have Robin Hood's men on the run, and we shall soon see who is master in this shire. I am only sorry that we let them have the golden arrow."

As he spoke a missive sped through a window, and fell clattering upon his plate, causing him to spring back in alarm.

It was the golden arrow, and on its feathered shaft was sewed a little note which read :

" This from one who will take no gift from liars, and who henceforth will show no mercy. Look well to yourself. R. H."

CHAPTER XX

HOW WILL STUTELY WAS RESCUED

Forth of the greenwood are they gone,
    Yea, all courageously,
Resolving to bring Stutely home,
    Or every man to die.

THE day set for the hanging of the outlaw dawned bright and sunny. The whole face of nature seemed gay, as in despite of the tragedy which was soon to take place within the walls of Nottingham town. The gates were not opened upon this day, for the Sheriff was determined to carry through the hanging of Will Stutely undisturbed. No man, therefore, was to be allowed entrance from without all that morning and until after the fatal hour of noon, when Will's soul was to be launched into eternity.

Early in the day Robin, finding the gates closed, had placed his men at a point, as near as he dared, in the woods where he could watch the road leading to the east gate. He himself was clad in a bright scarlet dress, while his men, a goodly array, wore their suits of sober Lincoln green. They were armed with broadswords, and each man carried his bow and a full quiver of new arrows, straightened and sharpened cunningly by Middle, the tinker. Over their greenwood dress each man had thrown a rough mantle, making him look not unlike a friar.

240

How Will Stutely was Rescued

"I hold it good, comrades," said Robin Hood, "to tarry here in hiding for a season while we send someone forth to obtain tidings. For, in sooth, 'twill work no good to march upon the gates if they be closed."

"Look, master," quoth one of the widow's sons. "There comes a palmer along the road from the town. Belike he can tell us how the land lies, and if Stutely be really in danger. Shall I go out and engage him in speech?"

"Go," answered Robin.

So Stout Will went out from the band while the others hid themselves and waited. When he had come close to the palmer, who seemed a slight, youngish man, he doffed his hat full courteously and said :

"I crave your pardon, holy man, but can you tell me tidings of Nottingham town? Do they intend to put an outlaw to death this day?"

"Yea," answered the palmer sadly. "'Tis true enough, sorry be the day. I have passed the very spot where the gallows-tree is going up. 'Tis out upon the roadway near the Sheriff's castle. One Will Stutely is to be hung thereon at noon, and I could not bear the sight, so came away."

The palmer spoke in a muffled voice ; and as his hood was pulled well over his head, Stout Will could not discern what manner of man he was. Over his shoulder he carried a long staff, with the fashion of a little cross at one end ; and he had sandalled feet like any monk. Stout Will noticed idly that the feet were very small and white, but gave no second thought to the matter.

" Who will shrive the poor wretch, if you have come away from him ? " he asked reproachfully.

The question seemed to put a new idea into the palmer's head. He turned so quickly that he almost dropped his hood.

" Do you think that I should undertake this holy office ? "

" By Saint Peter and the Blessed Virgin, I do indeed ! Else, who will do it ? The Bishop and all his whining clerks may be there, but not one would say a prayer for his soul."

" But I am only a poor palmer," the other began hesitatingly.

" Nathless, your prayers are as good as any and better than some," replied Will.

" Right gladly would I go," then said the palmer ; " but I fear me I cannot get into the city. You may know that the gates are fast locked, for this morning, to all who would come in, although they let any pass out who will."

" Come with me," said Stout Will, " and my master will see that you pass through the gates."

So the palmer pulled his cloak still closer about him and was brought before Robin Hood, to whom he told all he knew of the situation. He ended with :

" If I may make so bold, I would not try to enter the city from this gate, as 'tis closely guarded since yesterday. But on the far side no attack is looked for."

How Will Stutely was Rescued

" My thanks, gentle palmer," quoth Robin, " your suggestion is good, and we will get us to the gate upon the far side."

So the men marched silently but quickly until they were near to the western gate. Then Arthur-a-Bland asked leave to go ahead as a scout, and quietly made his way to a point under the tower by the gate. The moat was dry on this side, as these were times of peace, and Arthur was further favoured by a stout ivy vine which grew out from an upper window.

Swinging himself up boldly by means of this friendly vine, he crept through the window and in a moment more had sprung upon the warder from behind and gripped him hard about the throat. The warder had no chance to utter the slightest sound, and soon lay bound and gagged upon the floor; while Arthur-a-Bland slipped himself into his uniform and got hold of his keys.

'Twas the work of a few moments more to open the gates, let down the bridge, and admit the rest of the band; and they got inside the town so quietly that none knew of their coming. Fortune also favoured them in the fact that just at this moment the prison doors had been opened for the march of the condemned man, and every soldier and idle lout in the marketplace had trooped thither to see him pass along.

Presently out came Will Stutely with firm step but dejected air. He looked eagerly to the right hand and to the left, but saw none of the band. And though more than one curious face betrayed friendship in it, he knew there could be no aid from such source.

Will's hands were tied behind his back. He marched between rows of soldiery, and the Sheriff and the Bishop brought up the rear on horses, looking mightily puffed up and important over the whole proceeding. He would show these sturdy rebels—would the Sheriff—whose word was law! He knew that the gates were tightly fastened; and further he believed that the outlaws would hardly venture again within the walls, even if the gates were open. And as he looked around at the fivescore archers and pikemen who lined the way to the gallows, he smiled with grim satisfaction.

Seeing that no help was nigh, the prisoner paused at the foot of the scaffold and spoke in a firm tone to the Sheriff.

" My lord Sheriff," quoth he, " since I must needs die, grant me one boon; for my noble master ne'er yet had a man that was hanged on a tree :

> " Give me a sword all in my hand,
>   And let me be unbound,
> And with thee and thy men will I fight
>   Till I lie dead on the ground."

But the Sheriff would by no means listen to his request; but swore that he should suffer a shameful death, and not die by the sword valiantly.

> " Oh, no, no, no," the Sheriff said,
>   " Thou shalt on the gallows die,
> Ay, and so shall thy master too,
>   If ever it in me lie."

How Will Stutely was Rescued

" O dastard coward ! " Stutely cried,
  " Faint-hearted peasant slave !
If ever my master do thee meet,
  Thou shalt thy payment have.

" My noble master thee doth scorn,
  And all thy cowardly crew ;
Such silly imps unable are
  Bold Robin to subdue."

This brave speech was not calculated to soothe the Sheriff. " To the gallows with him ! " he roared, giving a sign to the hangman ; and Stutely was pushed into the rude cart which was to bear him under the gallows until his neck was leashed. Once his neck was secure within the rope, the cart would be drawn roughly away and the unhappy man would swing out over the tail of it into another world.

But at this moment came a slight interruption. A boyish-looking palmer stepped forth, and said :

" Your Excellency, let me at least shrive this poor wretch's soul ere it be hurled into eternity."

" No ! " shouted the Sheriff, " let him die a dog's death ! "

" Then his damnation will rest upon you," said the monk firmly. " You, my lord Bishop, cannot stand by and see this wrong done."

The Bishop hesitated. Like the Sheriff, he wanted no delay ; but the people were beginning to mutter among themselves and move about uneasily. He said a few words to the Sheriff, and the latter nodded to the monk ungraciously.

245

Robin Hood & His Merry Outlaws

" Perform your duty, Sir Priest," quoth he, " and be quick about it ! " Then, turning to his soldiers, " Watch this palmer narrowly," he commanded. " Belike he is in league with those rascally outlaws."

But the palmer paid no heed to his last words. He began to tell his beads quickly, and to speak in a low voice to the condemned man. But he did not touch his bonds.

Then came another stir in the crowd, and one came pushing through the press of people and soldiery to come near to the scaffold.

" I pray you, Will, before you die, take leave of all your friends ! " cried out the well-known voice of Much, the miller's son.

At the word the palmer stepped back suddenly and looked to one side. The Sheriff also knew the speaker.

" Seize him ! " he shouted. " 'Tis another of the crew. He is the villain cook who once did rob me of my silver plate. We'll make a double hanging of this ! "

" Not so fast, good master Sheriff," retorted Much. " First catch your man and then hang him. But meanwhile I would like to borrow my friend of you awhile."

And with one stroke of his keen hunting-knife he cut the bonds which fastened the prisoner's arms, and Stutely leaped lightly from the cart.

" Treason ! " screamed the Sheriff, getting black with rage. " Catch the varlets ! "

How Will Stutely was Rescued

So saying he spurred his horse fiercely forward, and rising in his stirrups brought down his sword with might and main at Much's head. But his former cook dodged nimbly underneath the horse and came up on the other side, while the weapon whistled harmlessly in the air.

"Nay, Sir Sheriff!" he cried, "I must e'en borrow your sword for the friend I have borrowed."

Thereupon he snatched the weapon deftly from the Sheriff's hand.

"Here, Stutely!" said he, "the Sheriff has lent you his own sword. Back to back with me, man, and we'll teach these knaves a trick or two!"

Meanwhile the soldiers had recovered from their momentary surprise and had flung themselves into the fray. A clear bugle-note had also sounded—the same which the soldiers had learned to dread. 'Twas the rallying note of the greenwood men. Clothyard shafts began to hurtle through the air, and Robin and his men cast aside their cloaks and sprang forward crying:

"Lockesley! Lockesley! A rescue! A rescue!"

On the instant, a terrible scene of hand-to-hand fighting followed. The Sheriff's men, though once more taken by surprise, were determined to sell this rescue dearly. They packed in closely and stubbornly about the condemned man and Much and the palmer, and it was only by desperate rushes that the foresters made an opening in the square. Ugly cuts and bruises were exchanged freely; and lucky was the man

247

who escaped with only these. Many of the onlookers, who had long hated the Sheriff and felt sympathy for Robin's men, also plunged into the conflict—although they could not well keep out of it, in sooth !—and aided the rescuers no little.

At last, with a mighty onrush, Robin cleaved a way through the press to the scaffold itself, and not a second too soon ; for two men with pikes had leaped upon the cart, and from that point of vantage were in the act of thrusting down upon the palmer and Will Stutely. A mighty upward blow from Robin's good blade sent the pike flying from the hand of one, while a well-directed arrow from the outskirts pierced the other fellow's throat.

" God save you, master ! " cried Will Stutely joyfully. " I had begun to fear that I would never see your face again."

" A rescue ! " shouted the outlaws afresh, and the soldiery became faint-hearted and began to give back. But the field was not yet won, for they retreated in close order toward the East gate, resolved to hem the attackers within the city walls. Here again, however, they were in error, since the outlaws did not go out by their nearest gate. They made a sally in that direction, in order to mislead the soldiery, then abruptly turned and headed for the west gate, which was still guarded by Arthur-a-Bland.

The Sheriff's men raised an exultant shout at this, thinking they had the enemy trapped. Down they charged after them, but the outlaws made good their lead, and soon got through

248

How Will Stutely was Rescued

the gate and over the bridge, which had been let down by Arthur-a-Bland.

Close upon their heels came the soldiers—so close that Arthur had no time to close the gate again or raise the bridge. So he threw away his key and fell in with the yeomen, who now began their retreat up the long hill to the woods.

On this side the town, the road leading to the forest was long and almost unprotected. The greenwood men were therefore in some distress, for the archers shot at them from loopholes in the walls, and the pikemen were reinforced by a company of mounted men from the castle. But the outlaws retreated stubbornly, and now and again turned to hold their pursuers at bay by a volley of arrows. Stutely was in their midst, fighting with the energy of two ; and the little palmer was there also, but took no part save to keep close to Robin's side and mutter silent words as though in prayer.

Robin put his horn to his lips to sound a rally, when a flying arrow from the enemy pierced his hand. The palmer gave a little cry and sprang forward. The Sheriff, who followed close with his men on horseback, also saw the wound and gave a great huzza.

" Ha ! you will shoot no more bows for a season, master outlaw ! " he shouted.

" You lie ! " retorted Robin fiercely, wrenching the shaft from his hand despite the streaming blood ; " I have saved one shot for you all this day. Here take it ! "

Robin Hood & His Merry Outlaws

And he fitted the same arrow which had wounded him upon the string of his bow and let it fly toward the Sheriff's head. The Sheriff fell forward upon his horse in mortal terror, but not so quickly as to escape unhurt. The sharp point laid bare a deep gash upon his scalp and must certainly have killed him if it had come closer.

The fall of the Sheriff discomfited his followers for the moment, and Robin's men took this chance to speed on up the hill. The palmer had whipped out a small white handkerchief and tried to staunch Robin's wound as they went. At sight of the palmer's hand, Robin turned with a start, and pushed back the other's hood.

" Marian ! " he exclaimed, " you here ! "

It was indeed Maid Marian, who had helped save Will, and been in the stress of battle from the first. Now she hung her head as though caught in wrong.

" I had to come, Robin," she said simply, " and I knew you would not let me come, else."

Their further talk was interrupted by an exclamation from Will Scarlet.

" By the saints, we are trapped ! " he said, and pointed to the top of the hill, toward which they were pressing.

There from out a grey castle poured a troop of men, armed with pikes and axes, who shouted and came running down upon them. At the same instant, the Sheriff's men also renewed their pursuit.

How Will Stutely was Rescued

" Alas ! " cried poor Marian, " we are undone ! There is no way of escape ! "

" Courage, dear heart ! " said Robin, drawing her close to him. But his own spirit sank as he looked about for some outlet.

Then—oh, joyful sight !—he recognized among the foremost of those coming from the castle the once doleful knight Sir Richard of the Lea. He was smiling now, and greatly excited.

" A Hood ! a Hood ! " he cried ; " a rescue ! a rescue ! "

Never were there more welcome sights and sounds than these. With a great cheer the outlaws raced up the hill to meet their new friends ; and soon the whole force had gained the shelter of the castle. Bang ! went the bridge as it swung back upward, with great clanking of chains. Clash ! went one great door upon the other, as they shut in the outlaw band, and shut out the Sheriff, who dashed up at the head of his men, his bandaged face streaked with blood and inflamed with rage.

CHAPTER XXI

HOW SIR RICHARD OF THE LEA REPAID
HIS DEBT

The proud Sheriff loud 'gan cry
And said, " Thou traitor knight,
Thou keepest here the King's enemy
Against the laws and right."

"OPEN the gates ! " shouted the Sheriff hoarsely to the sentinel upon the walls. " Open, I say, in the King's name ! "

" Why, who are you to come thus brawling upon my premises ? " asked a haughty voice ; and Sir Richard himself stepped forth upon the turret.

" You know me well, traitor knight ! " said the Sheriff ; " now give up into my hands the enemy of the King whom you have sheltered against the laws and right."

" Fair and softly, sir," quoth the knight smoothly. " I well avow that I have done certain deeds this day. But I have done them upon mine own land, which you now trespass upon ; and I shall answer only to the King—whom God preserve !— for my actions."

" Thou soft-spoken villain ! " said the Sheriff, still in a towering passion. " I, also, serve the King ; and if these

How Sir Richard Repaid His Debt

outlaws are not given up to me at once, I shall lay siege to the castle and burn it with fire."

" First show me your warrants," said Sir Richard curtly.

" My word is enough ! Am I not Sheriff of Nottingham ? "

" If you are, in sooth," retorted the knight, " you should know that you have no authority within my lands unless you bear the King's order. In the meantime, go mend your manners, lording."

And Sir Richard snapped his fingers and disappeared from the walls. The Sheriff, after lingering a few moments longer in hope of further parley, was forced to withdraw, muttering fiercely.

" The King's order ! That shall I have without delay, as well as this upstart knight's estates ; for King Richard is lately returned, I hear, from the Holy Land."

Meanwhile the knight had gone back to Robin Hood, and the two men greeted each other right gladly.

" Well met, bold Robin ! " cried he, taking him in his arms. " Well met, indeed ! The Lord has lately prospered me, and I was minded this day to ride forth and repay my debt to you."

" And so you have," answered Robin gaily.

" Nay, 'twas nothing—this small service ! " said the knight. " I meant the moneys coming to you."

" They have all been repaid," said Robin ; " my lord of Hereford himself gave them to me."

Robin Hood & His Merry Outlaws

" The exact sum ? " asked the knight.

" The exact sum," answered Robin, winking solemnly.

Sir Richard smiled, but said no more at the time. Robin was made to rest until dinner should be served. Meanwhile a leech bound up his hand with ointment, promising him that he should soon have its use again. Some half-score others of the yeomen had been hurt, but luckily none had received wounds of grave moment. They were all bandaged and made happy by bumpers of ale.

At dinner Sir Richard presented Robin to his wife and son. The lady was stately and gracious, and made much of Marian, whom she had known as a little girl and who was now clothed more seemly for a dinner than in monkish garments. The young esquire was a goodly youth and bade fair to make as stout a knight as his father.

The feast was a joyous event. There were two long tables, and two hundred men sat down at them, and ate and drank and afterward sang songs. Even Little John was already so much recovered of his wound as to sing a song to Robin's accompaniment upon a harp. A hundred and forty of these men wore Lincoln green and called Robin Hood their chief. Never, I ween, had there been a more gallant company at table in Lea Castle !

That night the foresters tarried within the friendly walls, and the next day took leave ; though Sir Richard protested that they should have made a longer stay. And he took Robin

How Sir Richard Repaid His Debt

aside to his strong room and pressed him again to take the four hundred golden pounds. But his guest was firm.

"Keep the money, for it is your own," said Robin; "I have but made the Bishop return that which he extorted unjustly."

Sir Richard thanked him in a few earnest words, and asked him and all his men to visit the armoury, before they departed. And therein they saw, placed apart, a hundred and forty stout yew bows of cunning make, with fine waxen silk strings; and a hundred and forty sheaves of arrows. Every shaft was a just ell long, set with peacocks' feathers, and notched with silver. And Sir Richard's fair lady came forward and with her own hands gave each yeoman a bow and a sheaf.

"In sooth, these are poor presents we have made you, good Robin Hood," said Sir Richard; "but they carry with them a thousand times their weight in gratitude."

The Sheriff made good his threat to inform the King. Forth rode he to London town upon the week following, his scalp wound having healed sufficiently to permit him to travel. This time he did not seek out Prince John, but asked audience with King Richard of the Lion Heart himself. His Majesty had but lately returned from the Crusades, and was just then looking into the state of his kingdom. So the Sheriff found ready audience.

Then to him the Sheriff spoke at length concerning Robin Hood; how that for many months the outlaws had defied the

Robin Hood & His Merry Outlaws

King, and slain the King's deer ; how Robin had gathered about him the best archers in all the countryside ; and, finally, how the traitorous knight Sir Richard of the Lea had rescued the band when capture seemed certain, and refused to deliver them up to justice.

The King heard him through with attention, and quoth he :

" Meseems I have heard of this same Robin Hood, and his men, and also seen somewhat of their prowess. Did not these same outlaws shoot in a royal tourney at Finsbury Field ? "

" They did, your Majesty, under a royal amnesty."

In this speech the Sheriff erred, for the King asked quickly :

" How came they last to the Fair at Nottingham—by stealth ? "

" Yes, your Majesty."

" Did you forbid them to come ? "

" No, your Majesty. That is——"

" Speak out ! "

" For the good of the shire," began the Sheriff again, falteringly, " we did proclaim an amnesty ; but 'twas because these men had proved a menace——"

" Now by my halidom ! " quoth the King, while his brow grew black. " Such treachery would be unknown in the camp of the Saracen ; and yet we call ourselves a Christian people ! "

The Sheriff kept silence through very fear and shame ; then the King began speech again :

" Nathless, my lord Sheriff, we promise to look into this

How Sir Richard Repaid His Debt

matter. Those outlaws must be taught that there is but one King in England, and that he stands for the law."

So the Sheriff was dismissed, with very mixed feelings, and went his way home to Nottingham town.

A fortnight later the King began to make good his word, by riding with a small party of knights to Lea Castle. Sir Richard was advised of the cavalcade's approach, and quickly recognized his royal master in the tall knight who rode in advance. Hasting to open wide his castle gates he went forth to meet the King and fell on one knee and kissed his stirrup. For Sir Richard, also, had been with the King to the Holy Land, and they had gone on many adventurous quests together.

The King bade him rise, and dismounted from his own horse to greet him as a brother-in-arms ; and arm-in-arm they went into the castle, while bugles and trumpets sounded forth joyous welcome in honour of the great occasion.

After the King had rested and supped, he turned upon the knight and with grave face inquired :

" What is this I hear about your castle being a nest and harbour for outlaws ? "

Then Sir Richard of the Lea, divining that the Sheriff had been at the King's ear with his story, made a clean breast of all he knew : how that the outlaws had befriended him in sore need—as they had befriended others—and how that he had given them only knightly protection in return.

257

Robin Hood & His Merry Outlaws

The King liked the story well, for his own soul was one of chivalry. And he asked other questions about Robin Hood, and heard of the ancient wrong done his father before him, and of Robin's own enemies, and of his manner of living.

" In sooth," cried King Richard, springing up, " I must see this bold fellow for myself ! An you will entertain my little company, and be ready to sally forth, upon the second day, in quest of me if need were, I shall e'en fare alone into the green-wood to seek an adventure with him."

But of this adventure you shall be told in the next tale ; for I have already shown you how Sir Richard of the Lea repaid his debt, with interest.

CHAPTER XXII

HOW KING RICHARD CAME TO SHERWOOD FOREST

> King Richard hearing of the pranks
> Of Robin Hood and his men,
> He much admired and more desired
> To see both him and them.
>
> .   .   .   .   .
>
> Then Robin takes a can of ale :
> " Come let us now begin ;
> And every man shall have his can ;
> Here's a health unto the King ! "

FRIAR TUCK had nursed Little John's wounded knee so skilfully that it was now healed. In sooth, the last part of the nursing depended more upon strength than skill ; for it consisted chiefly of holding down the patient, by main force, to his cot. Little John had felt so well that he had insisted upon taking part in the rescue of Will Stutely before the wound was properly healed ; and, in spite of the fact that the wound was doing badly in consequence, he would have taken no rest in his cot if the friar had not piled some holy books upon his legs and sat upon his stomach. Under this vigorous treatment Little John was constrained to lie quiet until the friar gave him leave to get up. At last he had this leave, and he and the friar went forth to join the rest of the band, who were right glad to see them, you may be sure. They

Robin Hood & His Merry Outlaws

sat round a big fire, for 'twas a chilly evening, and feasted and made merry, in great content.

A cold rain set in later, but the friar wended his way back, nathless, to his little hermitage. There he made himself a cheerful blaze, and changed his dripping robe, and had sat himself down, with a sigh of satisfaction, before a tankard of hot mulled wine and a pasty, when suddenly a voice was heard on the outside, demanding admission. His kennel of dogs set up furious uproar, on the instant, by way of proving the fact of a stranger's presence.

" Now by Saint Peter ! " growled the friar, " who comes here at this unseemly hour ? Does he take this for a hostelry ? Move on, friend, else my mulled wine will get cold ! "

So saying he put the tankard to his lips, when a thundering rap sounded upon the door-panel, making it to quiver, and causing Tuck almost to drop his tankard ; while an angry voice shouted :

" Ho ! Within there ! Open, I say ! "

" Go your way in peace ! " roared back the friar. " I can do nothing for you. 'Tis but a few miles to Gamewell, if you know the road."

" But I do not know the road, and if I did I would not budge another foot. 'Tis wet without and dry within. So, open, without further parley ! "

" A murrain seize you for disturbing a holy man in his prayers ! " muttered Tuck savagely. Nathless, he was fain to

How King Richard Came to Sherwood

unbar the door in order to keep it from being battered down. Then, lighting a torch at his fire and whistling for one of his dogs, he strode forth to see who his visitor might be.

The figure of a tall knight clad in a black coat of mail, with plumed helmet, stood before him. By his side stood his horse, also caparisoned in rich armour.

" Have you no supper, brother ? " asked the Black Knight curtly. " I must beg of you a bed and a bit of roof for this night, and fain would refresh my body ere I sleep."

" I have no room that even your steed would deign to accept, Sir Knight ; and naught save a crust of bread and pitcher of water."

" I' faith, I can smell better fare than that, brother, and must e'en force my company upon you, though I shall recompense it for gold in the name of the Church. As for my horse, let him but be blanketed and put on the sheltered side of the house."

And without further parley the knight boldly strode past Tuck and his dog and entered the hermitage. Something about his masterful air pleased Tuck, in spite of his churlishness.

" Sit you down, Sir Knight," quoth he, " and I will fasten up your steed, and find him somewhat in the shape of grain. Half, also, of my bed and board is yours this night ; but we shall see later which is the better man, and who is to give the orders ! "

Robin Hood & His Merry Outlaws

"With all my soul!" said the knight, laughing. "I can pay my keeping in blows or gold as you prefer."

The friar presently returned and drew up a small table near the fire.

"Now, Sir Knight," quoth he, "put off your sword and helm and such other war-gear as it pleases you, and help me lay this table, for I am passing hungry."

The knight did as he was told, and put aside the visor which had hid his face. He was a bronzed and bearded man with blue eyes, and hair shot with gold, haughty but handsome withal.

Then once again the priest sat him down to his pasty and mulled wine, right hopefully. He spoke his grace with some haste, and was surprised to hear his guest respond fittingly in the Latin tongue. Then they attacked the wine and pasty valiantly, and the Black Knight made good his word of being in need of refreshment. Tuck looked ruefully at the rapidly disappearing food, but came to grudge it not, by reason of the stories with which his guest enlivened the meal. The wine and warmth of the room had cheered them both, and they were soon laughing uproariously as the best of comrades in the world. The Black Knight, it seemed, had travelled everywhere. He had been on Crusade, had fought the courteous Saladin, had been in prison, and often in peril. But now he spoke of it lightly, and laughed it off, and made himself so friendly that Friar Tuck was like to choke with merriment. So passed the

How King Richard Came to Sherwood

time till late ; and the two fell asleep together, one on each side of the table which they had cleared to the platters.

On the morning Friar Tuck awoke disposed to be surly, but was speedily mollified by the sight of the Black Knight, who had already risen gay as a lark, washed his face and hands, and was now stirring a hot gruel over the fire.

" By my faith, I make a sorry host ! " cried Tuck, springing to his feet. And later, as they sat at breakfast, he added : " I want not your gold, of which you spoke last night ; but instead I will do what I can to speed you on your way whenever you wish to depart."

" Then tell me," said the knight, " how I may find Robin Hood the outlaw ; for I have a message to him from the King. All day yesterday I sought him, but found him not."

Friar Tuck lifted up his hands in holy horror. " I am a lover of peace, Sir Knight, and do not consort with Robin's bold fellows."

" Nay, I think no harm of Master Hood," said the knight ; " but much I yearn to have speech with him in mine own person."

" If that be all, mayhap I can guide you to his haunts," said Tuck, who foresaw in this knight a possible gold-bag for Robin. " In sooth, I could not well live in these woods without hearing somewhat of the outlaws ; but matters of religion are my chief joy and occupation."

" I will go with you, brother," said the Black Knight.

Robin Hood & His Merry Outlaws

So without more ado they went their way into the forest, the knight riding upon his charger, and Tuck pacing along demurely by his side.

The day had dawned clear and bright, and now with the sun a good three hours high a sweet autumn fragrance was in the air. The wind had just that touch of coolness in it which sets the hunter's blood to tingling ; and every creature of nature seemed bounding with joyous life.

The knight sniffed the fresh air in delight.

" By my halidom ! " quoth he ; " but the good greenwood is the best place to live in, after all ! What court or capital can equal this, for full-blooded men ? "

" None of this earth," replied Tuck smilingly. And once more his heart warmed toward this courteous stranger.

They had not proceeded more than three or four miles along the way from Fountains Abbey to Barnesdale, when of a sudden the bushes just ahead of them parted and a well-knit man with curling brown hair stepped into the road and laid his hand upon the knight's bridle.

It was Robin Hood. He had seen Friar Tuck, a little way back, and shrewdly suspected his plan. Tuck, however, feigned not to know him at all.

" Hold ! " cried Robin. " I am in charge of the highway this day, and must exact an accounting from all passers-by."

" Who is it bids me hold ? " asked the knight quietly. " I am not i' the habit of yielding to one man."

How King Richard Came to Sherwood

"Then there are others to keep me company," said Robin clapping his hands. And instantly a half-score other stalwart fellows came out of the bushes and stood beside him.

"We be yeomen of the forest, Sir Knight," continued Robin, "and live under the greenwood tree. We have no means of support—thanks to the tyranny of our overlords—other than the aid which fat churchmen and goodly knights like yourself can give. And as ye have churches and rents, both, and gold in great plenty, we beseech ye for Saint Charity to give us some of your spending."

"I am but a poor monk, good sir!" said Friar Tuck in a whining voice, "and am on my way to the shrine of Saint Dunstan, if your worshipfulness will permit."

"Tarry a space with us," answered Robin, biting back a smile, "and we will speed you on your way."

The Black Knight now spoke again. "But we are messengers of the King," quoth he; "his Majesty himself tarries near here, and would have speech with Robin Hood."

"God save the King!" said Robin, doffing his cap loyally; "and all that wish him well! I am Robin Hood, but I say cursed be the man who denies our liege King's sovereignty!"

"Have a care!" said the knight, "or you shall curse yourself!"

"Nay, not so," replied Robin curtly; "the King has no more devoted subject than I. Nor have I despoiled aught of his save, mayhap, a few deer for my hunger. My chief war is

265

against the clergy and barons of the land who bear down upon the poor. But I am glad," he continued, " that I have met you here ; and before we end you shall be my friend and taste of our greenwood cheer."

" But what is the reckoning ? " asked the knight. " For I am told that some of your feasts are costly."

" Nay," responded Robin, waving his hands, " you are from the King. Nathless—how much money is in your purse ? "

" I have no more than forty gold pieces, seeing that I have lain a fortnight at Nottingham with the King, and have spent some goodly amounts upon other lordings," replied the knight.

Robin took the forty pounds and gravely counted it. One half he gave to his men and bade them drink the King's health with it. The other half he handed back to the knight.

" Sir," said he courteously, " have this for your spending. If you lie with kings and lordings overmuch, you are like to need it."

" Grammercy ! " replied the other, smiling. " And now lead on to your greenwood hostelry."

So Robin went on one side of the knight's steed, and Friar Tuck on the other, and the men went before and behind till they came to the open glade before the caves of Barnesdale. Then Robin drew forth his bugle and winded the three signal blasts of the band. Soon there came a company of yeomen with its leader, and another, and a third, and a fourth, till there were sevenscore yeomen in sight. All were dressed in new

How King Richard Came to Sherwood

livery of Lincoln green, and carried new bows in their hands and bright short swords at their belts. And every man bent his knee to Robin Hood ere taking his place before the board, which was already set.

A handsome dark-haired page stood at Robin's right hand to pour his wine and that of the knightly guest; while the knight marvelled much at all he saw, and said within himself:

"These men of Robin Hood's give him more obedience than my fellows give to me."

At the signal from Robin the dinner began. There was venison and fowl and fish and wheaten cake and ale and red wine in great plenty, and 'twas a goodly sight to see the smiles upon the hungry yeomen's faces.

First they listened to an unctuous grace from Friar Tuck, and then Robin lifted high a tankard of ale.

"Come, let us now begin," quoth he, "and every man shall have his can. In honour of our guest who comes with royal word, here's a health unto the King!"

The guest responded heartily to this toast, and round about the board it went, the men cheering noisily for King Richard!

After the feast was over, Robin turned to his guest and said: "Now you shall see what life we lead, so that you may report faithfully, for good or bad, unto the King."

So, at a signal from him, the men rose up and smartly bent their bows for practice, while the knight was greatly astonished at the smallness of their targets. A wand was set up, far down the glade, and thereon was balanced a garland of roses. Whosoever failed to speed his shaft through the garland, without knocking it off the wand, was to submit to a buffet from the hand of Friar Tuck.

" Ho, ho ! " cried the knight, as his late travelling companion rose up and bared his brawny arm ready for service ; " so you, my friend, are Friar Tuck ! "

" I have not gainsaid it," replied Tuck growling at having betrayed himself. " But chastisement is a rule of the Church, and I am seeking the good of these stray sheep."

The knight said no more, though his eyes twinkled ; and the shooting began.

David of Doncaster shot first and landed safely through the rose garland. Then came Allan-a-Dale and Little John and Stutely and Scarlet and many of the rest, while the knight held his breath from very amazement. Each fellow shot truly through the garland, until Middle, the tinker—not to be outdone —stepped up for a trial. But alas ! while he made a fair shot for a townsman, the arrow never came within a hand's-breadth of the outer rim of the garland.

" Come hither, fellow," said Little John coaxingly. " The priest would bless thee with his open hand."

Then, because Middle made a wry face, as though he had already received the buffet, and loitered in his steps, Arthur-a-Bland and Will Stutely seized him by the arms and stood him before the friar. Tuck's big arm flashed through the air—

How King Richard Came to Sherwood

whoof!—and stopped suddenly against the tinker's ear; while Middle himself went rolling over and over on the grass. He was stopped by a small bush, and up he sat, thrusting his head through it, rubbing his ear and blinking up at the sky as though the stars had fallen and struck him. The yeomen roared with merriment, and as for the knight he laughed till the tears came out of his blue eyes and rolled down his face.

After Middle's mishap, others of the band seemed to lose their balance, and fared in the same fashion. The garland would topple over in a most impish way at every breath, although the arrows went through it. So Middle 'gan to feel better when he saw this one and that one tumbling on the sward.

At last came Robin's turn. He shot carefully, but as ill luck would have it, the shaft was ill-feathered and swerved sidewise so that it missed the garland by full three fingers. Then a great roar went up from the whole company; for 'twas rarely that they saw their leader miss his mark. Robin flung his bow upon the ground from very vexation.

" A murrain take it ! " quoth he. " The arrow was sadly winged. I felt the poor feather upon it as it left my fingers ! "

Then, suddenly seizing his bow again, he sped three shafts as fast as he could send them, and every one went clean through the garland.

" By Saint George ! " muttered the knight. " Never before saw I such shooting in all Christendom ! "

Robin Hood & His Merry Outlaws

The band cheered heartily at these last shots ; but Will Scarlet came up gravely to Robin.

"Pretty shooting, master!" quoth he, "but 'twill not save you from paying for the bad arrow. So walk up and take your medicine!"

"Nay, that may not be!" protested Robin. "The good friar belongs to my company and has no authority to lift hands against me. But you, Sir Knight, stand as it were for the King. I pray you, serve out my blow."

"Not so!" said Friar Tuck. "My son, you forget I stand for the Church, which is greater even than the King."

"Not in merry England," said the knight in a deep voice. Then, rising to his feet, he added: "I stand ready to serve you, Master Hood."

"Now out upon ye for an upstart knight!" roared Friar Tuck. "I told you last night, sirrah, that we should yet see who was the better man! So we will e'en prove it now, and thus settle who is to pay Robin Hood."

"Good!" said Robin, "for I want not to start a dispute between Church and State."

"Good!" also said the knight. "'Tis an easy way to end prattling. Come, friar, strike an ye dare. I will give you first blow."

"You have the advantage of an iron pot on your head and gloves on your hands," said the friar ; "but have at ye! Down you shall go, if you were Goliath of Gath."

270

How King Richard Came to Sherwood

Once more the priest's brawny arm flashed through the air, and struck with a whoof! But to the amazement of all, the knight did not budge from his tracks, though the upper half of his body swerved slightly to ease the force of the blow. A loud shout burst from the yeomen at this, for the friar's fist was proverbial, and few of those present had not felt the force of it in times past.

"Now 'tis my turn," said his antagonist coolly, casting aside his gauntlet. And with one blow of his fist the knight sent the friar spinning to the ground, where he lay gasping on his back.

If there had been uproar and shouting before, it was as naught to the noise which now broke forth. Every fellow held his sides or rolled upon the ground from uncontrollable laughter; every fellow, save one, and that was Robin Hood.

"Out of the frying-pan into the fire!" thought he. "I wish I had let the friar box my ears, after all!"

Robin's plight did, indeed, seem a sorry one, before the steel muscles of this stranger. But he was saved from a tumble heels over head by an unlooked-for diversion. A horn winded in the glade, and a party of knights were seen approaching.

"To your arms!" cried Robin, hurriedly seizing his sword and bow.

"'Tis Sir Richard of the Lea!" cried another, as the troop came nearer.

And so it was. Sir Richard spurred forward his horse and

Robin Hood & His Merry Outlaws

dashed up to the camp while the outlaws stood at stiff attention. When he had come near the spot where the Black Knight stood, he dismounted and knelt before him.

"I trust your Majesty has not needed our arms before," he said humbly.

"It is the King!" cried Will Scarlet, falling upon his knees.

All was confusion for a moment.

"The King!" echoed Robin Hood after a period of dumb wonderment; and then he and all his men bent reverently upon their knees, as one man.

The · Aged · Palmer · gives · Yovng · David · of · Doncaster · news · of · Will · Stvtely

CHAPTER XX

Robin and Marian passed out, man and wife.
(CHAPTER XXIII)

CHAPTER XXIII

HOW ROBIN HOOD AND MAID MARIAN WERE WED

" Stand up again," then said the King,
  " I'll thee thy pardon give ;
Stand up, my friend ; who can contend,
  When I give leave to live ? "

.   .   .   .   .   .

Then Robin Hood began a health
  To Marian, his only dear ;
And his yeomen all, both comely and tall,
  Did quickly bring up the rear.

YOUR pardon, sire ! " exclaimed Robin Hood. " Pardon, from your royal bounty, for these my men who stand ready to serve you all your days ! "

Richard of the Lion Heart looked grimly about over the kneeling band.

" Is it as your leader says ? " he asked.

" Ay, my lord King ! " burst from sevenscore throats at once.

" We be not outlaws from choice alone," continued Robin ; " but have been driven to outlawry through oppression. We have ever been your Majesty's faithful servants, and have but resisted the oppression of unfaithful servants of the Crown. Your deer we have slain—abbots we have relieved of their oft ill-gotten riches. Yet have we befriended the poor and aided the widow and fatherless. Grant us grace and royal

273

protection, and we will forsake the greenwood and follow the King."

Richard's eyes sparkled as he looked from one to another of this stalwart band, and he thought within himself that here, indeed, was a royal bodyguard worth the while.

" Swear ! " he said in his rich full voice ; " swear that you, Robin Hood, and all your men from this day henceforth will serve the King ! "

" We swear ! " came once more the answering shout from the yeomen.

" Rise, then, good Robin ! " said King Richard. " I give you all free pardon, and will speedily put your service to the test. For I love such archers as you have shown yourselves to be, and it were a sad pity to decree such men to death. England could not produce the like again, for many a day. But, in sooth, I cannot allow you to roam in the forest and shoot my deer ; nor to take the law of the land into your own hands. Therefore, I now appoint you to be Royal Archers and mine own special bodyguard. There be one or two civil matters to settle with certain Norman noblemen, in which I crave your aid. Thereafter, the half of your number, as may later be determined, shall come back to these woodlands as Royal Foresters. Mayhap you will show as much zeal in protecting my preserves as you have formerly shown in hunting them. Where, now, is that outlaw known as Little John ? Stand forth ! "

How Robin and Maid Marian were Wed

" Here, sire," quoth the giant, doffing his cap.

" Good Master Little John," said the King, looking him over approvingly. " Could your weak sinews stand the strain of an office in the shire ? If so, you are this day Sheriff of Nottingham ; and I trust you will make a better official than the man you relieve."

" I shall do my best, sire," said Little John, great astonishment and gladness in his heart.

" Master Scarlet, stand forth," said the King ; and then, addressing him : " I have heard somewhat of your tale," quoth he, " and that your father was the friend of my father. Now, therefore, accept the royal pardon and resume the care of your family estates ; for your father must be growing old. And come you to London next Court day and we shall see if there be a knighthood vacant."

Likewise the King called for Will Stutely and made him Chief of the Royal Archers. Then he summoned Friar Tuck to draw near.

" I crave my King's pardon," said the priest, humbly enough ; " for who am I to lift my hand against the Lord's anointed ? "

" Nay, the Lord sent the smiter to thee without delay," returned Richard, smiling ; " and 'tis not for me to continue a quarrel between Church and State. So what can I do for you in payment of last night's hospitality ? Can I find some fat living where there are no wicked to chastise, and where the work is easy and comfortable ? "

"Not so, my liege," replied Tuck. "I wish only for peace in this life. Mine is a simple nature and I care not for the fripperies and follies of Court life. Give me a good meal and cup of right brew, health, and enough for the day, and I ask no more."

Richard sighed. "You ask the greatest thing in the world, brother—contentment. It is not mine to give or to deny. But ask your God for it, and if belike He grant it, then ask it also in behalf of your King." He glanced around once more at the foresters. "Which one of you is Allan-a-Dale?" he asked; and when Allan had come forward: "So," said the King with sober face, "you are that errant minstrel who stole a bride at Plympton, despite her would-be groom and attending Bishop. I heard something of this in former days. Now, what excuse have you to make?"

"Only that I loved her, sire, and she loved me," said Allan, simply; "and the Norman lord would have married her perforce, because of her lands."

"Which have since been forfeited by the Bishop of Hereford," added Richard. "But my lord Bishop must disgorge them; and from to-morrow you and Mistress Dale are to return to them and live in peace and loyalty. And if ever I need your harp at Court, stand ready to attend me, and bring also the lady. Speaking of ladies," he continued, turning to Robin Hood, who had stood silent, wondering if a special punishment were being reserved for him, "did you not have a sweetheart who was once at Court—one, Mistress Marian? What has become of her, that you should have forgotten her?"

"Nay, your Majesty," said the black-eyed page, coming forward blushingly; "Robin has not forgotten me!"

"So!" said the King, bending to kiss her small hand in all gallantry. "Verily, as I have already thought within myself, this Master Hood is better served than the King in his palace! But are you not the only child of the late Earl of Huntingdon?"

"I am, sire, though there be some who say that Robin Hood's father was formerly the rightful Earl of Huntingdon. Nathless, neither he is advantaged nor I, for the estates are confiscate."

"Then they shall be restored forthwith," cried the King; "and lest you two should revive the ancient quarrel over them, I bestow them upon you jointly. Come forward, Robin Hood."

Robin came and knelt before his King. Richard drew his sword and touched him upon the shoulder.

"Rise, Robert Fitzooth, Earl of Huntingdon!" he exclaimed, while a mighty cheer arose from the band and rent the air of the forest. "The first command I give you, my lord Earl," continued the King when quiet was restored, "is to marry Mistress Marian without delay."

"May I obey all your Majesty's commands as willingly!" cried the new Earl of Huntingdon, drawing the old Earl's daughter close to him. "The ceremony shall take place to-morrow, an this maid is willing."

Robin Hood & His Merry Outlaws

"She makes little protest," said the King; "so I shall e'en give away the bride myself!"

Then the King chatted with others of the foresters, and made himself as one of them for the evening, rejoicing that he could have this careless freedom of the woods. And Much, the miller's son, and Arthur-a-Bland, and Middle, and Stutely, and Scarlet, and Little John, and others played at the quarter-staff, giving and getting many lusty blows. Then, as the shades of night drew on, the whole company—knights and foresters—supped and drank round a blazing fire, while Allan sang sweetly to the thrumming of the harp, and the others joined in the chorus.

'Twas a happy, care-free night—this last one together under the greenwood tree. Robin could not help feeling an undertone of sadness that it was to be the last; for the charm of the woodland was still upon him. But he knew 'twas better so, and that the new life with Marian and in the service of his King would bring its own joys.

Then the night deepened, the fire sank, but was replenished, and the company lay down to rest. The King, at his own request, spent the night in the open. Thus they slept—King and subject alike—out under the stars, cared for lovingly by Nature, kind mother of us all.

In the morning the company was early astir and on its way to Nottingham. It was a goodly cavalcade. First rode King

How Robin and Maid Marian were Wed

Richard of the Lion Heart, with his tall figure set forth by the black armour and waving plume in his helm. Then came Sir Richard of the Lea with fourscore knights and men-at-arms. And after them came Robin Hood and Maid Marian riding upon milk-white steeds. Allan-a-Dale also escorted Mistress Dale on horseback, for she was to be matron-of-honour at the wedding. These were followed by sevenscore archers clad in their bravest Lincoln green, and with their new bows unstrung in token of peace.

Outside the gates of Nottingham town they were halted.

" Who comes here ? " asked the warder's surly voice.

" Open to the King of England ! " came back the clear answer, and the gates were opened and the bridge let down without delay.

Almost before the company had crossed the moat the news spread through the town like wildfire.

" The King is here ! The King is here, and hath taken Robin Hood ! "

From every corner flocked the people to see the company pass ; and wildly did they cheer for the King, who rode smilingly with bared head down through the market-place.

At the far end of it he was met by the Sheriff, who came up puffing in his haste to do the King honour. He fairly turned green with rage when he saw Sir Richard of the Lea and Robin Hood in the royal company, but made low obeisance to his master.

Robin Hood & His Merry Outlaws

"Sir Sheriff," quoth the King, "I have come to rid the shire of outlaws, according to my promise. There be none left, for all have now taken service with their King. And lest there should be further outbreak, I have determined to place in charge of this shire a man who fears no other man in it. Master Little John is hereby created Sheriff of Nottingham, and you will turn over the keys to him forthwith."

The Sheriff bowed, but dared utter no word. Then the King turned to the Bishop of Hereford, who had also come up to pay his respects.

"Harkee, my lord Bishop," quoth he, "the stench of your evil actions has reached our nostrils. We shall demand strict accounting for certain seizures of lands and certain acts of oppression which ill become a churchman. But of this later. This afternoon you must officiate at the wedding of two of our company in Nottingham Church. So make you ready."

The Bishop also bowed and departed, glad to escape a severer censure for the time.

The company then rode on to the Mansion House, where the King held high levee through all the noon hours, and the whole town made holiday.

In the afternoon the way from the Mansion House to Nottingham Church was lined with cheering people, as the wedding party passed by. The famous bowmen were gazed at as curiously as though they had been wild animals, but were cheered none the less. Robin, who had long been held in secret

How Robin and Maid Marian were Wed

liking, was now doubly popular since he had the King's favour.

Along the way ahead of the King and the smiling bride and groom to be ran little maids strewing flowers ; while streamers floated in greeting from the windows. I ween, the only hearts that were not glad this day were those of the old Sheriff and of his proud daughter, who peered between the shutters of her window and was like to eat out her heart from envy and hatred.

At last the party reached the church, where the King dismounted lightly from his horse and helped the bride to alight ; while Will Scarlet, the best man, assisted Mistress Dale. Within the church they found the Bishop robed in state, and by his side Friar Tuck, who had been especially deputed to assist.

The service was said in Latin, while the organ pealed forth softly. The King gave away the bride, as he had said, and afterward claimed first kiss for his pains. Then the happy party dispersed, and Robin and Marian passed out again through the portal, man and wife.

Out through the cheering streets they fared, while the greenwood men ran ahead and flung gold pennies right and left in their joy, and bade the people drink the health of the young couple and the King. Then the whole party took horse at Will Scarlet's earnest wish, and went down to Gamewell Lodge, where old Squire George wept for joy at seeing his son and the King and the wedding party. That night they spent there, and feasted, and the next day Sir Richard of the Lea claimed them.

And thus, amid feasting and rejoicing and kingly favour, Robin Hood, the new Earl of Huntingdon, and his bride began their wedded life.

CHAPTER XXIV

HOW ROBIN HOOD MET HIS DEATH

" Give me my bent bow in my hand,
  And a broad arrow I'll let flee ;
And where this arrow is taken up,
  There shall my grave digg'd be."

NOW by good rights this story should end with the wedding of Robin Hood and Maid Marian ; for do not many pleasant tales end with a wedding and the saying, " and they lived happy ever after " ? But this is a true account—in so far as we can find the quaint old ballads which tell of it—and so we must follow one more of these songs and learn how Robin, after living years longer, at last came to seek his grave. And the story of it runs in this wise.

Robin Hood and his men, now the Royal Archers, went with King Richard of the Lion Heart through England settling certain private disputes which had arisen among the Norman barons while the King was gone to the Holy Land. Then the King proceeded amid great pomp and rejoicing to the palace at London, and Robin, the new Earl of Huntingdon, brought his Countess thither, where she became one of the finest ladies of the Court.

The Royal Archers were now divided into two bands, and one-half of them were retained in London, while the other

283

half returned to Sherwood and Barnesdale, there to guard the King's preserves.

Time passed on, and Robin began to chafe under the restraint of city life. He longed for the fresh pure air of the greenwood, and the rollicking society of his yeomen. One day, upon seeing some lads at archery practice upon a green, he could not help but lament, saying : " Woe is me ! I fear my hand is fast losing its old-time cunning at the bowstring ! "

Finally he became so distraught that he asked leave to travel in foreign lands, and this was granted him. He took Maid Marian, and together they went through many strange countries. Finally in an Eastern land a great grief came upon Robin. Marian sickened of a plague and died. They had been married but five years, and Robin felt as though all the light had gone out of his life.

He wandered about the world for a few months longer, trying to forget his grief, then came back to the Court, at London, and sought some commission in active service. But, unluckily, Richard was gone again upon his adventures, and Prince John, who acted as Regent, had never been fond of Robin. He received him with a sarcastic smile.

" Go forth into the greenwood," said he coldly, " and kill some more of the King's deer. Belike, then, the King will make you Prime Minister, at the very least, upon his return."

The taunt fired Robin's blood. He had been in a morose

How Robin Met His Death

mood ever since his dear wife's death. He answered Prince John hotly, and the Prince bade his guards seize him and cast him into the Tower.

After lying there for a few weeks, he was released by the faithful Stutely and the remnant of the Royal Archers, and all together they fled the city and made their way to the greenwood. There Robin blew the old familiar call, which all had known and loved so well. Up came running the remainder of the band, who had been Royal Foresters, and when they saw their old master they embraced his knees and kissed his hands, and fairly cried for joy that he had come again to them. And one and all forswore fealty to Prince John, and lived quietly with Robin in the greenwood, doing harm to none and only awaiting the time when King Richard should come again.

But King Richard came not again, and would never need his Royal Guard more. Tidings presently reached them of how he had met his death in a foreign land, and how John reigned as King in his stead. The proof of these events followed soon after, when there came striding through the glade the big, familiar form of Little John.

" Art come to arrest us ? " called out Robin, as he ran forward and embraced his old comrade.

" Nay, I am not come as the Sheriff of Nottingham, thanks be," answered Little John. " The new King has deposed me, and 'tis greatly to my liking, for I have long desired to join you here again in the greenwood."

Robin Hood & His Merry Outlaws

Then were the rest of the band right glad at this news, and toasted Little John royally.

The new King waged fierce war upon the outlaws soon after this, and sent so many scouting parties into Sherwood and Barnesdale that Robin and his men left these woods for a time and went into Derbyshire, near Haddon Hall. A curious pile of stone is shown to this day as the ruins of Robin's Castle, where the bold outlaw is believed to have defied his enemies for a year or more. At any rate King John found so many troubles of his own, after a time, that he ceased troubling the outlaws.

But in one of the last sorties Robin was wounded. The cut did not seem serious, and healed over the top; but it left a lurking fever. Daily his strength ebbed away from him, until he was in sore distress.

One day as he rode along on horseback, near Kirklees Abbey, he was seized with so violent a rush of blood to the head that he reeled and came near falling from his saddle. He dismounted weakly and knocked at the Abbey gate. The Abbess, shrouded in black, peered forth.

"Who are you that knock here? For we allow no man within these walls," she said.

"Open, for the love of Heaven!" he begged. "I am Robin Hood, ill of a fever and in sore straits."

At the name of Robin Hood the woman started back, and then, as though bethinking herself, unbarred the door and

How Robin Met His Death

admitted him. Assisting his fainting frame up a flight of stairs and into a front room, she loosed his collar and bathed his face until he was revived. Then she spoke hurriedly in a low voice :

" Your fever will sink, if you are bled. See, I have provided a lancet and will open your veins, while you lie quiet."

So she bled him, and he fell into a stupor which lasted nearly all that day, so that he awoke weak and exhausted from loss of blood.

Now, there is a dispute as to this Abbess who bled him. Some say that she did it in all kindness of heart ; while others aver that she was none other than the former Sheriff's daughter, who found her revenge at last in this cruel deed.

Be that as it may, Robin's eyes swam from very weakness when he awoke. He called wearily for help, but there was no response. He looked longingly through the window at the green of the forest ; but he was too weak to make the leap that would be needed to reach the ground.

> He then bethought him of his horn,
> Which hung down at his knee ;
> He set his horn unto his mouth,
> And blew out weak blasts three.

Little John was out in the forest near by, or the blasts would never have been heard. At their sound he sprang to his feet.

" Woe ! woe ! " he cried. " I fear my master is near dead, he blows so wearily ! "

Robin Hood & His Merry Outlaws

So he made haste and came running up to the door of the abbey, and knocked loudly for admittance. Failing to get reply he burst in the door with frenzied blows of his mighty fist, and soon came running up to the room where Robin lay, white and faint.

" Alas, dear master ! " cried Little John in great distress ; " I fear you have met with treachery ! If that be so grant me one last boon, I pray."

" What is it ? " asked Robin.

" Let me burn Kirklees with fire, and all its nunnery."

" Nay, good comrade," answered Robin Hood gently, " I cannot grant such a boon. The dear Christ bade us forgive all our enemies. Moreover, you know I never hurt woman in all my life ; nor man when in woman's company."

He closed his eyes and fell back, so that his friend thought him dying. The great tears fell from the giant's eyes and wet his master's hand. Robin slowly rallied and seized his comrade's outstretched arm.

" Lift me up, good Little John," he said brokenly. " I want to smell the air from the greenwood once again. Give me my good yew bow—here—here—and fix a broad arrow upon the string. Out yonder—among the oaks—where this arrow shall fall—let them dig my grave."

And, leaning heavily against Little John, with one last mighty effort Robin sped his last shaft out of the open window, straight

How Robin Met His Death

and true, as in the days of old, till it struck the largest oak of them all and dropped in the shadow of the trees. Then he fell back upon the sobbing breast of his devoted friend.

" 'Tis the last!" he murmured. " Tell the brave hearts to lay me there with the green sod under my head and feet. And—let them lay—my bent bow at my side, for it has made sweet music in mine ears."

He rested a moment, and Little John scarce knew that he was alive. But on a sudden Robin's eye brightened, and he seemed to think himself back once more with the band in the open forest glade. He struggled to rise.

" Ha! 'tis a fine stag, Will! And Allan, thou never didst thrum the harp more sweetly. How the light blazes! And Marian!—'tis my Marian—come at last! "

Once more the glazed look came over his brave blue eyes, and the death-sweat stood in great drops upon his forehead. Little John sobbed. A gentle pressure of the hand, and the noble spirit passed.

Robin Hood, truest and kindest of men, was no more.

So died the body of Robin Hood ; but his spirit lives on through the centuries in the deathless ballads which are sung of him, and in the hearts of men who love freedom and chivalry.

They buried him where his last arrow had fallen, and Little John set up a stone to mark the spot, that generations yet unborn

might know where the hero was laid to rest.   And on the stone
he had graven in bold, deep letters :

> Here lieth the body of Robin Hood :
> A better man there ne'er was one.
> Such archers as Robin and his men
> Will England never see again.

AZRAEL

Robin·shooteth·his·Last·Shaft:

H·P·

CHAPTER XXIV